Die Laughing

LOUISE STEVENSON

About Louise Stevenson

Louise Stevenson is a comedian and the author of *How to Be a Comedian* and *The New Comedians' Handbook*. Born in London in 1972 and raised in Glasgow, she holds a PGD and Master's degree in Creative Writing. Alongside her writing, Louise runs Brighton Comedy Course, teaching comedy and 1:1 coaching, and Speakeasy Coaching, where she helps clients with public speaking, confidence, and writing engaging speeches. She's also a keynote speaker, compère, and regularly appears on podcasts and after-dinner talks for corporate events and universities. Louise now lives in Brighton with her partner.

First published in 2025.

Paperback ISBN: 978-1-8381307-3-2

Disclaimer:

This is a work of fiction. Any resemblance to actual persons, living or dead, events, or locales is purely coincidental.

For Poddy,

Thank you for your encouragement, your laughter, and for enduring the rants and cursing that peppered the many edits of this novel. Got there in the end!

Prologue

The air inside the van is oppressive, thick with sweat and a sharp, chemical tang. Sharon stirs, her wrists aching against rough bindings. Her eyes flutter open.

A face looms over her, uncomfortably close, grinning with unsettling calm.

'Morning, sleepyhead,' he murmurs. His voice is soft, almost kind.

She jerks instinctively, but the restraints hold firm. The room tilts as panic claws its way up her throat. She tries to cry out, but the gag muffles her shallow gasps, the fabric scratchy against her dry tongue.

'Shh,' he soothes, brushing her hair with a tenderness that sends a shiver down her spine. 'No need for that. We're going to have fun.'

Standing tall, his shadow stretches unnaturally across the van walls, distorted by the dim light. He hums a jaunty tune while rummaging through a bag. Sharon's eyes dart to the details around her: the cramped van interior, the faint glow of a blinking camera light, and the unmistakable gleam of duct tape and tools. He turns back, holding a board painted in garish colours with a spinning arrow at its centre. 'This,' he says with a theatrical flourish, 'is how I'll know if you're enjoying yourself. Don't worry, I'll explain it all soon.'

The grin doesn't falter as he crouches beside her, tilting his head like a curious child. 'Showtime,' he whispers, his breath warm and cloying against her ear.

The camera light blinks as he reaches for her gag.

Chapter 1

The January afternoon hangs heavy, damp with drizzle that clings to George's duffel coat. Bare trees line the path home, their skeletal branches bending against a sharp breeze. His gloved fingers tighten around the straps of his bag as he moves through the park.

The shortcut isn't ideal—puddles pool in muddy patches, threatening to soak his trainers—but it's a quicker route home from school than by the main road. His mum will kick off if he's late again.

A sharp crack echoes behind him. George pauses, his breath misting in the cold air. He glances back, seeing nothing but empty swings swaying in the wind.

He shrugs it off and keeps walking, but his pace quickens. Another sound—a rustle in the bushes, faint but deliberate—sends his heart thudding. He spins around. A figure stands at the edge of the trees, hood pulled low, just far enough away to blur into the fading light.

'Hello?' George calls, his voice cracking.

No answer.

He forces a laugh. 'Bloody weirdo,' he mutters, turning away.

He doesn't run—he's not that kind of guy—but his steps come faster now, each one squelching in the mud. When he reaches the park's exit, he risks a glance over his shoulder. The figure is gone.

At home, George steps through the gate, shaking the rain off his coat. Inside, the house smells of damp washing and yesterday's dinner, a mix of boiled cabbage and potatoes lingering in the air. He hears his mother banging pots in the kitchen and his sister Sammy's laughter drifting down the stairs.

'George, is that you?' his mother calls.

'No, Ma, it's Jack the Ripper,' he shoots back, hanging his coat on the peg by the door.

'Don't get smart,' she warns. 'Where's the milk?'

'Ah, sorry,' he mumbles, hoping to slip upstairs.

'Sorry's no good to me. I need it for the cheese sauce!' She appears in the hallway, hands on hips, eyes narrowed. 'You'll need to nip round the shop.'

'It's pouring down out there!'

'You'll no melt,' she replies with mock sympathy, shoving a fifty-pence piece into his hand.

He storms back out, pulling his hood up against the cold Glasgow rain.

On his return, he sets the milk down on the counter. His mother glances at it but doesn't stop stirring her pot of… gravy?

'Thought you were doing a cheese sauce?' he asks.

She doesn't look up. 'Changed my mind.'

'You—' He stops himself, clenching his teeth.

Sammy storms into the kitchen. 'George! Been in my room again?' she asks, holding up her Primal Scream vinyl.

'No,' George mumbles, his voice strained. 'I've no idea how it got in my room.'

His mother turns, stirring her pot with theatrical innocence. 'Too easy,' she mutters.

He glares at her. 'Did you—'

'Don't look at me. I'm just making dinner.'

Sammy cuts him off. 'You're such a weirdo, George.'

He gives up and stalks upstairs to his room, slamming the door behind him. Flinging his uniform to the floor, he lies down on his bed. His private shoebox is slightly ajar. Heart pounding, he kneels beside it. He digs in the box, looking for his photo of Tracey—it's gone. Frantically, he tears through his belongings, magazines, clothes, everything.

'Where the hell is it?'

He finds it tucked in an envelope at the bottom of the pile and exhales in relief.

This photo of Tracey is his favourite. She's asleep, her face turned to the side, strands of her hair falling messily over her pillow. Her shirt has ridden up slightly—that had taken silent skill. She is dead to the world when she sleeps, she and Sammy have this in common. Makes sleepovers interesting!

George stares at it for a long moment, his fingers brushing lightly over the edge.

Sammy's voice screeches from the hallway. 'George, dinner's ready!'

Reluctantly, he shoves the box back under the bed and stands, running a hand through his hair. One day, Tracey Evans is going to see George—really see him.

Downstairs, his mother and Sammy are already halfway through their food, laughing at something he's not part of.

The sound of rain intensifies outside. George's gaze shifts to the window, his mind racing back to the figure in the park. Was it just a shadow, or had someone really been following him? He picks at his food, a knot tightening in his stomach.

The unease lingers with George into the next day, though he pushes it aside when he meets Will by the canal. Their banter, as always, keeps his mind occupied—for a while. The air hangs damp and heavy as George kicks a loose stone, sending it skimming across the path beside the canal. The water lies dark and still, reflecting the low-hanging clouds. Will ambles beside him, hands shoved deep into his jacket pockets, his breath visible in the cold.

They pass a few shady characters, their heads down to avoid eye contact.

'Did you watch *Dirty Rotten Scoundrels* last night?' Will asks.

'Missed the start. Ma had to watch *You've Been Framed*. God, I hate that show. It's like comedy for weans. What's funny about a cat falling off a chair half a foot off the ground? Now, a cat falling off a skyscraper—that's funny.'

'Not exactly family viewing, though, is it?'

'Too much crap pretending to be "family viewing". Take *Last of the Summer Wine*—I'd rather put a noose around my neck than sit through that.'

Ahead, a middle-aged couple passes, their argument loud and laced with swearing. George and Will stifle sniggers as the row escalates. The woman's hands gesticulate wildly, and the man's face twists with rage. Then—slap!

Their laughter dies instantly.

The man grabs her hair, yanking her close, muttering something low, before shoving her away. She stumbles, stunned and crying.

The woman pulls out a hankie and a small mirror, dabbing at her tears before reapplying lipstick. With a deep breath, she steadies herself and walks on.

Watching her retreat, a faint unease flickers in George—something he doesn't fully understand but doesn't push away.

At the end of the street, he and Will part ways. George hurries home, his pace quickening against the cold.

Approaching the front door, his heart stumbles. Pinned to the door, a photo—Tracey asleep—stares back at him.

He glances around the street, then rips it down, stuffing it into his pocket.

Through the living room window, he sees his mother asleep in her chair, the magazine she was reading lying on the floor.

Inside, more photos plaster the hallway mirror and kitchen door. He follows them up the stairs, tearing them down one after another.

Sammy's voice rings out, smug and gleeful. 'I wonder what kind of weirdo took those, eh?'

She stands in her bedroom doorway holding a fan of identical photos and waving them like playing cards.

'Give me those,' George demands, lunging toward her.

Sammy steps back, raising an eyebrow. 'You're such a creep, George. Tracey is going to be furious! She'll probably call the police! Only a matter of time before you find your natural home—a bloody cell!'

His fists clench, but he stops short. Sammy sneers and slams her door behind her.

Upstairs, George flings himself onto his bed, the tension in his jaw making his teeth ache. He closes his eyes for a moment.

A muffled scream jolts him awake.

He freezes, ears straining. His mother's voice—low and guttural—filters through the floorboards.

'Get away from me, ya bastard!'

His pulse quickens as he creeps to the top of the stairs.

Her voice rises, wild and frantic. 'Stay away from me, you hear me?'

The cries taper into quiet whimpers, then fade into the steady rhythm of sleep. His stomach knots tighter.

The next morning, George's 16th birthday begins with cheap socks, an aftershave set that reeks of Old Spice, and a sarcastic card from his mum. A £10 voucher from Auntie Anne rounds out the disappointment.

He puts his cards up next to the television, feigning gratitude.

'Do you like my gift?' his mum asks, slurping her tea.

'Erm... yeah, great.' He forces a smile.

An envelope arrives with the second post. A £50 note slips out, along with the familiar scrawl: *Happy Birthday. A chip off the old block! Don't forget where you came from. Thinking of you.*

George stares at it, his teeth grinding. He rips the card in half, marches to the bathroom, shreds it into tiny pieces, and flushes it down the toilet. At the bathroom sink, he splashes his face with cold water and breathes deeply. He stands there for a moment, seething, trying to calm the storm inside him. He lets it pass, throws on his jacket, and heads out to meet Will.

The queue outside The Warehouse stretches down the frosty street. George stamps his feet against the cold, his breath visible in the icy air.

'Don't look at Chris when we get to the front,' Will whispers. 'Just keep your head down.'

George nods, heart thudding as Will's neighbour, Chris, waves them through.

Inside, the bass thrums through his chest, the strobe lights painting flashes of movement across the packed dance floor.

The lager goes down quickly, and the pill Will slips him makes the world tilt pleasantly. George grins as the music swells, bodies moving in sync, arms raised, heads bobbing.

He jumps up and down, pogo style, bumping into someone behind him for the third time.

'Sorry, mate,' he says, turning.

Will bursts out laughing. 'Fuck, he looks like a nutter. You might be in trouble, G.'

George chances a look. A six-foot yucca plant stands tall beside the dance floor, minding its own business. George and Will collapse into laughter.

Rebel MC's 'Street Tuff' kicks in, and the crowd surges, bodies pressing closer. George loses himself in the music.

A girl in red hotpants catches his eye, her movements bold, her smile inviting as she dances closer. She leans in, her face inches from his, and shouts over the beat, 'First time?'

'Yeah,' he replies quickly, grinning back. But her eyes flick past him, landing on Will.

She laughs, louder now, catching Will's attention, and then winks—at him—before weaving through the crowd. *Tart.*

Hours blur into seconds. When the lights finally come up, George stands drenched in sweat but grinning from ear to ear.

'Best night ever,' Will shouts, his arm slung around George's shoulder.

'Fucking brilliant,' George replies, his heart still racing.

At home, George tiptoes through the dark, peeling off his damp clothes and collapsing into bed. His mind replays the night—the music, the drugs, the girl in red—eyes closed, dead to the world.

A smile creeps across his face as sleep pulls him under.

Chapter 2

Will is buzzing with excitement when he arrives at the pub. He insists on getting the drinks before revealing his big news.

'Alright, let's hear it before you pee yourself,' George says, taking a gulp of his pint.

'You'll never guess.'

'I won't have to, since you're dying to tell me.'

'It's brilliant… I'm moving to London.'

The words hit George like a punch. 'What? You're joking.'

'The company's opening a branch down there. I told my boss I was interested—didn't think he'd take me seriously, but he offered me the job today.'

'You've been there two months. Two! How does that even happen?'

'Guess they're desperate,' Will grins. 'It's brilliant, isn't it?'

George forces a smile, though everything inside him tightens. His job as a stagehand is crap, and now the only good thing in his life is leaving.

'You can come too,' Will says.

'Aye, right. How? I've no job there, and no money.'

Will's smile falters. He looks down at his pint. The excitement drains from his face, replaced with uncertainty.

George knows he's being selfish, but he can't stop. Will's his only anchor. Without him, there's nothing. They drink in silence for a moment before Will claps him on the shoulder.

'You'll figure it out, G.'

Time crawls by. George juggles his dead-end job, endless comedowns, and nights out with Robert, his workmate turned dealer. On the dance floor, with music pounding and arms in the air, George feels alive. Euphoria wraps around him like a warm blanket. But the high always fades. Back at home, he sinks into the familiar pit of loneliness.

London feels further away with each passing month. The money he saves vanishes on pints and pills. Will hasn't been home in over a year.

His manager, Karl, corners him at reception, face solemn. 'Follow me.'

George trails behind, dreading what's coming.

'Take a seat.' Karl folds his hands on the desk. 'When you started here, I thought you had potential—a bit of guidance, and you'd find your feet. But even after a written warning, things haven't improved.'

George stares at the floor.

'I've no choice but to let you go. Your P45 will be sent out today.'

Karl's voice drones on, but George stops listening. Standing, he mumbles a thank you he doesn't mean and walks out.

The chip shop bag feels cold in his hands as he inches open the front door. His mother's voice rings out, cackling with one of her cronies.

'I swear, Jean, he's the spit of him. Those cold blue eyes. The way he runs that comb through his hair, like The Fonz from *Happy Days*. Creeps me out!'

George freezes, blood pounding in his ears. His bag slips off his shoulder, clattering against the hallway table.

'Who's there?' his mother yells.

He forces his voice to stay steady. 'It's just me.'

She steps into the hallway, hands on hips. 'Why are you home early?'

'Half day,' he lies.

'You got your dig money?'

He hands over the cash, already plotting his next move. Upstairs, he grabs Will's number, heart racing. London. Can he make it work?

The phone rings three times before Will answers.

'Smith's Electronics, Will speaking.'

'It's me.'

'G! How's it going?'

'Got the sack.'

'Shite. What happened?'

'Boss was a prick. Never liked me.'

'What you going to do?'

George hesitates. 'Thought maybe I'd come down to London. Start fresh.'

The line falls quiet.

'Mate, it's expensive here. And I'm still bunking with workmates. I can't put you up.'

George's chest tightens. 'Aye, you're right. Never mind.'

'Save up and call when you're ready, yeah?'

George slams the phone down and collapses onto his bed. No one wants him. Not Will. Not anyone.

He wakes, hours later, to the sound of his mother singing loudly in the kitchen. Sliding out of bed, he stumbles downstairs.

'What's going on?'

'You'll never guess.' She claps her hands, swaying slightly. 'Won three hundred quid at the bingo!'

Her purse is stuffed with notes. She waves them in his face before counting out his dig money—with five pound extra on top.

'A rent-free week on me. Don't say I'm not good to you,' she cackles.

George forces a smile. He jogs upstairs, grabs his bag, and starts packing. Screw this place. Screw Will. He'll find his own way.

'Dancing Queen' blares from the living room as George creeps down to the kitchen. His mother's purse sits open on the counter.

He hesitates, eyeing a fifty-pound note. *She might not notice... In for a penny.* He grabs everything, stuffing the notes into his pocket, heart hammering.

Suddenly, the kitchen door swings open. Jean bursts in, startling him.

'Hiya, George. How you doing?' she asks casually, oblivious to his tension.

'Fine,' he mutters, gripping the counter behind him.

She grabs a bottle of wine and leaves without a second thought. George exhales sharply, shoving the purse back where it was, and bolts for the door.

He's nearly free when Sammy steps through the gate, catching sight of him.

'Where you going?' she asks, her gaze narrowing at the bag in his hand.

'Just returning this. Ma's looking for you. She won at bingo. She's feeling generous,' George says, forcing a smile.

Sammy doesn't hesitate. She bolts inside. George grins, slams the gate, and takes off running.

The rain pelts harder, and the cold seeps into his bones as George circles back toward the house, bag clutched tightly in his hands. Streetlights flicker, casting distorted reflections across the puddled pavement. He wipes the rain off his face with his sleeve, chest heaving, adrenaline coursing through him. He's freezing, soaked, and exhausted after two hours of failed hitching. *Hitching is much harder than in the movies*! *Maybe it's a sign—I'm not ready.* He'll wait until his mum finishes her bottle, sneak the money back into her purse, and make a new plan tomorrow. Sammy's at Aunty Anne's, one less obstacle.

Crouching behind a hedge facing the house, he surveys the street, eyes scanning the shadows. The faint orange glow from the living room flickers out, plunging the house into darkness.

Movement catches his eye at the corner. His body freezes. He's not alone. A hooded figure stands motionless behind the neighbour's shed. George holds his breath, ducking lower. *What the fuck?*

The figure strides toward the house, calm and deliberate. George presses deeper into the hedge, his breath catching as thorns scrape his skin.

Through the swaying branches, he watches the man slip through the gate with eerie precision. The figure pauses, scanning the windows. His shadow spills across the stone path leading to the front door.

George is frozen, a thousand questions racing through his mind. Time feels suspended as he struggles to process what he's just seen. Finally, he snaps out of it and inches closer, his body trembling. He crouches low by the fence, trying to steady his breathing. A tiny gap in the curtains offers a glimpse into the living room.

The window is slightly open, and he can hear muffled sounds. Candlelight flickers dimly within. He cranes his neck, trying to get a better look.

His mother is slumped in her chair, bound tightly by ropes. Her face is a grimace of fear and loathing. The man towers over her, his silhouette jagged and hulking. Cold, blue eyes catch the flicker of the candlelight, and a chill runs down George's spine. He freezes, dizzy, as memories flood back—those piercing blue eyes.

Her eyes widen, and she screams, the sound barely audible through the gag. Tears streak down her face. His father towers over her, intimidating, silencing her cries.

A sharp object glints in his hand.

'Miss me, love?' His low voice rumbles through the quiet.

George's mother's muffled reply is desperate, pleading. The man tilts his head, amusement flickering in his eyes, then leans in close, murmuring something George can't hear. The only word he catches is 'escape'.

George gasps, rooted in place, his body paralyzed by fear. He feels the warmth of urine running down his leg.

The man's head jerks toward the window.

George ducks instinctively, heart pounding, eyes squeezed shut. *Did he see me?*

A siren blares in the distance, growing louder, followed by the unmistakable sound of a helicopter, its spotlight cutting through the dark, moving down the street. The sound of propellers roars, growing closer.

The man freezes, alert, before hastily retreating toward the kitchen and vanishing from sight.

George bolts, running blindly down the street, the noise of the siren and helicopter pulsing in his ears. The man's looming figure burns into his mind as he sprints away from the flashing lights and the chaos.

Chapter 3

The rain falls, light but persistent, misting the air as George pulls his jacket tight against the vile Scottish weather. His boots crunch on the gritty pavement as he heads toward the motorway, trembling hands shoved deep into his pockets. As his breath returns to normal, his resolve hardens. He'll go to London. Get away from all this shit and never look back.

Cars barrel past without slowing. He edges closer to the road, thumb extended, his arm aching with the effort.

An idea strikes. At the next service station, behind a pile of discarded boxes, he finds what he needs. Flattening one, he scrawls *LONDON* in bold black strokes, going over the letters until they stand out. Back at the roadside, he holds the sign high, scanning faces through the rain-streaked windshields. Nobody stops.

'You're not looking for a lift to London by any chance?' A voice from behind him startles George. He turns to find a burly man with greying hair and an amused smile.

'I am, actually.' He keeps his tone casual.

'London, eh? Not running away, are you?'

'Nah, I've got a mate down there. Been begging me to join him.'

The man studies him for a moment, then nods. 'I'm heading to Manchester. You'll have better luck from there. Your call.'

Relief washes over him. 'That'd be great. Thanks.'

'Name's Jimbo.' He extends a hand, his grip soft despite the imposing size.

'George. My mates call me G.'

'Well, G, let's get you moving.'

The massive Eddie Stobart truck parked nearby looks like something from a movie. Climbing into the cab, George dumps his bag at his feet and takes in the dashboard clutter, walkie-talkies crackling with static.

'First time in a truck?'

'Yeah.'

'Your lucky day, then.'

The truck merges into the steady stream of motorway traffic. George stares out at the endless road ahead as Jimbo talks about everything and nothing. The chatter keeps the nerves at bay, though a faint unease lingers. Jimbo's friendliness feels genuine, but he doesn't let his guard down completely.

Hours later, the signs for Manchester tick down to two miles. At the service station, Jimbo pulls off. 'This is your stop, son. Good luck in London.'

George steps into the rain, shoulders hunched against the chill. 'Thanks. All the best.'

The next few hours pass in a miserable haze. His drenched sign smears, becoming unreadable. Hunger gnaws at him, but he'll need every penny he has for London. Back at the service station, he shelters under the awning, scanning the car park.

A burly, moustached man catches his eye, moving quickly and glancing around. He stops at a small van, rapping on the back window. A woman slides it open, and they exchange muffled words. Moments later, the man climbs inside, slamming the door.

Curiosity pulls George forward, his steps tentative. The van rocks, rhythmic groans cutting through the rain's patter. The curtains on the back windows hang loose, offering a sliver of a view.

The man's bare arse bobs above the woman, who lies pinned beneath him. The scene is sordid, animalistic—and yet there's a magnetic pull. The man groans, louder and louder, until he collapses onto the woman. George steps back quickly, retreating to the motorway.

The next truck that stops is driven by a man named Dave, who offers him a ride all the way to London. George doesn't hesitate, clambering into the warmth of the cab.

'You look knackered,' Dave observes. 'There's a bunk in the back if you need a kip. Long drive ahead. Don't be tugging off at my posters,' Dave jokes, gesturing at the wall plastered with nude women.

The exhaustion is too much to resist. George climbs into the cramped sleeping area; unease prickles at the back of his neck, but sleep pulls him under quickly.

He wakes to a blinding flash.

Dave looms over him, camera in hand, grinning. 'Flash works every time. You sleep alright?'

'Yeah... fine.' The explanation doesn't ring true, but he's too groggy to argue.

Hours later, they pull into a secluded road and park at a house, shrouded by tall hedges and overshadowed by a gnarled, leafless tree. The place looks deserted, with a single streetlamp flickering weakly.

'Not exactly London,' Dave admits with a sheepish grin. 'But close enough. You'll be alright here tonight.'

George hesitates, eyeing the house. It's too late to back out now.

The outside of the house is plain, with a red-painted door and a polished letterbox—presentable enough. Inside, the stench hits first—damp, decay, and something fouler. The living room is a chaotic mess of dirty mattresses, empty cans, and discarded food. A portable TV sits on the floor, its screen cracked, surrounded by tripods and cameras.

'That one's yours,' Dave says, gesturing to a mattress in the corner. 'Sleep tight, G.'

The door slams behind him, plunging the room into darkness. George gropes for a light switch but finds none. A faint glow seeps through a gap in the curtains, enough to reveal the squalor around him.

He lies stiffly on the mattress, desperately wishing someone knew where he was, every instinct screaming that he shouldn't be here.

A noise wakes him. Grunting, low and rhythmic.

His eyes adjust to the dark, finding the source—a naked woman astride a figure on the nearest mattress. Her gaze locks onto him, unblinking, cold.

The air grows thicker, stifling. He should look away, but he can't. The way she stares—like she knows something about him—pins him in place.

George squeezes his eyes shut, heart hammering in his chest. The smell of unwashed bodies fills the air, mixed with something metallic. He risks another look. The woman hasn't moved her gaze, her dark, emotionless eyes fixed on him as though sizing up prey.

She's small, wiry, and entirely detached from the act. Her hands clutch the shoulders of the man beneath her, whose grunting grows louder. George's stomach churns.

The red light of a camera blinks in the corner. He wills himself to stay calm.

The woman smiles—a slow, deliberate curve of her lips. She raises a hand and flips him off, her gesture defiant and mocking.

George shifts, slowly getting onto all fours and crawling towards the door.

'Looks like he's trying to escape,' she says, her voice a taunting singsong.

The man beneath her shifts, sitting up. It's Dave.

'George! Where you off to?' Dave's grin stretches wide, his teeth yellowed in the dim light. 'Meet the beautiful Sasia.'

She gives a little wave. Fear twists in his stomach, but his eyes don't leave the scene. Her mocking grin, the way she holds herself—unwavering, in control—draws his gaze despite himself.

Dave's smile sharpens, his eyes glinting. 'You can't leave already? We've barely started.'

The room feels smaller, suffocating. George scrambles to his feet, adrenaline spiking, but the woman moves with unsettling speed. Her hand grabs his ankle, and he stumbles back, landing hard on the filthy mattress.

'Easy now, little bunny,' she purrs, crouching low, her face inches from his. The stink of cigarettes and sweat rolls off her in waves. 'You're not going anywhere.'

'Playtime,' Dave says, his voice unnervingly calm as he steps past him.

Something hard slams into the back of George's skull. White-hot pain flashes across his vision. He collapses forward, instinctively putting his hands out. His body is flipped onto its back, and cold metal cuffs clamp around his wrists.

'Much better,' Sasia croons, tightening the cuffs with a vicious jerk.

George struggles against the restraints, but the effort is futile. His breathing grows shallow, panic clawing at his chest.

'There now,' Dave says, grabbing George by the shoulders and hauling him upright. 'This'll be fun.'

The words send a jolt of fear through him. He thrashes, wild and desperate, but Dave's grip is unyielding.

Sasia circles him like a predator, knife gleaming in her hand. She trails it down his arm with deliberate slowness, the cold metal biting his skin.

'Such soft skin,' she murmurs, her voice almost tender.

'Get the camera ready,' Dave calls over his shoulder, dragging George toward the centre of the room.

Sasia sets up a tripod, positioning it with meticulous care. Every movement feels rehearsed, deliberate.

Pinned to the floor, George's breath catches as Sasia kneels beside him, her face splitting into a wide grin. She presses the knife to his throat—not hard enough to draw blood, but close enough to make her point.

'Don't scream, little virgin. You'll ruin the show,' she says, her lips brushing his ear.

His mind races, searching for a way out. But amidst the terror, something stirs—a flicker of fascination. He hates them, but their twisted dynamic, their absolute control, grips him in a way he can't fully ignore.

Sasia backs away, raising the knife theatrically toward the camera. 'Rolling,' she declares.

Dave steps into the frame, his grin widening as he gives an exaggerated bow, like a theatre encore.

'This is insane,' George mutters, his voice raw.

Dave winks. 'Insane's just another word for fun.'

The humiliation burns deeper with every second. George's arms strain against the cuffs, muscles screaming. His gaze darts around the room, desperate for something—anything—he can use.

The knife glints on the edge of Sasia's mattress. She's too busy performing for the camera, waving a large dildo as if she's selling it on a shopping channel. His focus sharpens, zeroing in on the knife.

Lunging forward, he grabs the blade with his cuffed hands, the metal cutting into his palms. He spins, slashing blindly.

Sasia screams, clutching her arm as crimson seeps through her fingers.

'You little shit!' Dave roars, lunging forward.

George twists, driving the knife into Dave's thigh. Blood sprays across the mattress. Dave stumbles, collapsing to one knee.

'You're dead, you hear me boy?' Dave bellows, his voice raw with fury.

George doesn't wait for a second chance. He scrambles to his feet, yanking his wrists against the cuffs until the pain makes his vision blur.

Sasia charges, her face twisted in rage, but George swings the knife in a wild arc, catching her across the shoulder. She recoils, shrieking.

The front door looms ahead, tantalisingly close. He charges toward it, yanking the handle—but the door won't budge.

A hand clamps around his neck from behind. He spins, plunging the knife into soft flesh. Sasia gasps, her hands flying to her throat as blood gushes over her fingers.

Her knees buckle, her body crumpling to the floor. She stares up at him, her eyes wide with disbelief.

'You fucking… bastard,' she rasps before the light fades from her gaze.

George stares, frozen. His chest heaves, his mind a whirl of shock and disbelief. He just killed her.

The sound of movement jolts him back. Dave struggles to his feet, his wounded leg buckling beneath him.

'You're gonna pay for that,' Dave growls, staggering toward him.

George doesn't think. He grabs a heavy metal object from the floor—an engine part, maybe—and hurls it at the door's glass pane. The impact shatters the glass, shards cascading to the floor.

Ignoring the fresh cuts on his hands, George squeezes through the jagged opening, the cold night air biting his skin.

Rain pelts his face as he stumbles onto the pavement, his legs moving on autopilot.

Dave's voice roars behind him, muffled by the pounding rain.

He doesn't look back. He runs. Every muscle burns, his lungs scream for air, but he doesn't stop.

Chapter 4

George sits in his bedsit, watching the news. There's still no word on Sasia's death. After six months, his fear of arrest is subsiding. The bedsit is dark and musty. The wallpaper looks like it's been there since the place was built. He considered painting it but decided against it—better to avoid unnecessary interaction with his landlord. The carpet is threadbare and brown. It's a shithole in the worst part of London.

He checks his watch—ten to four. Another two hours to go. The shop is bustling with tourists hunting for cheap jeans. They've come to the right place—Mr Jeans is the cheapest and the nastiest in town. He edges towards the door for a bit of people-watching. Tottenham Court Road is always packed. Hidden behind rows of Levi jeans, he surveys the shoppers—more entertaining than searching for a thirty-inch waist in distressed denim. It's June, sunny, the best time for watching—more flesh, less haste.

'You're not staring through that window again?' Darren asks.

'No,' George replies, unconvincingly.

'Good… I'd have to report it to Mr Travis. He's already given you a verbal warning this week.'

'Because you grassed me up.'

'I'm your supervisor. I have a responsibility to report flaunting of working hours.'

'Five minutes late, hardly the crime of the century.'

'We've a business to run. Targets to make.'

George clenches his jaw. Roll on the weekend—the only thing that keeps him going. The raves, stomping about, off his face in muddy fields. He touches the ticket for tomorrow night's extravaganza: *Fantasia*, 30,000 people. London's rave scene is the best.

'Keeping my eye on you,' Darren says, smoothing his gelled hair from his gigantic head.

George resumes watching the crowd. Near the end of the day, he makes sure all the jeans are folded neatly. No unpaid overtime required if everything's tidy. At five to six, two petite women with loud European accents descend, tearing the place apart and keeping George there until half-past.

The tube is muggy, as usual. Sandwiched between a sweaty armpit and a heavy man with halitosis, George feels a familiar discomfort. The Northern Line is always packed. Fourteen suffocating stops later, he reaches Tooting Broadway.

The sky is heavy and grey over Garrett Lane. He hopes South London's criminal activity is paused until he's safely home. He picks up speed as he passes the cemetery and council estate. A bottle smashes from the estate's direction. A couple of hoodies yell profanities at their latest victim.

'Serves you right, you nonce!' the taller hoodie shouts, kicking a car on the way, setting off the alarm. George keeps his head down, walking faster.

Arriving home, he steps through the main door and listens for any sound. It's unusually quiet. He takes the stairs two at a time up to his bedsit.

'You can fuck back off to Romania if you're not happy,' his landlord yells, voice seeping through the floor.

Home sweet home. Another night below a domestic battlefield. Something crashes against the wall. Konstantinous's girlfriend screams, 'My mother bought me that, you pig!' The door upstairs slams, followed by heavy footsteps.

George takes a beer from the humming fridge, switches on the portable TV, and flicks through the channels, searching for something worth watching.

There's a knock at the door. He turns down the volume and stands still. It's someone he doesn't know—he hasn't met any of the other tenants. The knocking starts again, more forceful this time. A peephole in the door would be useful.

Konstantinous's girlfriend has a weak smile and panda eyes, her mascara leaving black snail trails down to her chin. She's pretty in an odd way. She hugs her cardigan tightly.

'Hi, can I help you?' George asks.

She takes it literally; her eyes fill with tears, and she invites herself inside. 'Don't know if you can help. You have booze?'

He needs her to leave. Konstantinous isn't someone to cross. 'No, sorry,' he says, holding the door open.

'Lucky I brought some,' she says, pulling a bottle of vodka from under her cardigan. 'Glasses?'

'Sorry, I…'

'It's okay. We drink out of the bottle.' She sits on his bed, takes a slug, and holds it out for him.

'I'm alright, thanks. Listen…' he stumbles, not sure of her name.

'Anka. My name is Anka. And yours is George. Stinky Kon talks about you. He calls you "the ferret". It's a furry animal, apparently.'

A ferret, the cheeky bastard! He closes the door. 'I think he looks like a gorilla.'

Anka's laugh is loud and surprising for such a small person. If Kon heard her laughter coming from his room, it would be disastrous. Apart from the beating, he'd lose his deposit.

'Anka, I think you should go,' he says, standing at the door.

'You don't like me?'

'It's not that. I'm sure you're very nice, but Kon won't be happy you're here.'

'He's a bloody coke head. That's all he cares about—the coke,' Anka spits, taking another slug.

'Okay.'

'He snores like a bear.'

'Or like a gorilla?'

Anka laughs again. George likes her laugh. The front door slams downstairs. Fuck. He puts his finger to his lips. Anka senses the need to be alert.

'You need to go now,' he whispers, opening the door. She slips out to the hallway. He quietly closes the door behind her. The bottle of vodka is still on the bed. He opens it, takes a swig, and grimaces. If there's ever a drink that needs a mixer, it's vodka. He returns to his beer and settles on a rerun of *Only Fools and Horses*.

The following night is warm and light. George meets his mate Gary in front of the tube station. His unruly hair and tall frame make him hard to miss.

'Hello, G. I've got a pocket full of drugs, and we're off to the event of the year.'

They chatter excitedly at Vauxhall, waiting for their lift. They hear it before they see it—house music booming from the open windows. Baz greets them with a wave. He's around forty, sporting a beard and a tie-dye T-shirt. George likes him instantly.

'I don't know where we're going exactly. We're relying on a pirate radio station for updates. Jump in.'

They drive, bobbing their heads in unison to the beat. Gary chops up white powder on the dashboard, rolls a note, and snorts a line then holds the wheel while Baz takes his. The vibe is electric. This is freedom. They follow signs for Leicester.

'I hear Groove Riders is playing. He's wicked. Saw him in Camden Palace—he blew the roof off,' Gary says.

'I saw him at Dungeons. Amazing set,' George adds.

'War stories from past raves, drugs, and music gigs keep the ride flying by. George chomps on his chewing gum as the anticipation builds.

'Fuck, I think we might be lost,' Baz says.

'It might be the next turning,' he adds, pressing on the gas. The road is empty. Baz frowns, checking the map.

'How's your map reading, George?'

'I'll have a go,' George says, taking the map. 'Think it's this road. Let's see what happens.'

Baz cranks up the music. Twenty minutes later, they're parked on the side of the road, trying to tune into the pirate station. Baz fiddles with the knob; they move the van a few metres at a time, hoping for better reception. George just wants to get there. He's ready to dance.

They stop for a piss. Loud beats rumble behind them, the bass heavy enough to swallow you whole. A car full of ravers approaches, beeping its horn and waving as it drives past.

'Fuck, fuck, Gary! Get in the van! Follow that bass!' George hollers.

Gary jumps into the van, and they pick up speed. Gary lights a joint, passes it to George. He takes a few puffs. 'Fuck, there's cars following us,' George says, waving out the back window.

The car behind beeps, then the one in front beeps. Baz joins in.

'We're in a fucking convoy,' Gary says. 'Brilliant.'

'Brilliant... if we're headed to the right place,' Baz laughs.

George turns the music down. 'Can you hear it?' There's music in the distance. They follow the road, which becomes narrower. A makeshift sign reads, *Turn left for the night of your life.*

'We're here,' George shouts, the excitement building. He can't remember feeling this pumped.

The music gets louder as they turn into a huge field. Hundreds of people dance around a giant sound system. Rows of cars line the edges, not blocking an inflatable bouncy castle.

'Cheers for the lift,' Gary says, pulling out a bag of pills and passing them around.

The warm night is illuminated by floodlights and a perfectly round moon. Ravers dance, hands in the air, eyes closed. The music speeds up, and a wave of euphoria sweeps over George as he throws his hands up.

Chapter 5

The strobe light freezes the crowd as they dance, their bodies changing colour with each flash. The field fills with ravers in acid logo T-shirts, flared jeans, and Happy Mondays T-shirts. The guy next to George is chewing gum so ferociously, it looks like he might swallow his tongue. Glow sticks are held high in the air or waved energetically in time with the music. And, of course, there's the standard guy in white gloves, blowing a whistle and throwing shapes—big fish, little fish, cardboard box.

George feels the E coming up and fights the urge to sit down and sink into it. He closes his eyes and focuses on the music. He feels himself rising and beyond, wanting to share the love.

'Can You Feel It' comes on, its rhythm pulsing as the lyrics echo through the speakers. The whole crowd explodes. George closes his eyes, his spine tingling as euphoria takes hold of his body. He immerses himself in the music and dances through the first ambush of E. When the rush subsides, he moves through the crowd looking for Gary, Baz, and water. People nod and smile as he passes by. High and happy. An old guy dances up a storm. A few are new to dancing, self-conscious and guarded. Drugs clearly not kicked in.

He buys a bottle of water and gulps it down in the designated chilling area. People are taking a break from dancing, smoking joints, and chatting shit. A girl sits alone on the grass with her head in her hands. She lifts her head up. Her eyes are red and wet. She catches him looking in her direction. He looks away.

In the Portaloo, a mirror is stuck to the back of the door. He looks like shit. His face is covered in dirt from stomping in the field. He blows his nose, and mud snot fills the toilet roll. It takes more energy than he has to clean his face. Smiling at himself, he decides that he's quite good-looking, even dirty.

Outside the loo, the girl is still there. Picking up another bottle of water, he takes it over to her, approaching slowly.

'Hiya. I thought you could do with a drink,' he says, holding out the water.

She takes it with a watery smile and mutters thanks. He lets the silence go on, takes out chewing gum from his pocket, and offers her one.

'Thanks. You must think I'm a mentalist.'

'Not at all.'

'I'm Mandy.'

'Pleased to meet you, Mandy. I'm George.'

'Where you from?'

'Glasgow. You?'

'Devon.' She takes a sip from her bottle and starts to perk up.

'You alright now?'

'I'm fine. Really. Need to splash some water on my face. Will you wait while I go to the loo, George from Glasgow?'

'I certainly will.'

Mandy gets to her feet and physically gives herself a shake. She passes him the bottle of water. 'Don't run away,' she says, with a wave.

'Alright, mate,' a young guy with a smiley face T-shirt asks George. 'You want to buy any uppers or downers?' he asks.

'What you got?'

'Speed or Rohypnol. Speed for now. Rohypnol when you want to get to sleep. Ten quid each, mate.'

What the hell. George fishes out twenty quid from his jeans and hands it over. The guy gives him a bag of white powder and a small bottle. 'You might want some of this too, mate,' he says, holding a bag of salt.

'Bath salts?'

'Na, mate, smelling salts. If you need to bring yourself sharply back to earth, this is what you need. They've got ammonia in them. Tell you what, have these on me, and tell your mates to come find me for anything else,' he says, exiting with a salute.

George dabs the powder and nods his head to the beat of the music, admiring the view. A whole different world where people are free to do whatever they want. The opening bars of his favourite song come on. Whistles and horns introduce the song. People around him stand up and make their way to the centre of the action. He stands and dances on the spot.

'Go for it,' Mandy says, looking much better than before. She dances next to him.

'Let's go,' she says, taking his hand and winding through the crowd to the front. Mandy dances next to him, in her own world. She's quite a good dancer. They dance till dawn breaks, shrugging off the darkness.

'Fancy a spliff?' she asks, holding up a little bag of weed.

'Don't mind if I do.' They walk back to the chilling area and sit down.

Mandy bobs her head to the music as she makes a joint. 'Shit, I don't have a light.'

'I'll get one,' George scans the groups of people squatted around him and heads towards a plume of smoke.

'Can I borrow a lighter, mate?'

'No bother,' the guy says in a Scottish accent. George recognises the voice vaguely.

'Thanks,' George says.

'Oh, my fucking God. George, is that you? George Mailer?' he says, jumping to his feet.

George is stunned. 'Fucking hell, Will!'

Will bear hugs him. 'It's so good to see you. Thought you were dead. Sit down, join us. I can't believe it's you.'

Will introduces him to the people sprawled about him. 'Pete, Tom… new mates… I lost mine within ten minutes of arriving,' Will says.

'So did I,' George admits. They both laugh.

Will shakes his head. 'What happened, G? Why did you disappear?'

George isn't quite sure how to answer. *You pissed me off. You left me.* 'Thought you'd found your own life… new mates, new flat and all that.'

'And I didn't want you as my best mate anymore?'

George is elated. *Will does care!*

'I phoned your mum a few times.'

'I imagine she had good things to say?'

'She said you ran away with her bingo money. She called you, what was it? A snivelling coward.'

A coward? What does she mean? Did she see him outside the window?

'She's mad. I didn't steal shit.'

'The second time I called, she said, "I have no son." A right one for the drama, your ma.' Will takes a deep puff of the spliff and hands it to George.

Dawn breaks, but no one moves to leave. A few die-hards remain dancing in the field, though most have found their way to the chill-out area, slipping into second gear, chatting and smoking with faces like coal miners—happy coal miners.

'Give me a hug, man. Honestly, brilliant to see you,' Will says, enfolding him. 'Where you staying?'

'Tooting.'

'No fucking way. I'm in Clapham. Not too far at all. How you getting back?'

'Not sure,' George laughs.

'These guys are giving me a lift. I'm sure they can squeeze in a wee one.'

The blond kid with dreadlocks nods his consent.

George and Will chat and laugh incessantly all the way home, like no time has passed.

The happy highs are replaced by lethargic lows as George drags his body out of bed the next day; eight hours of Rohypnol-induced sleep, and he still feels like crap. Two pints of water do nothing to quench his thirst. He flicks on the TV and lands on *Songs of Praise*. Seriously, who's watching this shit? Grannies? Christians? He finds a quiz show on another channel and wonders about the fascination with quiz shows in this country.

Food might make him feel better, but he's no appetite. There's the kebab shop downstairs, but he can't risk bumping into his shithead landlord. He opens a beer and lies back down, thanking his lucky stars that he has a full day to recover before Mr Jeans.

He hears raised voices upstairs—Kon's mainly. If he's up there, he can't be working in the shop. George shakily stands, picking up a T-shirt and a pair of jeans from the floor. The jeans are caked in mud, so he tosses them aside and grabs a pair of jogging bottoms. Shit outfit, but no one's going to see him. He locks up just as the door upstairs crashes open. 'Go back to your mummy, bitch,' Kon bellows, slamming the door.

George has no time to duck back inside.

'G the G mister. You're lucky you're gay. Women are trouble.'

'I'm not gay,' George mutters.

'You're not? Oh,' Kon says insincerely.

Cunt.

Kon takes him in. 'You look rough.'

George regrets feeding him more fuel with the yellow jogging bottoms. 'I'm fine. Bye, Kon.'

'Bye, G star,' Kon says, sniggering. 'Keep it real.'

How is it possible to find so many shitty variations of his name! G star, though, does have a ring about it.

The kebab is swapped for the chippy. Three lads play a computer game, noisily winding each other up. He orders a bag of chips and hears one of the lads mimicking him in a bad Scottish accent to laughter from his idiot friends. It's at this point in life he'd like to pull out a gun. Scare the shit out of them, teach them a lesson. He leaves the chippy to a barrage of cheers at the latest game victory.

Mr Jeans on Monday morning is life-affirming; his job is shit. He hangs around the counter waiting for Will to call. Private calls at work aren't allowed, but he's determined to reach the phone first. By four o'clock, hope starts slipping away. Was Will only happy to see him because he was off his face? The phone goes, George dives for it. It's not Will. It's for Darren.

Darren finishes his call. 'Are you on reception duties today, George?' he asks. 'Because, as far as I know, your title is sales assistant.'

'Just trying to be helpful.'

'Just do your job. Help those two girls over there.' He points.

With Darren's eyes heavily on him, George puts on a smile and approaches the customers. He feels like shit and needs to find a new job. The girls smile to indicate his assistance is appreciated, in contrast to British customers who automatically bark, 'I'm just looking,' thinking all sales assistants are sharks; they're right. They buy four pair of jeans and thank him for his help in broken English. George steps outside the shop to wave them goodbye.

'Please ask next time you want to leave the shop,' Darren snipes.

George ignores him, folding jeans with feigned enthusiasm.

Two weeks go by, still nothing from Will. He feels like an idiot. He's furious. They had a great time coming back from the rave, laughing and sharing school stories. The phone rings, George has given up answering it.

Darren swiftly moves behind the counter and answers. 'Can I ask what it's regarding? … Sorry, George isn't allowed to take private calls at work.'

George marches over and pulls the phone out of Darren's hand, his heart beating fast, full of anticipation. 'Hello.'

'Alright, G, it's me, Will. Who's that prick?' George puts his hand over the phone.

'I'll be two minutes, Darren… 'Alright mate, how you doing?' he whispers.

'Sorry I haven't called… I've been mad busy.'

'I know what you mean… not enough hours in the day,' he says, cursing himself for sounding like someone's granny.

'I've got a gig tonight at a pub in Camden if you're free?'

'Erm, I was meant to be going out with a few guys from work,' he lies.

'Don't worry. It was short notice,' Will says.

'Tell you what, I'll go for a few with them and meet you later. What time you thinking?'

'About half seven. We can have a drink first. I'll meet you outside Camden station.'

'No bother. I'll see you then,' George says, as casually as possible. He puts down the phone and fists the air in triumph.

'George, can you come into my office?' Darren says, his arms folded in front of him.

'You don't have an office, Darren.'

'The stockroom is my office. I think we both know that. Follow me.'

Darren sits behind a cardboard box he's made into a makeshift table. George would love to tell him what to do with his crap job.

'You know the company rule, no personal phone calls.'

George remains quiet and decides to let whatever's coming slip over him.

'You are now on a written warning. Do you understand that?'

'I do, Darren.' He wants to punch him in the face.

'You're on very thin ice. Back to the shop floor now.'

George leaves on the dot of six, without Darren's blessing.

Dressed in his best t-shirt and aftershave, looking and smelling good, he heads out and takes the tube to Camden. Ten minutes early, no sign of Will. Twenty minutes pass, and doubts begin to creep in. Glancing at his watch, he spots Will emerging from the turnstile, flustered and red faced. 'So sorry, G. Work thing came up. Hope I didn't get you into shit today.'

'Don't worry about it, the guys a tool. How's you?'

'I'm shitting myself about this gig.'

'Can't wait to see you in action. How many gigs you done now?'

Will's forehead creases in concentration, 'Thirty, I think.'

'A professional then.'

'A delusional pal, that's exactly what I need.' Will laughs. 'Let's go get a pint.'

Chapter 6

The pub is busy, a mishmash of people—girls in shabby chic attire, bordering on homeless, with holey tights and made-up faces heavy with eyeliner and mascara; guys sporting the classic bobbed hair and ripped jeans look, though a few upmarket office types are mixed in. The music is so loud they have to shout their drink orders.

They find a table in the corner. 'How's work then, G? Is the tosser on the phone your boss?'

'God, no. He's just filling in today. They want to promote me to manager but I'm not keen on the responsibility,' George says dismissively.

'Better money though, no?'

'I'm just too laid back to be anybody's boss, know what I mean?'

'I do,' Will nods. 'It's hard managing different personalities—thick ones, late ones, the "I didn't get the memo" ones. The permanently arsey ones are the worst.'

'Jeez, how many are you managing?'

'One of the managers left. I'm looking after two teams now.'

'Fuck… very adult. You must be earning a bucket?'

'I wouldn't go that far, but it pays alright. Enough work talk. You got a bird?'

'I couldn't possibly say.'

'Why's that? She a munter?' Will laughs.

'No, she's gorgeous. Eastern European.'

'Very exotic. Where's she from?'

'Romania. She's dead keen… we'll just see how it goes. You seeing anyone?'

Will smiles. 'Met Jemma last year. She's lovely and smart. A journalist, working in New York at the mo.'

'You're doing well, mate. I can't wait to see you do your thing tonight. Can't believe you're a comedian. I was the funny one at school.'

Will laughs good naturedly. 'I'm doing the support slot… I'm shitting it.'

'The support?'

'The slot before the headliner. A guy called Nick Sheppard. You heard of him?'

George hasn't. 'Rings a bell.'

'Better head off. It's just along the road but I want to check out the room, see what the vibe's like.'

Shady characters are out in abundance on the streets of Camden, looking for spare change or selling weed. They arrive at the pub before eight. Will reads his notepad, muttering under his breath as George gets in the drinks.

In a semi-dark function room, there's a solo mic stand and a few rows of chairs. Basic. George takes a seat at the front and watches Will approach a small clique of guys standing at the back of the room, they shake hands and clap each other on the back.

The carpet sticks underfoot as George heads to the toilet. Passing Will, laughter erupts from the guys. How long have they known him? Not fucking twenty years, that's for sure. On his way back, he tries, and fails, to make eye contact with Will.

A few new audience members sit in the back rows. Why didn't he sit in the back row? He feels like a spare part, sitting up at the front on his own, all he's missing is a 'Billy no mates' T-shirt. George finally makes eye contact with Will and waves him over.

'You alright, G?'

'Erm, you want another drink? I've saved a seat for you.'

'All comedians stand at the back, mate, sorry. They're going to start in a minute.'

Really? There's ten people here. Will smiles and disappears. George feels trapped and conspicuous so sneaks downstairs to the bar, orders a pint, and takes his time returning.

The show still hasn't started when he takes his seat. A tall character with a red woolly hat bounces onto the imaginary stage and takes the mic with a flourish. Hardly any need for a mic, the twenty audience members are practically sitting on his knee.

'Hello, everybody,' he says in exaggerated children's presenter style, 'How are we this evening?'

Dick. George tries not to make direct eye contact. He's seen audience participation with comedians on TV and wants no part of it.

'Great to see you all.'

Using 'all' quite loosely.

'Tonight, we've a wonderful line-up for you.'

A few more audience folk enter and take a seat.

'We were just waiting for you guys to turn up so we could start,' the MC says.

That gets a titter. 'As I was saying, we have a great line-up for you tonight. Nick Sheppard will be headlining this evening.'

Whistles and applause come from behind him.

'Our support act tonight is a Jock, yes, the best thing out of Scotland since Billy Connolly.'

No response from the audience. Why is no one cheering? He wants to, but doesn't want to look like a twat. The silence hangs. George can bear it no more; he whoops and claps enthusiastically. People turn to stare.

'Looks like your number one fan is here, Will.'

George looks at the floor, mortified. The audience laughs.

'Okay, on with the show. Our first act tonight is all the way from Balham, that's twelve tube stops, folks. Let's show him some love. It is the wonderful Allan Jerry.'

The audience clap timidly as the comedian, a forty-something guy with a bald head and a robust belly takes the mic. He introduces himself as the world's best lover. Silence follows. He explains his wife told him she was a virgin when they married. Not funny!Jerry's confidence doesn't falter as he talks *at* the audience. The silent response doesn't put him off. George shrinks lower in his seat, this is painful. Minutes stretch into months, years. It's a relief when he finally leaves the stage.

George's stomach is in knots at the possible downfall of his friend. Two more acts come on: a cheeky-chappy Cockney, who has moderate success, followed by a Geordie who stereotypes all Geordies for comedic effect. The MC returns 'on stage' and announces the interval.

Will is pacing around at the back of the room.

'Alright, mate?'

'Fine, G. Need to go over my material. I'll speak to you after.'

Dismissed, George returns to his seat for the second half of the show. The crowd's grown, with a handful of animated students chatting and gulping pints. George bites his nails, wondering how he'll look Will in the eye if he's crap?

The MC bounds on, snatching the mic. 'Okay, you lucky people, next on we have our favourite Sweaty Sock.'

Fucking Londoners and their rhyming slang.

'All the way from Scotland, to be with us tonight.' *Liar.* 'So, how about we start the applause from you, madam...' He points to a girl at the front. 'And go all the way around to you, sir. Let's give him a full-on, warm London welcome.'

Warm London welcome? The irony!

'For the sensational Will Devon.'

Will takes the mic from the MC and pauses. He looks confident. 'Hello, everyone. How are we?'

Will delves into his routine. George sits up as Will takes control of the room, pausing mid-sentence to take a sip of his pint. The audience loves him. Will laps it up, smiling and nodding, letting the laughter settle before starting a new joke. He is a fucking professional.

His gig comes to an end with a solid round of applause. George claps wildly, holding himself back from shouting 'That's my mate!' He ignores the MC on stage to go congratulate him.

'Well done. That was brilliant,' George gushes.

'It was alright?' Will asks, looking relieved.

'All fucking right? It was superb! You're a bloody natural,' George says, slapping him on the back.

He arrives at work in good spirits the next morning. Darren announces to the team with a sadistic smile that someone will be spending the day in the stockroom. George volunteers. Darren is disappointed to have a willing participant.

He puts on the radio and starts unpacking the boxes thinking about Will's performance. So cool. George has always fancied himself as a comedian.

'Hi, my name is G and I'm from a country that's so hard, it batters Mars bars.' A huge round of applause from his adoring audience. 'I've just come down from the Isle of Skye,' he sings, 'Donald, where's your trousers?'

The audience goes wild. He tips his head back laughing, nearly falling off the ladder.

'What the hell are you laughing at?' Darren barks.

'Erm, the radio.'

'Two boxes need to be emptied by home time, laughing boy,' Darren snarls.

George bites his tongue and tunes back into his audience. 'More, more!' He starts writing his award speech in his head.

George is dying for a beer. He buys a six-pack of Carlsberg on the way home and walks briskly, averting eye contact with the local psychos and criminals. He takes the stairs two at a time to his bedsit, hoping to avoid Kon, the resident psycho.

The beer tastes good, though his place looks worse than usual with dirty dishes and a pile of clothes on his bed. A large cockroach scuttles out from under the toaster. 'Fuck!' George yells. The insect moves at speed and disappears behind the fridge. He feels dirty and scummy. He wants to pack a bag and leave.

There's a knock at the door. He holds his breath; they'll go away. The banging increases in volume till he's forced to open it.

'Hi, George,' Anka says, smiling. 'I heard a scream, sounded like it came from here.'

'A scream? No. We're fresh out of screaming women I'm afraid.'

'You drinking beer?' Anka says, peering behind him hopefully.

How to get rid of her. 'No Kon tonight?'

'He's at the casino. I'm all alone,' she says, looking desperately sad.

He concedes and opens the door, inviting her in, handing her a beer.

'I could have sworn I heard a scream,' she says, a smile playing on her lips as she crosses her legs, skirt hitching up to reveal honey-coloured thighs. 'What have you been up to?'

'Not much.'

'I don't believe that. You seem like an interesting guy to me.'

George blushes slightly and straightens up. 'I did go see my mate do stand-up comedy last night.'

'Any good?'

'He was brilliant.'

'You would be a great comedian, George.'

'Well, erm…' *Take the plunge.* 'I'm thinking about it,' he confesses, waiting for her to laugh at him.

'That's exciting,' she claps. 'Tell me a joke.'

'Not had a chance to write any.'

'No time like the present. You write, I get the vodka, will help the creative process,' she says, her accent strong and determined. She throws him a pen before darting out the door.

At the sink, he rinses out two glasses. It feels good that Anka has faith in him. She's quite cute too.

She returns with a full bottle of vodka and a gossip magazine. 'What you doing just sitting there?' she says, hands on hips. 'Write. I'll pour. You write.'

Anka pours two glasses of vodka and settles back with her magazine.

What to write about? Work? No. Childhood? No. London? No… or maybe. Annoying people in London, the tubes, rush hour, the rudeness.

An hour passes, and the vodka works its magic as he scribbles furiously, trying to get it all down. Four pages later, he runs out of ideas and looks up to find Anka watching him.

'Okay, let's hear it,' she smiles encouragingly.

'What! Now?'

'Yes, now. Stand over there.'

He stumbles to his feet and steadies himself. The vodka and the expectant blue eyes of Anka give him confidence, though he still feels like a prat. Anka pretends to hold a mic to introduce him. 'Okay, let's welcome to the stage, the very funny, George.'

He clears his throat and struggles to read his own notes. 'Ladies and gentlemen, it's nice to see you. My name is George and I'm from Glasgow. Known for the worst diet in Europe, the

Proclaimers, and shit weather. It's great; you should go.' George waits.

Anka laughs, loud and heartily. She has a good laugh. He's delighted and ploughs on. 'You know, there is a fine line between telling a joke and being a joke. It's good for you to know that.'

Anka laughs again.

'You know, I love Londoners… when they're six feet under and I don't mean on the tube.'

Anka rolls about laughing. *Fuck, I'm really good. I knew I would be.* He goes through his material and Anka laughs in all the right places.

'That's it,' he says, sitting down.

'What you mean, that's it? It's brilliant. You're brilliant,' she chirps, pouring two large vodkas and raising her glass. 'To George, the best comedian in the world!'

He clinks the glass and swallows it back, elated. Anka straddles him and plants a long deep kiss on his mouth. George doesn't resist. The fear of Kon's wrath is replaced by hard vodka and a soft body.

Chapter 7

George arrives at work ten minutes late, head pounding, stomach churning. What if Kon finds out about him and Anka? He'll either kill him or make him homeless. Bloody vodka. Darren pounces the minute George walks in.

'What time do you call this?' Darren points to his watch.

'Ten past nine,' George growls, not in the mood for Darren's shit.

'And what time do you start?'

'Nine.'

'That's right. Come with me.'

The other staff edge closer, sensing a scene. Darren turns up the volume. 'You can't just walk in here anytime you like, enough is enough.'

'Fuck's sake Darren, I'm ten minutes late. There's no customers... what's the problem?'

'You're the problem. Follow me into my office,' Darren retorts, marching toward the stockroom. George stays put, smirking at the staff who pretend to be busy. Darren reappears, bristling. 'The office. Now,' he shouts.

'I'll tell you what, why don't you take your job and stick it up your arse?' George steps forward. 'You're a fucking twat and your head's the size of a football. If it were any bigger, you'd have to drag it along the ground.'

Darren stands, stunned, mouth open.

'Oh, and while we're at it, you shouldn't wear jeans cos you look shite in them. Arsehole!'

The staff smile and nod as George passes, head held high. Darren's face will be a memory he'll treasure forever.

Two hours later, sitting in McDonald's, George wonders if he's done the right thing. The elation fades. Rent? How's he going to pay it? An ad for a courier job catches his eye. He circles the number.

The phone box smells like piss, but he holds his breath and dials.

'Oh hello, I'm calling about the courier job. Is it still going?'

'It is. We need someone ASAP.'

'I'm free now for an interview, if you have time?'

'Okay, come. We're just off Oxford Street, before M&S, 164 Baker Street. Ask for Ron, that's me.'

A large sign proclaiming 'Stand and Deliver' stands out. The Adam and the Ants song plays in his head as he steps inside. Waiting in the rundown entrance is Ron, a burly man in his fifties, who introduces himself with a hearty handshake.

'George? I'm Ron Stone, not to be mistaken with Rhine Stone, the cowboy.' He leads him to a small office.

'What experience do you have with bikes and mopeds?'

'Not much, but I've been driving for five years.'

'You have a clean licence?'

'Yes. Passed first time.'

'What's your knowledge of London like?'

'Great,' George lies. 'I'm a comedian. I drive all over London to gigs.'

Ron looks impressed. 'You kidding me? A comedian? Tell me a joke.'

'Erm…' George squirms.

'I'm just kidding.' Ron laughs. 'Bet you get people saying that all the time, eh?'

'Just a bit,' George replies, relieved.

Ron hands him a key and helmet. 'Let's see what you can do.'

George follows Ron outside to a battered moped. He's never been on a bike, but how hard can it be? He sits, turns the key, and the engine roars to life.

'Take it around the block to get a feel for it.'

George revs the bike and jerks it forward, trying to control it. The bike lunges slightly, but he keeps steady pressure on the throttle. Traffic's light, so he takes his time, then revs it up on the way back, enjoying the speed before slowing down and entering the small car park.

'Not a bad little runner,' George says confidently.

'Okay,' Ron says. 'You can start Monday for a week's trial. Be here at nine.'

The days and weeks pass in a flash. Nerves begin to settle in as George prepares for his comedy debut. He paces the room, going over his lines. The material's solid, but the order keeps slipping away. Checking the time again, he mutters, 'Fuck, can't be late.' Stomach in knots, the day's been spent in the loo. He's determined not to use notes on stage—Will never does, and neither will he. A small list of bullet points sits in his back pocket, just in case.

After changing clothes twice, he settles on jeans and a shirt. Sweating profusely, he splashes water on his face. 'Come on, you can do this,' he mutters. His material is original, a cut above some of the crap he's heard. He drinks two swallows of beer, puts on his jacket and checks himself in the mirror. His black hair frames bright blue eyes, his best feature, even with a few laughter lines. His teeth are remarkably white.

'You're going to be fucking superb,' he says with conviction. Bring it on.

A hard knock at the door freezes him. The knocking turns to kicking at breakneck speed. He pounces to open it.

Anka stands in the doorway, hands on hips, dressed in a tight gold skirt and matching top, her navel exposing a silver belly-ring. Her heavy makeup frames the malice in her eyes. Her long red hair is unwashed and unruly.

'Well?'

'Well what?'

She slams the door, pushing past him. George can't believe her timing.

'Where the fuck were you last night?' Anka demands, voice shrill.

'I told you, I was staying at Will's.'

'And I told you, I'd tell Kon if you did.'

'And did you?'

'You wouldn't still be breathing if I had, mister.'

'Neither would you.'

'You know how much he loves me. I'm all he has. He'd never hurt his precious angel. You though? The pain-in-the-ass, late-paying tenant. I think he'd enjoy hurting you. Especially when I tell him about you stealing his mail. That'll really piss him off.'

George reaches for her hand. 'Come on now, Anka. You know I'm crazy about you. We've just got to wait a little longer.'

Her eyes widen in fury. 'A little longer,' she mimics, mocking his accent. 'It's been months. You said you were going places, that you'd take me with you, that I'd be rich and famous.'

Just months? Feels like years. Two months of puppy-like adoration followed by mood swings, demands, and threats. Exhausting. Why get involved? Ignoring the warning signs—the late-night screaming battles with Kon, the highs one minute, the violence the next. A clear sign of a nutcase.

George smiles, trying to calm the situation. 'Listen, tonight's the night. I've got a big show lined up. This is the beginning. This is it. This is what gets us out of here and onto bigger and better things.'

'Heard it all before. You're not going anywhere, you bloody loser. You take me away this Friday, or I'm telling Kon when he gets home.' She points at him. 'I fucking mean it this time,' she spits.

She picks up a mug and throws it at his head. It catches him above the eye, smashing on the floor. Blood trickles down as she darts out, singing, 'Friday, Quick-fuck. Last chance.'

George closes the door behind her, hearing her stomp back upstairs. He worked hard to stay calm, now he's a bloody, sweaty mess. A solution will have to be found, but for now, he must focus on the big picture: his comedy career.

He cleans up and heads to Highgate station. Will's already there, looking cool in Stan Smith trainers and an old-school Adidas cardi. Women are drawn to him—six-foot tall, blond, blue-eyed.

'Alright G. How you feeling?'

'Good,' George replies, though butterflies swarm his stomach.

Will rants about work as they walk down the street. George tunes him out, finally understanding Will's silence before gigs.

'Do you know what I mean, G?'

Please shut the fuck up, Will. 'Sorry mate, what did you say? I was just thinking about my material.'

'Shit, sorry G. I'm babbling like an eejit. I think I'm more nervous than I was on my first gig.'

'That's helpful.'

'Shit, ignore me. Honestly, you'll be brilliant.'

George runs through his lines in his head. What if the audience hates him? *They won't.* What if there's a heckler? He'll annihilate them. *Focus.* They finally reach the venue.

'That's Dave May, the compere,' Will says, pointing to a bald guy.

George introduces himself. Dave nods, pointing to a light above the bar. 'When the red light comes on, that's your five minutes. Finish your set and get off. You're on second.'

Later would be better—the audience isn't drunk enough early on. George heads to the toilet, splashing his face. Time to shine.

He runs through his material again and joins Will at the bar. 'Hope more people turn up. I don't fancy playing to ten people.'

'When you start doing shows at the Edinburgh festival, audiences can be small. This is good practice.'

His own Edinburgh show. Yes! He gulps his beer, scanning the room. It's seen better days. No stage, just a space at the front with a mic stand.

The MC informs them they're waiting for a stag do.

George bristles at the delay and knocks back his pint.

'Go easy, G. You don't want to be hammered,' Will warns. 'Got any blokey material for the stag do?'

'Like what?'

'I don't know, footy, rugby, nagging girlfriends?'

'None of that. Fuck it. I'll do my stuff, and they'll enjoy it.'

Will slaps him on the back. 'That's the spirit.'

George relaxes after another pint. The audience doesn't seem bothered by the delay. Finally, the stag party arrives—loud and drunk. George takes a deep breath, trying to steady himself.

'Piece of advice,' Will murmurs. 'Listen in, find out what they're talking about. Might be some material there.'

George inches closer, taking out a scrap of paper. He scribbles notes as he listens.

Dave May greets the stags like a Magaluf holiday rep, high-fiving and joking. They're mostly from Essex.

'Buckle up. We're ready to start,' Dave tells George.

The stag party shuffles to the front row. The spotlight hits the stage. The music stops. George holds his breath.

He wipes a hand over his face. *Why am I doing this?* The audience quiets.

Dave introduces the first act, a young comedian who manages to connect with the stags right away and keeps them laughing throughout his set. Bastard.

George waits for his name to be called, his nerves building. The Big Funny judge sits in the front row. Sweat trickles down his forehead as he steps closer to the stage.

Focus. You can do this.

Will catches his eye and gives him a thumbs up. George breathes deeply.

'Please welcome, for his first-time gig, George Mailer.'

He steps into the spotlight. First ever gig. Prick.

'Hello folks, how we doing?'

A single response from the back, 'Good thanks.'

'For the record, this is my first London gig, not my first ever gig. Londoners! Think they're the centre of the world. Don't get me wrong, I do like a Londoner. Preferably when they're six feet under, and I don't mean on the tube.'

The Essex crowd laughs. That's all he needs. They're the loudest.

'Essex lads, I hear someone pissed himself last night.'

They laugh hard, pointing to the culprit, who looks pleased with himself.

'Now, ladies and gents, that's not the worst of it! A dorm full of bunk beds. Guess who was sleeping on top?' He pauses.

'He pissed all over his mate's face. Taking one for the team to a whole new level.'

The group roars with laughter. George has them in the palm of his hands.

'I bet you woke up with a hangover this morning.' They nod in unison. 'My hangovers get worse every year. Never got hangovers in my teens… but the comedowns were vicious.'

He continues, getting a few laughs. When the exit light comes on, he wraps it up.

'I've been George Mailer, and you've been great. Thanks very much.'

The audience claps. A brilliant debut. He stands on stage, soaking in the applause until Dave May pries the mic from his hand.

Will raises his glass. 'Welcome to the club, G. Amazing!'

The stag party leader, Liam, pats him on the back. 'Mate, when you mentioned Sudsy pissing himself—fucking hilarious.'

George waits for more handshakes and booking offers, but they don't come. People are too intimidated to approach him.

Will nods toward James Hay, knee-deep in comedians. 'Go introduce yourself.'

'Nah. I'll meet him at The Big Funny competition.'

'What? You're going to do The Big Funny? Heats start in a month, G.'

'I'll be ready. Don't worry about that… it's in the bag.'

He arrives home just before midnight to find a note pinned to the door: *TICK TOK, TICK TOCK...*

Chapter 8

Loud banging startles George awake. Anka is stamping on the floor above his head, in a full-throttle hissy fit. The bare lightbulb sways, its weak light flickering. She's desperate for a fight.

Teeth clenched, George pulls a pillow over his head. A moment of peace. He needs this—needs to bask in his comedy glory, uninterrupted. If she tells Kon, it won't be just a kicking. Kon's already escaped two assault charges, and an attempted murder charge this year. Anka has him cornered, and his promises no longer carry weight. Swallowing a sleeping pill, George chases it with a stale can of Coke, shuts his eyes tight, and waits for silence.

The fading afternoon light signals his return to consciousness—a slight improvement. He grabs a lager from the fridge and flicks on the TV.

Immediately, the banging resumes. Fuck. The hallway door slams open. Anka's high-pitched voice fills the space. 'Hey, Quick-fuck, get out here,' she screams, pounding on the door.

Reluctantly, George slides out of bed and opens the door.

'Time's up, mister. I've got a plane ticket out of here. I'm telling Kon everything. I'll call him from the airport,' she spits. 'I've left him photos too. Don't want anything left to the imagination, do we now, Quick-fuck?' She smiles sweetly.

George snaps and pounces, clamping his hand over her mouth, and shoving her onto the bed. '*Enough!*' he screams.

Her mouth drops open in shock.

'This is over. Your threats end here. You'll get on that plane, and I'll never hear from you again. Understand?'

Anka nods, her defiance shattered, eyes now filled with fear. A cold rush runs through George. The surge of power is intoxicating. A flashback hits him so vividly that he can almost smell the damp and decay from that disgusting house. His fingers brush the skin around his wrists, recalling the cold, rough texture of the cuffs, the tightness around his wrists, and Sasia's evil smile. This time, he's the one in control.

He leans in, voice low, a whisper full of venom. 'If you tell Kon anything, I'll find you, Anka. And you'll regret it.'

He removes his hand from her mouth and lifts his weight off her. She stands, no longer smiling, and stumbles toward the door. Then she turns, her face twisted with rage.

'Your jokes aren't funny, and neither are you, bastard. Kon's gonna kill you,' she spits.

She pulls the door open, and dashes into the hallway. Fuck. He rushes after her, grabbing her by the neck and yanking her back inside. Smothering her screams with his hand, he kicks the door shut and forces her to the ground. His heart races with adrenaline as he straddles her, pinning her arms to the floor. Her body bucks beneath him, but her thin frame offers no real resistance.

The fear in her eyes evaporates, replaced by cold, steely resolve. Was she pretending before? Hard to say, but now there's no mistaking her intent. She's going to tell Kon. She's going to get him killed. *Fuck.*

Energy surges in a frenzy as he wraps his hands around her throat. Her body squirms violently, but he tightens his grip. Her eyes burn with hate, malice—he's seen that look before. A fresh wave of rage crashes through him.

Her mouth opens and closes, gasping for air. He controls her breath, squeezing tighter. She claws at his hands, but nothing gets through. Her body goes limp beneath him. He checks for a pulse—nothing.

Why couldn't she have just left quietly? *Shit!* He paces the room, thinking frantically. He can't go to prison. They'll have a field day with a pretty boy like him.

Think, think. Kon's back tomorrow. Yes, that's it—Kon! No time to waste.

George inches the door open, listening for movement. The old man at the end of the hallway is as deaf as a corpse. He's relieved to find Anka's door propped open with an ancient Yellow Pages.

Inside, an empty vodka bottle and beer cans litter the table. Mindful of fingerprints, he grabs a pair of bright yellow marigolds from the kitchen and slides them on. He takes the vodka bottle and smashes it against the wall. Glass sprays across the floor. He flips the coffee table, throws cushions to the ground, and dumps the heavy ashtray from the counter, spilling ash and cigarette butts across the light carpet.

Perfect. It looks like an almighty bust-up.

In the silence of the hallway, George dashes back to his room, dragging Anka's body across the floor. Struggling up the stairs, her weight grows heavier in death. Dropping her onto the couch, George rummages through Kon's wardrobe for a tie. The fabric slips around Anka's neck, pulled tight. A crime of passion. That fits Kon's personality.

God, the look in her eyes before she went limp. Fear. Real fear. The sensation surges through him. No one fucks with George Mailer.

Grabbing a set of keys from a tacky cuckoo clock, he pockets them.

In his room, he strips off, tossing his clothes and the marigolds into a bin liner. He washes himself thoroughly at the sink.

Sitting on the bed, brow furrowed in concentration, George weighs his next move. *Shit, an alibi.* He needs one, fast. Rushing to get dressed, he jogs downstairs to the phone booth, praying Will picks up.

'Alright, Will? I'm having a drink with a mate, not far from your place. Might swing by,' he says, forcing casualness into his tone.

'Cool. Just got in. Come round.'

George races back to his room, pulls on a jacket, and sprints down Garrett Lane. The station clock reads 7:40 p.m. He keeps his head down, avoiding eye contact on the train. Not hard in London.

He exits Balham station just after eight, running through the park and up the long road to Will's house. He pauses to catch his breath before ringing the bell.

Will greets him with a beer in hand. 'Alright, mate. How you doing?' he says, ushering George inside.

'Top of the world.'

Will hands him a can of lager. 'Guess who got you a gig at the Comedy Café next Friday?' He beams with excitement.

'The Comedy Café? Never heard of it,' George replies, disappointment creeping in. 'Another open mic night?'

'Seriously, mate, it's your second gig,' Will bristles. 'Open mics are how you get experience.'

George wants bigger clubs, bigger laughs. 'Yeah, sorry… I need to start somewhere,' he says, not believing it. 'Alright if I crash here tonight?'

'No probs. Nick's away. Sleep in his room.'

'Cool. Any tequila left? I feel like celebrating.'

'Coming up,' Will says, getting to his feet.

George snatches the clock from the bookcase, moving it back an hour to seven, and slumps heavily on the sofa, letting out a long, deep sigh. Happy days.

Chapter 9

George wakes up in the mid-afternoon to an empty house. Nice of Will to let him sleep in while he's at work. He wonders if Anka's been found yet. Searching for any feelings of guilt, he finds none. Instead, he feels empowered. He had a problem, and he dealt with it.

He smiles at his reflection in the bathroom. 'George Mailer. I know him. Doesn't take shit from anybody.' Faking modesty, he holds his hands up. 'What can I say? I just don't take shit!'

Laughter bursts from him as he steps into the shower, helping himself to the expensive products while singing and soaping up. Dressed and feeling invincible, almost reborn, he whistles a forgotten song on his way to the station. The streets are quiet, save for a young mum and her baby. A small brown teddy falls from the pram. The mum, engrossed in her phone, keeps walking. George picks it up and chases after her.

'Hi there,' he smiles, waving at the baby. 'I think you've lost a little friend.'

'Thanks,' the mother says, her smile brief, returning to her conversation.

George hands the teddy back, ruffling the baby's hair. 'No problem.'

He grabs a newspaper from the newsstand at the station. Skimming the pages on the tube, he finds nothing about Anka.

Arriving on Garrett Lane, he walks home, head held high. The police car parked outside his building stops him in his tracks.

Breathe. Look confident. He has a cast-iron alibi.

Yellow tape across the front door signals a crime scene. A young policeman stands by it.

'What's happened?' George asks, his brow furrowed in confusion.

The policeman gives him a long look before the front door opens, and a tall man with thick eyebrows and greying hair steps outside.

'Can I help you, sir?' he asks.

'I live here. What's going on?'

'I'm Detective Inspector Tanner.' The man pulls out a pad and scribbles. 'Can I have your name?'

'George Mailer. I live in number two, first floor.'

Tanner writes it down. 'Right, can you accompany me to the station?'

'To the station? Why?' George's unease spikes.

'We can talk there, if you don't mind.' Tanner nods toward the parked police car.

'Erm... well... I've got things to do,' George stammers, panic creeping in.

Tanner opens the back door of the car. 'Won't take too much of your time, Mr. Mailer.'

'Eh, anything I can do to help,' George says, swallowing hard. Cast-iron alibi.

The detective studies him in the rearview mirror as the car moves. George maintains a nonchalant face. At the station, a man with tiny eyes and a receding hairline leads George into a small interview room, then silently sits across from him. Tanner joins, introducing his colleague, DC Stone.

'Where were you between 7 p.m. and midnight last night?' Tanner asks.

'I was at my friend Will's in Balham. Just got back.'

'Can your friend confirm that?'

'Yeah.'

'What time did you arrive?'

'Around seven.'

'Around seven?'

George wonders if the room echoes. 'Maybe just before.'

'Right. Just a casual visit?'

'Yeah. No particular reason, well…' George hesitates.

'Mr. Mailer, this is a serious investigation. If you have something to say, spit it out.'

George rubs his forehead, pretending internal struggle. 'They were fighting upstairs. I just needed a break.'

'Who was fighting?'

'My landlord, Konstantinous Demetri, or Kon, as he's known, and his girlfriend, Anka. I got home at six, heard them going at it, so I went back out.'

'They fight often?'

'It's like Bosnia up there. Screaming, smashing things.'

'Why didn't you call the police?'

'Would've made it worse. Kon's violent. I try to stay out of it.'

'How do you know he's violent?'

'I've seen her with black eyes, bruises.'

'You a friend of Anka's?'

'No. I see her in the hall sometimes, but we don't speak.'

'You don't speak?' he repeats.

'No. She doesn't talk to anyone. Every time I see her, she looks... fragile. Petrified.' George glances from one policeman to the other. 'Can you please tell me what this is about?'

'Anka was found dead this morning.'

'Oh my God,' George whispers, shaking his head. 'How did she die?'

'We don't know yet.'

'Did Kon kill her?' he asks, forcing a shaky voice.

'We're following several lines of enquiry, including speaking to Mr. Demetri.'

'It's terrible, really terrible. Erm... if you need my mate's number, I can give it to you?'

'That's all for now. We'll contact you if we need anything else.'

George stands to leave.

'One more thing—has Anka ever been in your room?'

Careful.

'Not while I've lived there. She cleans when tenants move out, so probably.'

Tanner glances at Stone, his face unreadable. 'The top flat's cordoned off, but you can enter your room now.'

At reception, Tanner takes Will's number and hands George a business card. 'If you think of anything else, give us a call.'

George holds eye contact and shakes his hand firmly.

The sun hits him as he steps outside the station. He takes a moment to feel the heat on his face before replaying the interview in his head. He did well. Other tenants will corroborate the fighting, unless they're scared.

At home, George calls Will. It rings out. *Please be home.* Another minute passes before he picks up.

'Hello, Will?' George asks, anxiety creeping in.

'Hey, G. Was out in the garden. You alright?'

'Not really. Someone's been murdered in my building.'

'No fucking way. What happened?'

'Don't know. The landlord and his girlfriend always fight.'

'You said.'

'She's dead now.'

'Fuck's sake, man. That's unbelievable. Did he do it?'

'They think so. They're holding him for questioning. They took me in too.'

'You're kidding?'

'No, just routine. Happened last night while I was at yours. Glad I wasn't home alone; you know what coppers are like.'

'I'll tell them you were here. No problem.'

'I got to yours just before seven. I gave them your number.'

'Right, just before seven. That's fine. You want to stay here tonight?'

'They've got him in for questioning. I'll be fine.'

'They might let him go.'

'I'll ring the cops and ask. I'll come over if he's out. Thanks for the offer.'

'Don't be daft.'

'Cheers, mate.'

George hangs up the phone. Surely they won't let Kon out. He must be the prime suspect after George's interview. *Better safe than sorry.* He takes out the card and calls the police station.

'Hello, this is George Mailer from 108 Garrett Lane. There was a murder, and you have my landlord in for questioning. I live in the building, and I was wondering if he's going to be released tonight. Just want to make sure I'm not in any danger.'

'I can't give you that information, sir.'

'I came to the station today... voluntarily. Giving up my valuable time to help your investigation, and you can't tell me if I might be murdered in my bed tonight?'

The policeman sighs. 'Hold on.'

A few minutes later, the phone crackles back to life. 'Konstantinous Demetri will be held overnight for questioning. It's unlikely he'll be released before court the day after tomorrow.'

'Right. Thanks for your help.' *Twat.*

George grabs a piece of paper and a 10p coin, making one last call to the Comedy Café to secure his next gig.

Back in his room, he turns on the TV and cracks open a beer. Thoughts swirl through the last 24 hours. Something niggles at him. Unanswered questions. Does Kon know about him and Anka? Will he suspect I've set him up? Will he come after me when released? Paranoia creeps in. His mind drifts back to last night, to the final moments of Anka's life. Those eyes. The fear. The power. Will that power ever return?

Chapter 10

The phone rings in the hallway. George curses, gets up and goes downstairs to answer it, knowing that none of the other lazy bastard tenants will bother.

‘George Mailer?’

‘Yes.’

‘It’s DI Tanner here. I understand you called the station last night. We wanted to let you know we’ve charged Mr Demetri with Anka’s murder… though we will need your help to secure a conviction. We need your statement in court, and it’s likely we’ll have to call you as a witness for the prosecution.’

‘What if he gets off with it? He’ll come after me.’

‘Mr Demetri will be going straight to jail, I suspect. He’s got no alibi, and one of the other tenants confirmed the fighting. The problem is they aren’t willing to testify. It would help significantly if you did. Will you testify?’

George feels like playing hard to get. ‘It’s a lot to ask, detective. He’s a complete psycho. The kind of guy who would hold a grudge and they won’t put him away forever.’

‘Can I just remind you, Mr Mailer, that a young lady’s life has been taken? A young lady in her prime.’

Oh, she was in her prime alright! George feels himself getting excited, thinking about it.

‘Look, Mr Demetri is going to be locked up for a very long time, 15 years minimum.’

‘OK, DI Tanner, you’re right. I have a moral responsibility to put this man behind bars. I will testify.’

‘Great. A date will be set at the Magistrates’ Court tomorrow for the Crown Court. Until then, we expect he’ll be held in remand. You’ll receive a witness summons with the date soon after the hearing.’

Will is unusually flustered when George arrives with a six-pack of beer tucked under his arm.

In the kitchen, a recipe book is propped up against the toaster next to an explosion of ingredients. Will dabs at a large red stain on the front of his t-shirt.

'You don't have to go to this much effort on my behalf,' George says. 'You know a frozen pizza works for me... preferably cooked but you know.'

'It's a special night, G. I've a surprise for you later.' Will looks nervous.

'What kind of surprise?'

'You'll see. Now, give me one of those beers and finish chopping that onion.'

George has rarely seen his friend this excited. Maybe they've landed a big gig, or a TV appearance!

His stinging eyes stream as he chops the onion. 'The police called me today and asked me if I'll testify against Kon. I'm going to do it.'

Will manically beats eggs in a bowl. 'You sure? From what you've said, he sounds like a mad bastard. You don't want to be looking over your shoulder the rest of your life?'

'I know, but I need to do what's right.'

'You're a braver man than me.'

'Just doing what any decent guy would do. I thought spag Bol was the height of your culinary skills. You're really going for it tonight.'

Will takes a deep slug of his beer and gives George a look he can't make out. The doorbell rings.

'You expecting someone?'

Will looks uncharacteristically coy and checks himself quickly in the mirror. 'Let me get it.'

The hallway is filled with an excitable, high-pitched voice. George pops his head round the door. Will is snogging a tall, dark-haired woman. *What the fuck?* George coughs lightly. Will turns round, beaming, radiating happiness.

'George, this is Jemma. Jemma, this is George.'

On the first day of autumn, George exits the shop with his new purchase, pulling his coat tighter as he squeezes through the crowds. The streetlights cast a glow over Oxford Street as he inspects his new phone, when suddenly, two youths on skateboards appear out of nowhere. One of them knocks the phone from his hand, sending it splashing into a puddle.

'Little bastards,' he yells. A few shoppers pause to watch the commotion, though most keep their eyes ahead and move on. The smallest skater boy turns and gives him the finger before continuing to weave his way through the crowds. George picks up the phone from the puddle and finds the screen is cracked. Shit. He runs back to the store but finds it closed. He taps on the window to grab the attention of the sales assistant who served him. The spotted teenager gesticulates towards the clock and draws a finger across his throat in an overly dramatic fashion.

A woman with a large pram appears from nowhere and rams it into the side of his leg. George winces but utters a 'sorry' before he can stop himself. The woman fixes him with a hard stare and walks on. How fucking dare she? She barges through the throng of shoppers, completely oblivious to others, striding confidently in her bright red coat with the matching pram.

She pauses to buy a *Big Issue* from a bearded vendor, hands over the money and is about to put the purse back in her bag when the two skater boys whiz by, knocking her into the vendor's arms.

The woman springs back to an upright position. 'Come back here!' she demands in a public-school accent.

The skater boys ignore her. She curses, takes her *Big Issue* and marches down the street. Her purse falls out of her unzipped bag. George moves quickly to pick it up. So does the vendor.

'You giving that back?' he asks, in a gruff northern accent, pointing at the purse.

'Of course, I am,' George says, indignantly.

'You better hurry then or you'll lose her,' the vendor states, craning his neck in her direction.

'Lose her? She's dressed like a double-decker bus, mate. I'll catch her up. I'll take a *Big Issue* off you.'

The bearded man looks at him suspiciously but hands him a copy. 'One pound eighty,' he grumbles, hand out.

George hands over the money.

'Catch her up then, mate,' he goads, layering heavy sarcasm onto the word 'mate.'

George spots her farther up ahead and takes off at a run. When he reaches the side road, he turns sharply left, ignoring the curses and shouted obscenities from the *Big Issue* guy as he ducks into a shop doorway and checks the purse. One crispy fifty-pound note. Nice. He pockets it and tosses the purse into the nearest bin. Checking his watch, he swears under his breath. Fuck. He takes off again, dodging puddles to keep his new trainers intact.

Two heavy doormen block the entrance of Othello's wine bar. George tries to get past them, but the biggest one steps into his space. 'Can I help you?' he asks, feigning a smile that doesn't mask the malice.

'I'm meeting an associate here at 8:00 p.m. I'm running late. Is there a problem?' George replies, returning his fake smile.

'An associate, eh?' The doorman looks him up and down and sneers. 'We have a clear door policy—no trainers.'

'What? No sneakers. That's mental.'

'We have standards. You won't get in here wearing *sneakers*,' he sneers.

A well-dressed couple reach the doorway and shake out their umbrellas. The doorman greets them and holds open the door. They glide past, all smiles.

'No shoes. No entry,' he states, turning to mutter to his colleague.

'Look, I really need to speak to the person I'm meeting. Could I at least pop in and let him know I'm here?'

'Nope.'

'Can you give him a message from me? His name is Steven Trent. He has his own table here.'

'We know Stevie T.'

George grabs a piece of paper from his pocket and scribbles a short note with his telephone number and gives it to the doorman. 'He's expecting me. Can you make sure he gets this?'

The doorman takes the note. 'We'll pass it on. Good evening.'

Beaten, he walks back onto the street. *Bastards.*

He heads towards the Comedy Café, hoping to rescue the night by picking up a gig. He needs more gigs before the Big Funny competition. Success is just around the corner! He puts his collar up and strides through the wet streets.

It pisses him off having to pay to get into the Comedy Café. He's not gigging tonight, but still, it's insulting. The club is warm and half full, and the MC is doing his best to build rapport with the small audience. He buys a drink and makes his way over to a few comedians huddled at the back of the room at their assigned table.

'Alright,' George says, holding his pint up in a cheers gesture. Two of the comedians nod indifferently then turn their attention back to the stage.

Will emerges from the backstage area. 'Hey G, how you doing? Did you manage to ambush Trent?'

'No, I couldn't get in… fuckers… because I had sneakers on. Fucking bouncers are the biggest pricks in the world.'

'Second only to chefs.'

'Nope. Bouncers win every time. I'll try and contact Trent tomorrow. Talking about pricks, I've got the court hearing for my psycho landlord tomorrow.'

'You want me to come with you, for support?'

'I'll be fine.' George eyes up the other comedians. 'Any no-shows tonight?'

'No, everyone's here I think, though Big Paddy has a right hangover. You might get lucky.'

George finds Big Paddy in the gents, bent over the toilet pan, vomiting and hugging the bowl for dear life. *Opportunity knocks.* He dashes to the bar for a double rum and coke and a double whiskey and tips them in the same glass.

'Here Paddy. Drink this, mate. Hair of the dog, it's the way forward,' he says, patting Paddy on the back.

Paddy swallows the drink in one go. George gives him an encouraging thumbs up before leaving him to it. The MC works the audience, asking questions, fishing for laughs. At the comedians' table, George excitedly tells Will about his new material. The MC clears his throat and scowls in his direction. George lowers his voice as the compère introduces the first act. A man in his early twenties takes the stage and confidently works through his set. The audience sporadically rewards the young comedian with half-hearted titters. No sign of Paddy. George looks at his lines—they're brilliant. He's going to knock it out of the park. He briefly considers writing for bigger comedians in the future, but this material—these absolute gems—need his delivery.

Big Paddy appears at the table considerably perked up. 'What's your name?' he asks, slapping George on the back. 'You're a lifesaver. Feel much better. I owe you.'

'No problem,' George mumbles, looking around the room. *Now let's wait for the crash and burn.*

He spots the promoter, Susanna, sitting at the back and makes his way over.

'Hi Susanna,' he beams, slipping in the seat beside her. 'You know I'm reluctant to tell you… but I feel it's my duty as a performer. I just found Big Paddy cuddling the toilet pan, vomiting. I'd be happy to step in if you need me.'

Susanna eyes him with a bemused smile. 'That's kind of you, George.'

'Can I get you a drink?'

'I'll have a large chardonnay please, and if Big Paddy does keel over, you'll be first on the list.'

George delivers the overpriced drink with a flourish and goes back to the comedians' table. One shit comedian after the other takes the stage. This audience needs him. The final act of the first half receives a lukewarm response. George scans the venue for Paddy and finds him completely spark out, snuggled into a ball in a toilet cubicle. He steps over him, fishes his material from his hand and reads. What a fucking amateur. He rips it into tiny bits, flushes it down the toilet and starts rehearsing his lines.

Satisfied, he goes back to watch the show with a mixture of fear and excitement. He won't tell Susanna till after the interval. It will be too late for anyone else to step in, and he'll be the knight in shining armour who saves the day. Timing, it's all about the timing.

George makes his way over to Susanna. This is it, and I'm ready. There's a commotion at the back of the room, and a few audience members turn to look toward the entrance. A stocky man sitting at the front does a comical double take and nudges his friend. Whispering excitedly, he points. George follows their gaze. Steve Jenkins breezes in, larger than life, leaning in the doorway. A few comedians promptly make their way over to shake his hand. He smiles and waves at the comedians' table, bestowing fake humility and grace. Susanna springs out of her seat, looking as if Father Christmas has come early. Is this going to jeopardise his gig? George creeps toward the entrance to listen in.

'Just down to try out some new material,' Jenkins chirps, running his fingers through his hair.

Susanna assures him of as much stage time as he wants then scurries over to the bar to buy him a drink. George follows her.

'So, Susanna am I still ok to do a spot? Paddy's gone.'

She looks over towards Jenkins. 'Sorry, it doesn't look as if we're going to have time to put you on tonight, John.' She picks up the drinks and joins Jenkins.

John, who the fuck is John? 'It's actually George, not John,' he says to no one. He's seething. Nearly five fucking quid for a chardonnay! Jenkins is a bloody prick. His new material will be shit.

Jenkins sits at the table flirting with Susanna for the remainder of the show, completely ignoring the other performances. The MC comes on stage looking panto-excited. 'We have a huge treat for you tonight folks.' He pauses for effect then introduces Steve Jenkins. Jenkins rises to his feet and swaggers to the stage.

George glares at him as he swooshes by to a huge round of applause. Since appearing on *Whose Line Is It Anyway*, Jenkins' profile has rocketed on the London circuit. He's super confident, striding around the stage with the air of a man who has conquered the world. It was only a bloody TV appearance, hardly international success!

Jenkins delivers one joke after the other to an appreciative audience. Furious, George stuffs his material in his pocket. Enough. He moves to the front of the room to say bye to Will. Jemma appears from nowhere and plants a kiss on Will's lips. Will lights up like a Christmas tree.

'Sorry I'm late, love. Work's hectic. Have I missed your gig?'

'I'm afraid so. Don't worry about it,' Will smiles, looking into her eyes.

George takes a closer look at her. She's average height, though not average in looks; she's a knockout with big brown eyes and full luscious lips.

'Hi, George,' Jemma chirps.

'I'm just leaving. Sorry, Jemma, work in the morning.'

'Stay for a drink please. Would be nice to get to know you a little. Such a shame you had to rush off the other night. Will's toad in the hole was interesting,' Jemma says, mock grimacing.

Will gives him a pleading look and George relents. Jenkins finishes his set to a loud round of applause. Will goes to the bar.

'So, George, what do you do?' Jemma asks.

'I'm a comedian. Did Will not say?'

'Yes, he mentioned you did a few gigs.'

'More than a few,' George snorts.

'I thought stand up wasn't well paid.'

'It's not at first,' George stammers, wondering where this line of questioning is going.

'How do you get by then?' she asks, looking at him intensely.

'I work part time as a motorbike courier,' George retorts.

'Oh really! Who for?'

'Just a little firm at the back of Oxford Street,' George responds shortly. Jeez, what's with the third degree?

'Called?' she presses.

'Stand and Deliver.'

'Good to know. We use couriers all the time. I'll be sure to keep you in mind.'

Will hands them a drink. 'Is she badgering you, George? Journalists! Trait of the job I'm afraid. She asked me a hundred questions the night we met.'

George manages a tight smile.

'I just want to know everything about your best friend,' she says, kissing Will on the cheek.

'Isn't she great?' Will beams, kissing her hand.

'Yeah, she's great.' *Really fucking great.*

George knocks back his drink, makes his excuses, and leaves the club.

There's a light drizzle on Oxford Street. He zips up and heads to the tube station. The tube is packed with people working hard to avoid eye contact with one another.

He enjoys people-watching on the tube. He takes out his pad and looks around for potential sources of material. It's better when there's a group of friends. He likes to listen in on their conversations. And it's especially entertaining when drunk tourists attempt to strike up a conversation with London's unfriendly inhabitants. The girl facing him is texting incessantly on her phone. Her facial expressions suggest a romantic exchange as she smiles smugly then looks up dreamily, looking into the middle distance, her face beaming. George would love to be on the other end of the text and reply 'Look I've had my fun with you. I'm bored now so moving on to your friend Stacy who seems up for it. Bye, bye.' Would she cry? Or shout and swear? Before he can work it out, the girl gets up and moves towards the train door.

He puts his notepad in his bag and gets up, too. Standing behind her, he's close enough to smell the cheap perfume she's generously splashed on. The tube doors spring open. They're the only ones to exit. She takes her ticket from her bag and climbs the escalator in front of him. At the turnstile, she slows and puts the ticket in the machine. He speeds up to exit directly behind her. The station is quiet and deserted. As she reaches the top of the stairs, a teenager in a bright pink jogging suit screams, 'Shut up!' and runs toward her, hugging her tightly and dragging her over to join a scruffy group of kids hanging around the entrance. Tooting. Possibly the worst place in London.

Chapter 11

George goes over his statement in his head on the train journey, practising facial expressions and postures for the jury. He's never been to court before—it's quite exciting!

DI Tanner stands at the court entrance puffing a fag.

'There you are!' he grumbles, looking at his watch, although George is ten minutes early. 'Come. I need you to meet the prosecutor, Mr Farrell.'

Brief introductions are made, and George and Mr Farrell sit on a bench in the large hallway going over his statement. Mr Farrell asks him questions that the defence might ask. There's nothing too tricky. He's confident he'll be a credible witness.

'Now, Mr Mailer, there's a fifty-fifty chance that you'll be asked to take the stand. Do you understand that?'

I'm not flipping thick, you patronising wanker. 'I do,' he says, nodding and trying out his earnest, frightened look.

'You've nothing to worry about, George.' *Guess it worked.* 'This man is definitely going to jail.'

'Right,' George says softly, biting a nail.

'The case starts soon. If you're called, it'll be in the next hour or so. Just relax and remember to only answer the question you're asked.'

'Okay.' *I know that! Everyone knows that!*

An hour later, George is still waiting outside the courtroom. He walks up and down the dull corridors with the shiny floors.

A young policeman appears. 'You've been called. Are you ready?'

I was born ready. 'I think so.'

As he enters the courtroom, all eyes are on him. The attention feels great. Journalists are clustered together, notepads ready. He's disappointed the court is half-empty; he'd prefer a bigger audience. He pictures himself performing his set as a warm-up and fights off a smile. He takes the witness stand, catching a glimpse of Kon despite trying to avoid eye contact. He feels Kon's hostile glare, weighted with menace, directed his way. Kon is suited and booted, staring right at him. What was Kon's nickname for him? Anka liked to call him it, too. He taps his chin... The ferret, the bloody ferret. Let's see what this little ferret can do now.

Mr Farrell stands at the side of the witness box and swears George in. The judge nods to proceed.

'What is your name?'

'George Mailer.'

'And where do you live?'

'108 Garrett Lane, Tooting, South London.'

'What is your relation to the defendant, Konstantinous Demetri?'

'He's my landlord,' George states solemnly.

'On July 25th, can I ask where you were?'

'I was at work during the day and got home at 6:00 p.m.'

'And what happened then?'

'I went to my bedsit. I could hear an argument going on upstairs.'

'Did you recognise the voices?'

'Yes. It was my landlord, Konstantinous Demetri, and his girlfriend, Anka Gabor.'

'What happened then?'

'I heard things smashing and voices getting louder and louder.' George grimaces for the audience. 'It was out of control.'

'What did you do then?'

'I couldn't bear it anymore, so I went to stay at a friend's.'

'Was this the first time you heard arguing?'

'No.'

'How often would arguments occur?'

'At least once a week, sometimes more.'

'Did you have any reason to believe that there was any physical violence between Mr Demetri and Miss Gabor?'

George doesn't hesitate. 'She often had bruises and sometimes she had a black eye too.'

'Thank you,' Mr Farrell concludes, taking his seat.

The defence lawyer stands, a tall man with a lazy eye and an expansive belly, fixing George with a look of disdain. He nods at the judge and turns back to George. 'My name is Mr Driscoll. Can I ask you if you ever actually saw Mr Demetri hit Miss Gabor?' He looks confident.

Let's do this right, for all the ferrets out there. George pauses, letting the anticipation build. 'Yes, I did.'

Mr Driscoll looks taken aback and repeats the question. 'You saw Mr Demetri hit Anka?'

'Yes.'

'When did this happen?'

'About a week before her murder. I heard commotion in the hall. I was frightened but I edged open my door and… and… I saw Kon sitting on top of Anka. Her arms were pinned to the ground.' George tries for tears; he gulps and steadies himself. 'He had his hands around her neck.'

George covers his eyes with his hands, bobbing his shoulders up and down for good measure. He's trying desperately for tears, but they're not coming. A vision of his own hands tightening around Anka's throat flashes in front of him. A bolt of arousal and power floods through him.

'And what did you do, Mr Mailer, while you allegedly watched a woman practically being strangled?'

George sobers and digs deep. The tears come, trickling down his face. 'Nothing. I did nothing. I was a coward,' George cries. 'There's no excuse. I'll never forgive myself for not helping her to get away from that monster.' For the first time, he looks directly at Kon.

'You fucking lying bastard,' Kon bellows, bolting to his feet, spit flying from his mouth.

Two security guards jump to action. Kon struggles wildly in their grip, shouting 'You lying bastard. I'll get you. I swear I will!'

'Mr Demetri, control yourself or you'll be removed from this court!' the judge shouts.

Kon shrugs the guards off him, glares in George's direction and slowly sits back down.

'Mr Mailer, you may step down,' the judge concludes.

George allows himself a grin as he leaves court. He was brilliant, there's no other word for it—brilliant. And the Oscar nomination goes to... drum roll... George Mailer—huge round of applause!

DI Tanner greets him with a pat on the back and ushers him to the nearest bench.

'Will he be found guilty?'

'It looks likely. Once the jury have deliberated, he'll be brought back for sentencing. Thanks, Mr Mailer.'

'I just did what I had to do,' George shrugs. 'Erm... I have a question, when Kon is locked up, will he be able to collect rent?'

'He won't be conducting any business from prison, that's for sure.'

'Thanks,' George chirps, shaking his hand enthusiastically.

Rent free, Kon free, and Anka free. Life is good. Life is bloody good!

The next morning, DI Tanner calls George to tell him that Kon has been sentenced to fifteen years. George is delighted! The flat upstairs is sitting empty. It's time to make a new home for himself. He picks up the keys and a roll of black bin bags. He shuts his door and steps into the deserted hallway. One of the tenants moved out directly after Anka's murder, just one remains, the old man who locks himself away in his room. He wonders if he's still paying rent.

George lets himself into Kon's musty-smelling flat and opens the window to let the air in. The room is exactly how he left it. He places the cushions back on the sofa and picks up the glass ashtray, and butts from the floor. He shakes open a bin bag and swipes a load of nick-knacks, photo frames, and ornaments into it and tears the shabby net curtains down. The kitchen cupboards are well stocked with tins, rice, and pasta.

George flicks on the radio and moves swiftly through the flat like a tornado, filling five black bags in an hour. The bedclothes come off, and the bedroom window is opened. In the wardrobe, an assortment of Kon's ties catches his eye. Rubbing the silk between his fingers, he hopes the one he tightened around Anka's neck was Kon's favourite. A shiver of glee runs through him as the memory of her final look flashes in his mind. All of Kon's clothes are emptied into a large holdall found under the bed. Anka's things lie neatly folded in the drawers: three of clothes, one of underwear. He picks up a small lacy bra, running his fingers over the cups, replaying her last moments as he choked the life out of her. He wishes he'd filmed it to watch again and again. Maybe next time... Next time—interesting! Her clothes go into the bag, but the underwear stays in the drawer.

Dumping the bags in the spare room, George stands to survey his work. Better, though it could do with a lick of paint. He opens the hallway cupboard and finds what he's looking for: rollers, brushes, a large pot of white paint, and a smaller pot of lemon. In the spare room, he fishes out a t-shirt and trousers from Kon's clothes.

Turning up the radio, he gets stuck in, painting until late afternoon. He stands back to admire his work only when it's finished. It looks fresh.

After changing clothes in his bedsit, the phone rings. He runs downstairs to answer it.

Ron apologises for the lack of work this week. 'You still looking to buy a van? I'm selling mine.'

'How much for?'

'It's seen better days. I'd take £300.'

'I'm interested. I'll be in touch, Ron.'

He comes off the phone excited. A new van and new flat in the same day! Things are looking up. With wheels, he'll get more gigs. Might come in handy for other things too. He calls Steve Trent and gets his answer machine again. He leaves a message, wondering how promoters ever book any acts when they don't answer their bloody phones. He tries not to let it dent his good mood.

Will assures him that the chances are good for a gig tonight. Apparently, the promoter, a woman in her fifties, just loves young, good-looking guys. The charm will be laid on heavy, starting with a generous splash of aftershave.

He finds himself chuckling on the way to the tube station but reverts to automatic neutral on boarding the tube, not wanting to be the odd one out with a sunny disposition. He meets Will on Tottenham Court Road, outside the venue.

'Alright, bud. You looked pleased with yourself.'

'It's been a good day, Will. My psycho landlord was sent down for fifteen years.'

'Brilliant. Creepy as fuck to think that you were living in the same house as a murderer. A bloody murderer, unbelievable!'

A suited man hurries past them talking loudly on his phone.

'I'm trying not to think about it. My new flat and van are helping,' he beams, waiting.

Will looks shocked. 'Fuck! You've been busy. How've you managed that? Where's the flat?'

'Not far from my old place.'

'Must have cost a bit. Where'd you get the money?'

'Working, Will,' he retorts, slightly put out by the question. 'I pick up the van Monday. My boss wants next to nothing for it. A bit run down, but it'll be fucking great for gigs. We can go anywhere, start building our reps further afield. I mean, when I win the Big Funny, I'll be in demand so touring will be a must.'

'Right,' Will mumbles. 'A wee bit to go before that, G. We'll make a plan.'

'And I'll get on tonight?'

'Hattie loves a bit of boyish charm, just work it.'

'Don't worry about that,' George winks, running an imaginary comb through his hair.

'Still doing Fonzie? Nice!' Will laughs.

'Ayy!' George grins, giving a thumbs up—the trademark Fonz catchphrase and move.

The stairway to the club is dark, vaguely lit by an exhausted strip light. Inside the candlelit room, there's a stage with people sat in small clusters around it. George is delighted to see that it's a proper stage. Will heads towards a red-headed lady and taps her on the shoulder.

'It's my favourite Scottish comedian,' she purrs, eyeing Will up like he's prey.

'This is George, the comedian I was telling you about, Hattie.'

She gives him the once-over and smiles. 'Pleased to meet you, George,' she says, extending her hand.

George kisses it lightly. She smiles coyly. Putty in his hands. He offers to buy a drink; she opts for a large white wine. *Why do they never want half a fucking lager!*

He drops the wine in front of her. 'I hope you don't mind me popping in, Hattie. I've new material to try out for my Edinburgh show. Would love your opinion.'

'Five minutes in the second half. Don't let me down.'

'You're a beautiful woman,' George says, throwing her a cheeky wink. She smiles before switching her focus to a young man leaning in for air kisses. They take their leave.

'You laid that on thick,' Will laughs.

'Who can resist the Fonzie magic?'

'Absolutely no one,' Will chuckles. 'It's usually a nice crowd in here. Should be a good night.'

They take a seat at the back of the room and watch the audience filter in. The buzz of chatter fills the air, the clink of glasses adding to the typical nervous anticipation of a comedy night. George scans the crowd, his eyes landing on a girl near the front. She's nervously biting her nails, tugging at her skirt as if trying to stretch it over her legs. He wonders what her terrified look would be like. Her neck, delicate, pulls his attention away from his scribbled notes. The noise of the room fades, replaced by the sudden focus of the spotlight. He forces his attention back to the material in front of him, but the quiet intensity of the girl clings to him, drawing him in.

Chapter 12

The comedy night is in full swing. Some comedians get a quiet response, but deservedly so—they're shit. George can't stop looking at the girl. Small, perfectly formed, with mousy brown hair tied in a ponytail. He wonders what she'd look like, dead. His mind drifts, struggling to focus on the gig ahead. The MC announces a break, and the lights come up.

George moves closer. She catches his eye, looks away, and disappears into the ladies' toilets. Shy. Interesting.

'See anything you like?' Will asks, appearing by his side.

'Don't know what you mean,' George says, playing dumb.

'Ask her for her number.'

'Will, I'm not looking at anyone. I've no time for women, it's all about the comedy. You getting the pints in?' He nods towards the bar, keen to get rid of him.

Will takes the hint, parting with a wink.

George keeps his eyes fixed on the toilet door. She steps out. Close enough to smell her. Peachy. Nice.

The lights dim, and the MC takes the stage.

Will puts down his drink. 'Aren't you on next?'

'Shit, shit,' George mutters, weaving his way to the side of the stage. The MC introduces him. Calm and in control, he locates the girl, delighted to find her attentive. *Let's show her what I've got.* He winks in her direction, takes the mic, and delivers his lines without hesitation. Her laugh surprises him—deep and full, as if it belongs to a much bigger body. He laps it up, pausing to milk the audience's laughter. His detachment gives him extra confidence. The stage light flickers on at the back of the room, signalling his time. He thanks the audience, lingering on her just a beat longer before making his exit.

'Well done, mate,' Will says, patting him on the back.

'An easy crowd.'

'An easy crowd? Listen to you. Comedy expert! Right, I'm on.'

'Break a leg.'

Will starts with a joke about being a Scottish refugee, fleeing from poll tax and deep-fried Mars bars. The audience warms to him immediately.

George keeps an eye on the girl, watching what makes her laugh. He needs to speak to her. Why won't her stupid mate fuck off to the bar or the loo?

Will leaves to a good round of applause. They stay for the last act, a young northern lad who looks too young to be in a pub, never mind on stage. He does alright but lacks George's timing.

Her mate finally goes to the toilet. Time to make his move. George glides towards her, closing in. She lifts her head as he approaches. That swan-like neck. For a moment, he's speechless. The girl blushes.

'Hi, I'm George,' he smiles. 'You are?'

She fidgets, nervous but pleased that he's talking to her. 'Shelly,' she says softly.

'Nice to meet you, Shelly,' George recovers, his composure steadying. 'I hope you don't find this too forward, but would you like to go for a drink sometime?'

'Oh… erm… yes… sounds good. You were very brave, getting on stage tonight.'

Brave? What the fuck does that mean? That she wasn't impressed?

George locks eyes with her. 'I hope you enjoyed it?'

'Oh… I did,' she stutters.

'Great. If you want to give me your number, I'll give you a call,' he says, as casually as possible.

He wants her now. Wants to take her home tonight. She writes down her number on a napkin in neat, tidy handwriting just as her friend exits the toilet.

'I'll call,' he assures her hastily, with a quick wave and smile.

He finds Will at the bar with Hattie.

'George, there you are. Just in time to buy me a drink,' Hattie pouts.

'Anything for you, Hattie. Anything.'

She giggles. 'Flattery will get you everywhere. In fact, I might just have a couple of gigs for you both.'

'Excellent. A large glass of chardonnay coming up.'

As they walk briskly to the tube station after the gig, Will glances at George and asks, 'Did you get her number?'

'You've got a right imagination, honestly.'

'Whatever.' Will laughs. 'Listen, come over to mine tomorrow, and we'll book some out-of-town gigs. I've got a few northern ones we can try.'

'Cool,' George says, feeling ecstatic about the opportunities. What will Shelly be like at the end? Passive or aggressive? Will she accept her fate?

George wakes early, driven by purpose. As he sings along to the radio, he inspects the fresh paint job in the living room, satisfaction settling in. Moving the wardrobe against the wall, he lifts the set of drawers. One drawer slips free, tumbling onto his foot. Pain shoots up his leg, and he howls, dropping to the floor. Cursing, he rubs his foot, willing the pain to fade.

Placing the drawer against the runners, he spots a brown envelope strapped with masking tape on the back panel.

The envelope feels heavy. It tears open, revealing a wad of £50 notes and a bag of white powder. £1,000... £2,000... £3,000... £4,000. Fucking hell. A sharp gasp of delight escapes him.

Dipping a finger into the powder, the bitter taste makes him wince. It must be worth a fortune.

What to buy? Clothes, a flashy watch, things for the bachelor pad. Maybe a trip to IKEA. Transport—he needs that. The van. He'll go pick it up. A smart shirt goes on, and excitement buzzes through him as he heads downstairs to make a call.

Ron tells him he can collect the van today. George punches the air in triumph, counting out the cash from the envelope. Life is good.

He strides to the tube station with vigour, arriving at Stand and Deliver just after lunchtime.

Ron grabs the keys and shows him to the van. 'Passed its MOT a few months ago. It's automatic, easy to drive.'

George feels a mix of relief and nerves. 'I'll take it for a spin around the block.'

Ron briefs him on the controls and hands over the keys. George waits for Ron to walk away before putting the key in the ignition. He's never driven before, but he's played enough driving games. It can't be that hard. Perspiration gathers on his forehead as he turns the key.

Clutching the gear stick, he pushes it into drive. The van starts moving slowly. He puts his foot down, crawling cautiously out of the car park.

A large truck blocks the entire street ahead, the driver unloading stock at the back of a shop. George tries to go around it, but the road's too narrow. Reluctantly, he reverses, narrowly avoiding the car behind him. The driver doesn't get out, but she reverses and disappears. Ten minutes later, the truck moves off. George drives around the block, determined to get the hang of it, and begins to enjoy himself.

He meets Ron back at the office. 'It'll do fine.' Ron takes the £300. The van's perfect—a licence to freedom.

A few near collisions later, George reaches IKEA. The smell of hotdogs hits him immediately, so he buys one, drenched in chilli sauce, and eats it in two bites.

Inside, he picks up trendy lamps, retro curtains, and pictures, including a large print of a VW Kombi at sunset. In the garden section, he grabs a spade.

In and out in an hour, everything he needs.

The rush hour traffic is miserable, and the trip home involves more time stationary than moving. By the time he reaches Garrett Lane, it's dark. The street behind the graveyard is eerily quiet. Parking's trickier than driving—forward, back, forward, back.

He grabs the shopping from the back seat, feeling exhilarated, then picks up the last of his things from the bedsit. For a moment, he lingers by the spot where Anka's life ended. Something stirs inside him.

The fresh smell of paint greets him as he enters the flat. Home sweet home! He drops the car keys on the kitchen counter, hangs the pictures, and shakes his head, standing back to admire the transformation. It screams accomplished young bachelor.

He'd love to call Shelly but hesitates. He doesn't have Kon to pin it on this time. His efforts to distract himself fail. Giving in, he jogs down to the phone. She picks up on the second ring. Keen.

'Hi, is that Shelly?' he asks.

'Yes,' she stammers.

'It's George here, the comedian from the other night.' He loves calling himself a comedian. He imagines her face colouring, that delicate neck. 'I was wondering if you'd like to come over for dinner tomorrow night. I'm a mean cook.'

'Erm… oh… yes, that'd be nice.'

'I'll meet you at Tooting Broadway station at eight. Okay?'

'Great… that's a date then,' she says, grateful glee in her voice.

Waves of excitement swell through him. The next playdate is set.

He sets off for late-night shopping, whistling a merry tune as he heads to the tube station. Passing the graveyard, he notices not one, but two freshly dug graves at each end, with mounds of dirt—indicating the imminent arrival of new residents. A graveyard. There's surely no better place to hide a body. *Opportunity knocks.*

He stops, taking in the scene with a calculating look. The place is close to home, easy to get to. He could slip in, dig deeper, bury a body, then pile the dirt on top, pat it down—all under the cover of night. No one would be the wiser. And there would always be new arrivals, new holes already dug, keeping the backbreaking work to a minimum.

His mind works overtime as he makes plans on the whole tube journey to town.

The phone shop's bright contrast from the dark outside feels like a football pitch at night. The assistant greets him with a warm smile, quickly replaced by a frosty frown when an exchange is mentioned. She directs him to Simon, the manager, with a silent point.

Simon's short, moustached, and unkempt. His elbows are leant on the counter, absorbed in his phone.

'Hello, Simon. How are you?'

Simon looks up, his face unreadable. 'Yes?'

'I recently bought this phone,' George says, holding up the box. 'Some twat on a skateboard knocked it out of my hand. Now it doesn't work.'

'Did you buy insurance?'

'No.'

'Sorry, if it's not faulty, there's not much I can do,' Simon shrugs, returning to his phone.

'I'd like to upgrade. Money's no issue.'

The magic words. Simon jumps to attention, showing George several phones and explaining their functions. George picks a big, chunky black model, the kind that feels solid and heavy in his hand, with thick buttons and a design that's built to last.

A few more items later, he's feeling accomplished—with the car, the flat, and now the phone. On the way to Will's, he picks up premium beer and tequila, all while planning Shelly's visit and considering where to hide her when it's over. If he can make a quick trip to Will's like he did with Anka, he'll have an alibi.

A tall, blond guy answers Will's door.

'Erm… hello. Is Will in?' George asks.

'Come in. I'm Nick, Will's flatmate,' he says, shaking George's hand briefly before taking his leave.

Will appears. 'Alright, mate? How's it going?

'Good. I brought some goodies.'

'Premium beer and tequila, you flush mate?'

'Just a little something. No big deal,' George says, brushing it off.

'I've got a pizza in the oven,' Will says, frowning. 'This prick at work's really pissing me off. He's an absolute arsehole!'

'He's really rattled you,' George observes, surprised. 'Why don't you just sack him?'

'Can't. Disciplinary procedures. Gave him a verbal warning. You should've seen the look he gave me.'

'I have something to help,' George says, grabbing the shot glasses.

They knock back shots until the smell of pizza fills the kitchen.

Nick appears in the doorway. 'Have a good night, guys. You still up for tomorrow?'

'I am mate,' Will shouts to Nick's retreating figure.

'What's on tomorrow?' George asks.

'His girlfriend's having a party. Invited me and Jemma.'

'Right. Sounds fun.' *There goes my alibi!*

Chapter 13

'The party's in Camden, if you fancy it?' Will asks.

'Nah, I'm good. A quiet night in my new place for me,' George replies, his eyes flickering to the oven.

'Fuck, the pizza!' Will slurs, opening the oven door to a cloud of smoke. The alarm goes off. George grabs a mop and swats at the ceiling.

'Shit,' Will hiccups, staring at the charred pizza. 'Think it's fucked!'

'Nah, another tequila and it'll be fine.'

They settle into the sitting room with the bottle of tequila and the burnt remains.

George picks at it. 'I've had worse. I went to IKEA. You were right—great bargains. Picked up the van too. Ready to hit the road, mate.'

'We should make a few calls before we get too drunk. You speak, your blagging skills are better than mine.'

They dial the first venue, the Frog and Bucket. The phone rings... and rings. George balances it on his shoulder and takes another bite of pizza. 'How do you fuck up frozen pizza? Unbelievable.'

'Oh, hello, is that the Frog and Bucket?' George coughs, almost choking. 'Can I speak to John who books the comedy nights?'

'He's only here on weekends. Call back then,' the voice cuts him off and hangs up.

'Fucker,' George mutters, throwing the phone down. 'They don't know who they're dealing with.'

He dials the second number.

'Oh, hello. I was hoping to book a gig.'

'Where have you been gigging?'

'Scottish circuit. Now on the London scene.'

'What's your name?'

'George Mailer.'

'Not heard of you.'

'Been mostly in Scotland. Placed in a few big competitions, and I'm a regular at The Stand.'

'Mmm. Hold on a sec.'

George nods at Will, who lifts his beer in a silent toast.

The man comes back. 'Got a couple of unpaid spots on the 11th of March. If you're any good, we'll talk more.'

'Perfect. My mate Will Devon does support gigs for big headliners. We could drive up together—two for the price of one.'

With the gigs confirmed, George grins, and pours two more shots. 'We're on. Here's to hitting the road.'

They knock them back. 'Now, tell me, how's work? Dan the Man still giving you grief?'

'Oh, don't get me started. He's a pain in my arse.'

'I hope it's a pleasant pain, and he wears a condom,' George quips, grinning.

'Hilarious,' Will snorts. 'Thanks for bringing up work. I need to crash, or I'll be fucked tomorrow.'

'Condoms next time,' George teases.

'Sleep well on that sofa, mate,' Will says, tossing a blanket at him.

George settles into the couch, running through the next 24 hours, feeling the excitement build.

George makes the tube journey from Will's, feeling rough and thirsty. Arriving home, he crashes onto the sofa, dozing off.

He jolts awake at 7:00 p.m.—the playdate.

A ten-second shower, a quick change into dark clothes and a black cap, and he's out the door. Shelly's already waiting at the station. He lingers in a shop doorway, watching her. Her delicate neck, exposed by a high ponytail, catches his attention. She's young, innocent-looking in her white dress and blue cardigan. So fucking naive.

He licks his lips, adjusts his cap, and approaches.

'Hi there,' he says, planting a kiss on her cheek.

'Oh hello,' she replies, smiling shyly.

'How are you?'

'Good, thanks,' she stammers.

'I don't live far,' George says, setting off with her at his side. 'I wanted to cook something special, but I've had to work on my material all day. Got gigs coming up, maybe a TV spot. Hope takeaway's alright? Indian?'

'I like Indian,' she smiles, 'just not the spicy stuff.'

'Let me guess—a korma girl?'

She beams. He picks up the pace, passing the estate.

'This is me,' George announces, opening the door. 'Penthouse suite. Bit of a hike though.'

'Welcome to my humble abode,' he says with a flourish, as he invites her inside the flat.

'It's really nice, very modern,' she says, stepping inside.

'Thanks. What do you want to drink?'

'Wine, if you have it?'

'Of course. Take a seat.' He gestures to the sofa, pouring wine as he watches her, heart racing. He slips one of Anka's Valiums into her glass, stirring it casually with his finger.

'Cheers,' George says, handing her the glass.

She smiles, a little unsure, but still trusting.

He flicks through the CD collection, putting on 'Love Anthems'. Marvin Gaye's voice fills the room with his needs for sexual healing. George suspects a song about murdering healing wouldn't be as popular. He moves to the sofa, patting the seat next to him.

'Come on, take a seat. Tell me about yourself?'

She looks embarrassed. 'Erm…what do you want to know?'

Does anyone know you're here? How long before people start to look for you? 'Oh, I don't know, what's your favourite colour? What kind of music do you like?'

'My favourite colour is pink. My favourite music is country. I know it's dead old fashioned, but me and my mum used to listen to it all the time,' she says, her eyes tearing up. *Information drop.*

'Are you alright?' George asks, stroking her hand.

She puts her wine down on the table. 'Yes. It's just she died last year… I still miss her.'

'That's terrible. And your dad, he still alive?'

'He did a runner when I was a baby.'

'Any brothers or sisters?'

'One brother, older. He lives in Australia.'

Perfect.

'Must be hard him being so far away?' George says, picking up a takeaway menu from the counter. 'Choose whatever you like,' he says, admiring her slim wrists; everything's so bird-like.

He nods to the glass of wine. 'Drink up. Now, what was your friend's name, the one you were with the other night?'

'Sarah.'

'She'll be calling you tomorrow for the goss? I know what girls are like.'

'I didn't tell her I had a date. To be honest, I like to keep my love life private.'

A gift from the gods.

'And you live at home?'

'No, I live on my own. It's tiny, but I like it.'

Perfect.

'So, what would you like to eat?'

'A chicken korma, please.'

'I'll order some rice and bits too. The phones in the hallway. I won't be long,' he smiles his best smile.

On the way past his old bedsit, he stops to glance at Anka's sacred spot, promising himself to take it slowly with Shelly. No hurry. He climbs back upstairs, titillated.

'There's an hour's wait. Saturdays are busy for them.'

Shelly looks confused, holding up the menu. 'Don't you need this?'

'Erm. No…No. I call so often I've the number memorised. Sad, I know.'

He takes the wine out of the fridge and tops up her glass, wiping a bead of sweat from his forehead.

Will I enjoy it as much as last time? Will she put up a fight like Anka?

He rests his hand on her thigh. She doesn't move it. He moves it further up; she looks at him with trusting eyes. Heartbreaking, really. He leans in and kisses her. She barely responds, but it doesn't put him off.

She pulls back. 'I just need to go to the little girls' room,' she stammers.

'It's just at the end of the hall,' he says, smiling sweetly at her.

When the toilet door closes, he picks up her handbag and rummages through it. A pink lipstick, a small purse, no mobile. He hears the toilet flush and throws the bag down. She comes back into the living room and sits next to him.

'Erm, George. I'd like this to be something special.'

Oh, so do I.

'Do you mind if we just take it slowly?'

'Of course not. Let's just drink and be merry,' he says, picking up the bottle to fill her glass.

She puts her hand over the top. 'I've probably had my limit now. I'm a bit of a lightweight with alcohol, I'm afraid.'

Let's see how you are with Valium. He looks at the glass, it's nearly empty. It should be enough. Maria Carey bursts into a song about needing a friend. He takes her hand and looks into her trusting eyes.

She smiles. 'I never asked you what your favourite colour is.'

'Red. It's passionate, you know.'

'Mmm,' she mumbles, her eyelids fluttering slightly.

He keeps up the idle chit-chat, waiting for the drug to take effect. It doesn't take long before her eyes drift shut. Leaning in, he whispers her name in her ear, but she remains still. That's his cue.

Lifting her up, she feels light as a feather. He lays her on the bed and clumsily removes her clothes. Underneath, she's wearing matching underwear—cotton, white, simple, and functional. It's no surprise, but it's not what he wants.

He finds a more suitable option in Anka's knicker drawer, a cheap red lacey number. He wraps the bra around her and fiddles with the clasp to fasten it, and changes over the knickers. They fit perfectly. Taking the belt from his jeans, he binds her feet then loops a silk tie through the belt, tying it to the bed legs. He binds her hands and selects a tie to wrap round her neck.

'There! You look very pretty.'

What he needs is a video camera—he daren't use his phone. Too risky. A camcorder would be perfect, though. More planning, less haste. He smiles, a long, lingering grin, knowing there'll be more opportunities.

He picks up a roll of gaffer tape and sits on the bed next to her. He tilts her head and tapes her mouth, kicking himself for missing such precious moments that should be captured.

He drinks his wine, savouring the moment till he can wait no longer. He downs his glass and walks slowly to the side of the bed where she waits for him. He strokes her thigh. He's ready now! He sings into her ear, 'Shelly, oh Shelly. It's time to play.' He puts his two hands on each side of her face and gives a gentle slap, 'Wake up Shelly.'

Nothing. He puts smelling salts under her nose. She recoils but opens her eyes, momentarily smiling, pleased to see him. Then her expression changes as the big picture kicks in. Her eyes widen, her face drains of colour as she takes in the ties, and her near nakedness.

'I got you a present. New underwear, I hope you like it?'

Muffled sounds come from behind the tape. She wiggles her body slightly but can't move.

'Shelly, Shelly, Shelly. What are we going to do with you?' He takes his finger and runs it down the side of her face. Bingo. She's terrified.

He steps back, framing her with his fingers, mimicking a photoshoot, his tongue clicking in rhythm. She thrashes on the bed, her eyes darting wildly, searching for a way out. George wants to drag it out, but he can't wait any longer. He strips off, straddling her, his hands tightening around her neck. Her pupils flare. At first, he squeezes lightly, fighting the urge to rush. A flash of Anka's wide, pleading eyes comes to mind. Shelly's gaze mirrors the same helplessness, the same silent surrender. He grins down at her as he squeezes harder.

Chapter 14

George lies beside Shelly for a while, replaying every moment, indulging in the rush over and over. Waves of euphoria pulse through his body, leaving him electrified.

In the early hours of the morning, he gently lowers Shelly's lifeless body into the bath. He washes her with a sponge, wishing he could bring her back, just to experience it all once more.

After laying a towel on the floor, he dries her, dressing her in her underwear and clothes—the shoes are the hardest. Finally, he props her against the bathroom wall, her eyes still open, staring blankly.

He throws on a black hoodie and dark jeans, then empties a large holdall onto the floor. Carefully, he lowers her freshly scented body into the bag, tossing her handbag in after. It zips up easily, though it's a snug fit. The wheels make it easier to drag down the hallway. He pauses at the door, listening—nothing. He pulls the holdall down the stairs, swaying under its weight.

He drags the bag down the communal hall, peeking out the main door. The streets are deserted, shops closed. Moving quickly towards the graveyard, he keeps an eye out for any signs of life. He retrieves the spade from the van, closing the door lightly, then slowly pulls open the cemetery gate. The gate's loud creak cracks the silence.

He stands still, listening for movement. It's dark, and his eyes take a moment to adjust. He treads carefully, relieved to find one of the holes he spotted yesterday still empty. Dropping the bag to the ground, he begins digging. The adrenaline surges through him, making light work of the task. It feels like he has superpowers.

When he's satisfied with the depth, he unzips the bag and tips Shelly's body into the pit. Sweat beads on his skin, but there's no anxiety—he isn't meant to be caught.

He pushes a mound of dirt over Shelly, shovelling enough soil to refill the hole to its original depth, then pats it down with the spade, ensuring it looks undisturbed—no hands sticking out, no spare limbs showing.

With his hands in a prayer position, he bows his head. 'May you rest in peace, Shelly. Amen.' The words feel hollow, but for some reason, he says them anyway. He finishes with the sign of the cross, a good Catholic boy.

He exits the graveyard, closing the gate behind him, pausing to throw the holdall and shovel in the van. Scanning the road and nearby houses, he feels sure the residents of Garrett Lane are sound asleep. He bounces up the stairs to the flat, cleans up, and stuffs down a cheese and pickle sandwich before bed.

Late afternoon the next day, George receives a call from Will.

'Mate, you won't believe the news,' Will says, excitedly.

'What?'

'I've booked us gigs in Glasgow and Edinburgh, at The Stand.'

'No way. How'd you manage that?'

'I did a gig in Edinburgh for this wee club a few years back… bumped into the promoter at another gig, mentioned my desire to perform at The Stand. He put in a good word… and hey presto, they took my call and gave me gigs at both venues.'

'When is it exactly?'

'Tomorrow, in Edinburgh. Saturday, in Glasgow.'

'Tomorrow, Will? Fuck's sake.'

'They had a cancellation, so I jumped at it. This is a great career move, as you would say, G.'

'I'm not staying at my mum's. I don't want to see them.'

'Stay at ours. I've booked a day's holiday. You up for it?'

The idea of conquering his old patch appeals to him.

'Come on,' Will says. 'We'll have a laugh, and it'll mean you don't have to blag it anymore… You can say honestly that you've performed at The Stand.'

'I'm in. Fuck it. What time shall I meet you?'

'Be at mine about nine-ish.'

'You're full of surprises, Will,' George says, hanging up, immediately unsure of his decision.

George struggles to sleep, his emotions shifting from enthusiasm to dread. Can he be just two streets from his childhood home and not bump into his mum and sister? On the upside, imagine the front row of The Stand filled with his old classmates—George delivering his lines, the audience roaring with laughter, bent over, unable to breathe, tears running down their faces. They'll be impressed, no snide comments now. He puffs out his chest and stands tall. 'Yes, I am a comedian. What do you do? Painter and decorator? How exciting for you!' He smiles.

In the morning, he throws his best jeans and shirts into a bag, grabs a slice of toast, and leaves the flat. Will's waiting outside when he pulls up, cheerful and smiling. He tosses George's bag into the back of the van.

'Alright, mate. I've got a bag full of food and a load of CDs for the journey.

'No CD player, just the radio.'

'Just as well I'm here.' Will pulls out a portable CD player and two small speakers and sets them up in the glove compartment. The opening lines of Happy Mondays' 'Step On' fill the van.

George starts the engine. 'Fuck, what a tune. You know there's a big rave happening in Bristol next weekend. Fancy it?'

'Next weekend?'

'Yep.' George puts his foot down.

'Sorry, can't. Taking Jemma for dinner.' Will smiles, chuffed. 'I can't believe how funny she is… and sexy as fuck.'

George forces a smile, 'Bristol for one then.'

They reach the motorway and stay on it for most of the journey. For five hours, Will alternates between ranting about Dan the Man at work and crowing about his amazing girlfriend.

'Imagine me with an investigative journalist. Pretty classy, eh?'

'Yeah, classy.' George turns up the music.

'Just tell me if I'm boring the arse off you,' Will chuckles.

They pull into The Stand car park just after 7:00 p.m. It's dark. George's arse is killing him. He gets out of the car and stretches his legs. They enter the busy club, asking the woman on the door where to go. She points to a tall man with dark hair and bushy eyebrows. 'Speak to Jeff, he's MCing tonight'.

Will heads in his direction while George makes his way to the bar. A smiling barmaid greets him and quickly pours his drink. Hospitality—can't beat Scotland.

'There's a green room at the back of the stage,' Will says, joining him at the bar. 'A green room! We're going up in the world, eh? We're on the second half. You're opening and I'm doing the support spot.'

The audience is loud, talking excitedly, laughing, and drinking in small groups.

They go backstage and introduce themselves. Some acts are friendlier than others.

Apart from one comedian from Liverpool, all the acts are Scottish. Will shares London promoters' phone numbers and is rewarded with handshakes and pats on the back. George has no interest in mingling. He paces the back of the room, going over his lines.

His first time in front of a home crowd, and Edinburgh fuckers. They're always a bit up their own arse. The first half of the show drags by. George doesn't get involved in the back slapping banter of post-performance highs.

The MC welcomes the audience back for the second half and quiets them down. George takes another gulp of his pint as he's introduced and receives an enthusiastic round of applause—much friendlier than London audiences. He steps onto the stage, starting with his new Scottish material, hoping to connect with the crowd.

'I'm working in London at the moment and had to fly up for this gig,' he lies. 'I saw a couple with a matching set of Gucci luggage at Glasgow Airport. You see Gucci luggage on TV, and you think celebrity. In London, you think success. In Glasgow, you think shoplifters.'

Each joke lands with more laughter than all his previous gigs put together. He leaves the audience whistling and cheering and bounces back into the green room.

'Fucking hell, totally top crowd.'

'They loved you mate,' Will says, shaking his hand. 'Excellent work.'

George receives a head nod from another comedian but nothing else. *Jealous bastards!* The MC introduces Will to the stage to a good reception.

Will's first line goes down well, and his set is punctuated with laughter throughout. He leaves the stage, smiling from ear to ear. 'That was fucking tops.'

'You know, if we worked up here, I reckon we'd clear up. Big fish, little pond,' George says, as they set off for Glasgow. A Stone Roses CD is chosen, and they blast it, singing at the top of their lungs for most of the hour's ride back. They pull up to Will's just after 1:00 a.m.

'Looks like everyone's gone to bed,' Will says, quietly opening the front door. George is glad, he's knackered.'

'Blankets. Sofa. You're set mate,' Will says. 'See you for more showbiz fun tomorrow.' He salutes and goes upstairs.

George wakes up and sniffs the air, a smile spreading over his face. Square sausage and potato scones; Scottish food, the best in the world! The unhealthiest, but the best! He throws off a blanket, slips into his jeans and makes his way to the kitchen. Will and his sister are sitting at the table.

'Morning, George,' Kathy sings.

Her features are the total opposite to Will's. She's short and slightly plump with dark hair. She has a sunny disposition and a face bordering on pretty.

'Hiya, Kathy. How's it going?'

'I'm alright. Can't wait to see you two on stage tonight. I'm bloody nervous for you.'

'Oh, don't be, we're professionals,' George assures her. 'You'll be impressed, just no autographs, alright? That kind of shit embarrasses us.'

Kathy laughs, dishing up breakfast onto plates. *How can a heart attack look so good?* George takes the plate offered to him and sits down at the table.

'Ma and Da went into the toon. New curtains for the living room, I think,' Kathy says. 'What you two up to today?'

'No plans. We could go into the town,' Will suggests.

'Town? Kathy mimics. 'Your accents are totally Englified.'

'No, they aren't,' Will says, adopting his poshest voice. 'We must adapt to our surroundings, dear Katherine, or the English folk won't understand us.'

'Are you going to see Sammy and your ma, George?' Kathy asks, buttering a thick slice of toast.

'Maybe tomorrow, before we head back to London,' George lies, keeping his eyes fixed on his breakfast.

'Why didn't you bring Jemma up with you, Will? I'm dying to meet her.'

'I invited her, but she had work.'

This is news to George. Thank fuck she couldn't make it, a road trip with Jemma does not appeal.

Feeling refreshed after a shower, they leave the house and walk to the bus stop. A face from the past freezes George to the spot. Skeener, his tormentor from school. His shaved head and track suit and trainers makes George wonder why slobs are always kitted out in aerodynamic sportswear when they haven't exercised since school sports day. He stares at him, tightening his fists. *He's not ageing well.*

'Look who it is, Will! Skeener, fucking arsehole,' George hisses.

Will glances in Skeener's direction. 'Looks rough, eh?'

George is shocked to hear pity in Will's voice.

'His mum died last year from cancer, Kathy was saying. She reckons he's on heroin now.'

'Really?' George says, perking up. 'Couldn't happen to a nicer guy.'

Will raises his eyebrows.

'What? He made my life a fucking misery. I've no sympathy.'

'Here's the bus coming now,' Will says.

George feels a dark mood descending. Will didn't suffer like he did, he sits down heavily, clenching his jaw.

The town looks the same, though the big Boots at the dizzy corner has been replaced by a KFC. There's a Wimpy on the opposite corner. Enough fast-food places to make George wonder if they've overtaken the chippy in popularity—surely not.

They pass some high-end retailers. George doesn't remember Glasgow being so designer. The Glasgow he recalls was all jogging bottoms, shell suits, and dungarees.

'They've got some cracking stuff in Moschino. I went in there last time I was up. Couldn't afford a thing, but it's nice stuff,' Will insists.

George pushes open the glass door 'Let's have a look.'

The sales assistant looks like he's been dipped in a bucket of fake tan. He pounces early.

'We've been here less than a minute. We'll give you a shout if we need you,' George retorts. The orange man stomps off.

'Bit harsh mate. What's up with you?' Will asks.

'Seeing that arsehole, Skeener.'

'Well, I wouldn't say he's long for this world, G.'

'Here's hoping.' George picks up a black woollen jumper with an orange pocket. 'This is pretty cool.' He looks at the label. Ninety-five pounds. 'Fucking hell, they should be wearing masks in here, the robbing bastards.'

'Calm down mate, will you?'

'Fuck it.' He hands it to a hovering assistant. 'I'll take this.'

They stop at the chippy on the way home.

'Scottish chips are the best,' George says, savouring the vinegary taste. 'Don't know why they can't make them like this in London.'

George beats Will to the shower when they get back, donning his new top and generously splashing on aftershave. He finds Will's mum in the living room.

'Hello, George, how are you?'

'Great, Mrs Devon. How's yourself?'

'Aw, much the same. Not a lot changing up here, no like London. Are you enjoying it down there?'

'Aye, it's fine,' George says. *Aye?* He can't remember the last time he said aye.

'And do you have a job?'

'I'm a comedian first and a motorbike courier second.'

'Sounds dangerous.'

'Danger's my middle name, Mrs Devon.'

'Really? I thought it was Joseph,' Will says, coming down the stairs to give his mum a hug. 'Did you get your curtains?' he asks, picking up a bottle of Irn Bru and pouring a glass.

'Aye, they had a sale in BHS, got them half price.'

'Always the bargain hunter, Ma.'

'That's me. We're so excited to see you on stage tonight, boys. We'll be the ones at the front, laughing the loudest.'

Will hugs her. 'I'm sure you will, Ma. I'm sure you will.'

The Stand is a good size, with plenty of seats—few of which are empty. A huge improvement on the twenty seats in a basement bar in Camden. He goes over his lines as the rising volume of the audience fills the room. George peeks out from behind the stage curtain and sees Will's family seated in the front row, chatting animatedly.

The music stops, and the MC pounces on stage to build a rapport with the audience. George paces around the room until, at last, he's introduced. He strides onto the stage and takes the mic. The audience gives a half-hearted round of applause. The opening act has to work hard, and he does, until the laughs become more frequent. In full flow, he moves towards Will's family to share an inside joke he knows they'll love. A familiar face sits with them. What the fuck? It's his sister, Sammy. His confidence falters, leaving him momentarily silenced before he slips into autopilot for the rest of the gig. He can't wait to finish. Aware he's rushing his punchlines, he forces himself to slow down, eventually exiting to a respectable, though unenthusiastic, applause. He shoots his sister a cold stare and leaves the stage.

Chapter 15

Will brings drinks into the greenroom. George is fuming.

'What the fuck is Sammy doing here?' George spits.

Will puts his hands up in front of him. 'Calm down G. She's matey with our Kathy. I didn't know she was coming.'

'She put me right off,' George spits.

Instead of leaving like he wants to, George forces himself to stay for Will's gig. He stands at the bar, staring at the back of his sister's head. *She's got some fucking front.* Will shines on stage, his exit met with loud and clear applause. The MC announces the interval.

'I messed up that London joke,' Will says to George at the bar.

'It went well. Don't worry about it,' George mutters, gulping down his beer.

'Oh my God, you were brilliant,' Kathy screeches, giving Will a bear hug.

Sammy steps in front of George, leaning in for a hug—more for show than any real warmth. 'Hello, stranger.'

'What are you doing here?' he growls. He pulls away from her, steps back, and flashes a smile at Kathy.

'Surprise, surprise,' Kathy sings, 'Just call me Cilla Black, bringing families together, making people happy. You two must have loads to catch up on.'

Will's parents walk over, offering congratulations.

'Great surprise, George, to see Sammy, eh? Kathy's been talking about it all day,' Will's mum says, looking genuinely excited.

Wouldn't it just be nice if everyone minded their own fucking business? George slides his arm around Sammy and kisses her head. 'Brilliant. Thanks, Kathy.'

'You wouldn't come to Glasgow and not see your big sister, would you?' Sammy pouts.

'Don't be daft. I was going to visit tomorrow,' he lies.

'My wee baby brother,' she pinches his cheek roughly. 'Let's go for a drink and catch up. We'll pop back at the end of the show?'

'Of course, love. Enjoy,' Will's mum waves them off.

They step outside to the dark, wet night. George pulls his coat tighter, fighting off the wind.

'There's a pub at the corner,' Sammy says, walking briskly in that direction.

They step into The Grand, an old-fashioned pub. There's very little that could be described as grand inside—two old men prop up the bar. The fireplace crackles with a roaring, spitting fire, and the blood-red carpets wouldn't look out of place in a theatre.

'A whisky and coke for me,' Sammy says, taking a seat near the fire. Maybe he could throw her in.

A burly bartender with a red nose serves George. He looks affronted when George asks for a Beck's.

'We don't do Beck's. Tenants or Kronenbourg?'

When in Rome... 'Tenants, thanks.'

He watches Sammy. She hasn't changed much. Her hair is different, cut in a modern bob, but she's still self-assured, confident, and smug.

'One whisky and coke,' George says, putting the drink down in front of her. 'What are you doing here, Sammy?'

'I haven't seen you for over two years. I didn't even know if you were still alive.'

'We're not exactly a close family.'

'That doesn't mean you can just up and leave without saying a word. It was weird.'

'I had to go,' George says, gulping a drink of his pint.

'Why?'

'Erm, it's hard to explain.'

'Stealing my ma's bingo money was a shitty thing to do. She was absolutely distraught. She went right into herself after that!'

George struggles to control his breathing. He doesn't want to talk about this. 'Sammy, it was a long time ago.'

'I overheard Betty next door gossiping about the week after you left. She said the police were all over the place. She loves to exaggerate, that woman. I hardly think there would have been a big police operation for stolen bingo money—hardly Strathclyde's biggest priority,' Sammy says, downing half her drink before continuing. 'Betty said, "Good riddance to bad rubbish." Which was a bit weird, because I always thought she was quite fond of you. Anyway... she went as white as a ghost when she realised I was standing behind her and just shut up.'

George keeps his expression neutral.

'I couldn't believe it when Kathy mentioned you were in London with Will. You know, a postcard would have done.'

'Look, Sammy, I have my own life!'

'You're a callous bastard, George, sitting there in your designer top, thinking you're Mr Hoity Toity. You sound English.'

'Bit of an exaggeration. I just don't sound like I'm from the slums of Glasgow.'

'You saying I do?' Sammy says, sitting forward.

George holds her gaze. 'Does my ma know I'm here?'

'Aye. You should go and see her. She's changed so much. She's a nervous wreck now. A right curtain twitcher.' Sammy furrows her brow in concentration.

George fights a storm of emotions. 'Need to go to the toilct.'

The toilet is empty. He presses his palms to the sink, squeezing his eyes shut, willing the image of his mum—mouth gagged, her eyes wide with fear—to vanish. It doesn't. He splashes cold water on his face, breathing deeply, trying to ground himself. Keep it together. You can handle this.

Sammy jumps in the moment he puts the drinks down. 'I think that there's something you're not telling me. What happened the day you left?'

He remains silent, struggling to breathe.

'Did you two have a barney?' she says, taking a sip of her drink. 'Jesus, that's strong.'

'It's a double. You're welcome. So, tell me, Sammy, what have you been doing with yourself? Boyfriend?'

'I was seeing this guy for about a year, then found out he was cheating on me, so I had to chuck him. Are you seeing anybody?'

'I am. Been seeing her for a while now. She's a model.'

'Aye, right. Where are you living in London?'

'Penthouse flat in South London. You still at home?'

'Aye, though my ma's driving me mad. She's flaky—left the frying pan on the other day, nearly burnt the bloody place down.'

George distracts her by encouraging her to talk about herself. He can't wait to leave Glasgow and return to the cool indifference of London.

The next morning, after a round of toasts and goodbyes, they hit the motorway to London, arriving in the late afternoon.

George is delighted to be home. He opens a beer, flops down in front of the television, and begins channel hopping, amazed at how many inane scenarios can be the basis for a reality show. Nurses, cops, sales assistants, my pet, my weight, my cosmetic surgery, the removal men. Seriously, this can't be what the British public want. And where have all the actors gone? Probably queuing up at the dole office.

George settles on a documentary about role models and the fascination with celebrity. This isn't new. People have always been captivated by celebrities, dating back to the fifties with Marilyn Monroe—the Madonna of her day. People need someone to look up to. George has always known admiration would come. It's prepared him for the stage and the TV and film career ahead.

Wandering into the bedroom, George sits on the bed where Shelly lay. Picking up the sheets, he sniffs. The faint smell of her lingers, still present. Next time will be even better. Grabbing a pad and pen, he makes a list.

Camcorder

Rope

Tarpaulin

More neck ties too. All his girls will be smartly attired with a tie to match their personalities. *Interesting*. A bold red for the fiery ones, a subtle blue for the calm ones maybe. What will the next lucky lady look like? Small and thin? Delicate neck with a great laugh. He reminisces about Shelly laughing at his gig. She had really enjoyed his material. She had taste.

After a night of restless sleep, George wakes up late. He grabs a wad of cash, then picks up the shopping list on the way out. The graveyard is quiet and uneventful, everything looking as it should.

On Oxford Street, George heads to Dixons, eager to buy a camcorder. After a brief demo, he selects one of the pricier models, picturing the end result with a smile.

At Frasers, he picks up tarpaulins and red silk from the haberdashery, avoiding rope that might damage the goods. He buys five blood-red ties, stroking them on the way home. George Mailer has taste.

Later, George scans property ads, resting his eyes for a minute before his phone rings. Will's name flashes on the screen.

'Alright mate. Nodded off on the sofa.'

Will laughs. 'You're not getting any younger. Got us a gig in Salisbury.'

'When?'

'This Saturday.'

'Any money?'

'Um… no. They don't pay open spots.'

'Right,' George says, disappointed.

'I'll buy you a few pints. They're putting us up overnight too.'

'Really? I've got new material to try out. Fancy meeting up Friday?'

'I've got work drinks.'

'I'll tag along. Your work mates sound like twats, but I'll cope.'

'Actually, Jemma's coming. She wants to meet them.'

Of course she does. 'No bother, another time.'

'How about Thursday?'

'I've got a gig.'

'Alright, Friday it is. The Horse and Hound, six o'clock. See you then.'

George arrives at the pub fifteen minutes early. It's a Pitcher and Piano pretending to be an old man's pub—no old men in sight, just office types, with Will in the middle of a large group of them.

Will waves him over. 'Everybody, this is my best mate, George.'

George beams with pride.

The group greets him with a loud 'Hello, George,' in perfect unison, then laugh uncontrollably.

Proper wankers. George smiles. 'Can I get anyone a drink?'

'Work-kitty's sorted. Grab your own.'

George orders a pint, scanning the group. He guesses which one is Dan the Man before rejoining them. Will is mid-story about an angry customer, the team laughing at all the right moments. George notes—with pride, but a hint of envy—that his friend has their respect.

The shortest one elbows his way in with a Christmas night out story.

'Dan the Man?' George asks.

'The very one.'

Short, weedy, effeminate. Dan the Man indeed.

Jemma arrives in a fitted suit, her hair twirled up in a clip, looking every bit the young professional. Will kisses her hello. George offers a drink, and of course, she orders a large chardonnay.

As the bar fills up and people get drunker, George listens to a string of work stories that lack punch. Dan the Man, noticeably drunker than everyone else—likely due to his short frame—makes sly digs at Will when he's out of earshot.

Dan spills some beer down his shirt, to the others' amusement.

'Fuck, this is Giorgio Armani,' he mutters, rushing to the toilet.

George sets his pint down and follows. Dan is at the sink, scrubbing at his shirt with a handful of wet tissue.

'Unlucky,' George says, stepping up to a urinal.

'£300 this shirt cost me.'

George zips up his jeans and stands next to Dan at the sink, glaring at him in the mirror.

'Dan, is it?'

'Yes, that's me,' Dan says, distracted.

'Dan, Dan, Dan… a word of warning. If you give Will any more shit at work or anywhere else, I'm going to hunt you down and it won't be beer stains on your shirt. You get my drift?'

George steps closer, forcing Dan to look up at him. 'One more fucking snide remark and I'll snip your dick off.' He mimics scissors with his fingers.

Dan's mouth hangs open, eyes wide, completely frozen.

George smiles, repeating the cutting action and leaves the bathroom.

Will is at the heart of the work crowd.

'I hear your landlord got put away for murder,' Jemma says, appearing beside him.

'Yep, he's a head case.'

'You testified. Were you in the house when the girlfriend was killed?' she asks, sipping her wine, eyes fixed on him.

'No, I was at Will's.'

'Lucky for you. He could've killed you too.'

'Yeah, a lucky escape. How's the job?'

'Long hours, little thanks. I miss New York. I'm trying to get Will to come with me.'

'What?' George splutters. 'New York? He can't—he's got his comedy career to think of.'

'They have comedians there too.'

'Of course,' George smiles, masking his alarm. He can't let Will leave again. He won't allow it.

Chapter 16

George goes through his checklist. Silk tie—check. Rohypnol—check. Camcorder—check. Smelling salts—check. Alcohol—check. The scissors from the kitchen drawer glide through the red silk, making beautiful silk binds. He plans his on and off-stage performances in his head and eventually tracks down a crucial part of the plan in the *Loot* ads.

'Private storage space, no questions asked, £100 per month.'

George calls the number on his mobile and it's answered immediately by a gruff voice with a strong European accent.

George tries out his new name. 'Hello, I'm Gary Thompson. I'm calling about the storage space. Is it still available?'

'Yes. You'll need to be fast though, good price that. It's just outside Morden.'

'Can I come and see it this morning?'

'If you can make it by ten, I'll meet you there.

George takes down directions, pulls on Kon's baseball cap, and drives to the industrial estate. Unit seven is at the end of the row, tucked behind the main road with a Donatello's ice cream sign above the yellow shutter. He tries to lift it, but it won't budge. A car approaches. George steps back, hands in pockets, casual.

A black BMW pulls up and a stocky man climbs out. 'You must be Gary. I'm Vince,' he says, offering a firm handshake. The shutters lift to reveal a dark, musty unit, almost empty except for a chest freezer at the back.

'£100 a month, £100 deposit, and it's yours.'

George points to the freezer. 'Is that staying?'

'Comes with the unit. Need me to move it?'

'No, no,' George stammers, eyeing it. 'I'll take it for four months to start.'

Vince scribbles £100 deposit and £400 rent on a receipt. George signs and counts £500 from his wallet.

Vince pockets the money and slaps George on the back. 'Let me know if you want longer. Bye.' Vince waves a goodbye.

The freezer comes to life with a loud hum. It's empty and clean, though a little smelly.

On the way home, George pulls into Tesco. The wail of a child greets him as he steps inside. He hurries through the aisles, grabbing what he needs and picking up two bottles of wine.

At home, he struggles upstairs and dumps his shopping on the counter. He loves coming back now—amazed he ever lived in a shabby bedsit. This is what he deserves. Surroundings fit for a man on the rise.

After putting the shopping away, he gets dressed and inspects himself in the mirror. Not bad—handsome, smart. He winks at his reflection and grabs his coat.

On his way to visit Will, George passes Shelly's grave, hidden among the sea of headstones in the deserted graveyard. Still no mention of her missing in the news.

Traffic is light, and he arrives at Will's early.

Will throws his bag in the back and hops into the passenger seat. 'Fucking hell, two bags? It's only one night. What've you got in there, G?'

'My make-up,' George replies, cursing himself for not hiding it.

Will turns on the radio. 'Much needed, mate.'

George hasn't seen him since the New York bombshell and needs to know what's going on. 'I hear you're off to New York?'

Will raises his eyebrows. 'And leave the friendly people of London? Never!'

George starts the engine. 'Jemma practically has your flight booked.'

'I said I'd think about it, but I'll never get a working visa.'

George feels a weight lift. They drive on, radio up, windows down, singing along to 'Dirty Cash' by Stevie V.

'You were good at carpentry at school, Will?'

'Not bad. Why?'

'I'd like a bench seat built in the van. Can you do that?' George needs a secret compartment.

'I'll have a look. Should be easy enough… and I've got the tools.'

They stop at a service station for pasties and snacks. George scans the newspaper headlines, relieved to see no mention of a missing girl. Tonight's going to be amazing.

Will is reading the *Express* newspaper, sitting on the bonnet, when he gets to the carpark.

'Comfy, mate?' George asks.

'I'd prefer a deckchair, G, but I'm making the best of it.' He taps the newspaper. 'You know a girl went missing in London?'

'What? Shit. Erm.' *Composure!* 'I suppose it's not unusual in London?'

'Says she was twenty. Fucking scary,' Will holds up her picture. 'Weird… she looks familiar.'

George feels his heart stop. Staring back at him is a young Shelly. 'Familiar how?' he croaks, throat tightening.

'I'm not sure.'

George digs deep. 'There's a lot of fucking weirdos out there,' he growls. 'If I had a daughter, I'd keep her tied up inside.'

'You've got to let them live, though.'

'I suppose,' George says. *Where would be the fun in that?*

They sit in heavy traffic for an hour due to an accident. George wants to look, but the area's cordoned off with yellow tape. He wonders if he'll be creating his own incident scene tonight.

Drumming his fingers on the steering wheel, George says, 'I bought a camcorder. It'll be great to watch my gig back and see if any material needs editing. Will you record it for me?'

'No bother.' Will clears his throat. 'What do you think of Jem?'

George pauses. 'Seems nice.'

'Seems?'

'You know her better than I do. She's probably a cracking girl.'

'But?' Will turns to face him. 'Spit it out, G.'

He bites his lip, feigning a battle of conscience. ‘I don’t know. I just don’t trust her.’

‘What do you mean?’

‘I can’t put my finger on it.’ *She asks too many questions... and wants to take my best mate to America.*

George gets the silent treatment the rest of the way. His attempts at conversation are met with one-word answers. He gives up.

They arrive in Salisbury and find the venue easily. George grabs the camcorder from his bag and locks the van. Will stretches his legs while George scans the area for CCTV cameras. None are visible.

Large posters outside feature Will’s name in bold letters. George spots his own at the bottom in tiny font. Bristling, he follows Will inside.

The Comedy Cellar is a classy wine bar with high padded stools and oversized sofas. Two women at the bar sip prosecco, deep in conversation. George asks the barman loudly where the comedians should go, flashing a smile at the women. They ignore him and keep chatting.

The barman directs them downstairs to the gig, where they’re checked off a list and shown inside. It’s a decent-sized room with a well-lit stage. Most seats are already filled. George spots a group near the stage and guesses it’s the comedians.

‘Hiya, how you doing?’ Will says, introducing himself. ‘Looking for Sean Phillips?’

‘That’s me,’ Sean says, stepping forward and shaking Will’s hand.

‘Been hearing good things about you,’ Sean adds.

‘Really?’ Will replies, surprised. ‘This is George, George Mailer. He’s on too.’

‘Right,’ Sean says, no handshake for George. ‘You’re on first in the second half. Five minutes max. Will, feel free to do fifteen to twenty.’

George, seething, stomps to the bar.

As he gulps down his pint, he scans the audience for a special lady. The music stops, the spotlight hits the stage, and Sean takes the centre. Laid-back, chatty, he speaks to a few audience members.

Will asks him if he's alright.

'I'm fine,' George mutters.

The first act comes on stage; he's tall and confident with an Irish accent. He exudes the Irish charm. One girl laughs so heartily that the comedian asks her name, Jade. *Nice.* George angles his position to get a better look. She's a petite brunette with a big smile and she answers the comedian's questions shyly. George very much likes the look of her.

At the interval, George approaches Sean, who's laughing with the Irish comedian.

'Alright, Sean. Will mentioned drink tokens for the acts?'

'Don't think there's any left.' Sean pulls one from his pocket. 'Just one, sorry mate.'

George waits for him to hand it over, but Sean resumes his conversation. Heat floods George's face; his fists tighten.

'Same again,' George demands at the bar, forcing his breath to slow. Men aren't part of his plan, but maybe he could make an exception for this prick.

Sean Philips takes the stage for the second half, giving George an introduction fit for a disease.

George switches to cheeky-chappy mode, cracking self-deprecating jokes about being Scottish, hoping for the same rapport the Irish comedian had. Will is filming, and George desperately wants to deliver his best. The crowd laughs in parts, but his main jokes miss the mark. One bright spot: Jade laughs at everything he says. It's enough to keep him going, and he finishes to a mild round of applause.

'Fucking no sense of humour at these fucks,' George growls, taking the camera from Will to watch his performance. He looks great on screen.

Will takes the stage and nails his gig. The biggest laughs come from Jade, which annoys him. Is she laughing more for Will than for him? Possibly.

Will exits to a rapturous round of applause.

George slaps him on the back. 'Job well done.'

'Cheers, G. Sean said there's a bar in the hotel. Want to join them?'

'I'm knackered. Might hit the hay, mate,' George says, forcing a yawn. 'You go. I'll check in.'

'I'll do it,' Will says, looking guilty.

'Why?' The penny drops. 'The room's booked just for you, not me?'

'G, it doesn't matter. We're sharing anyway. I'll grab the key and be back in two minutes,' Will says, leaving his drink.

How dare they. The tight bastards!

George scans the room for Miss Laughter and spots her outside the toilets, talking to a friend who's swaying unsteadily. The friend staggers towards the ladies' room, covering her mouth. George moves in.

'Hi, how you doing? Is your friend okay?' he asks, his face a mask of concern.

'She'll be fine in a minute,' Jade says confidently.

'You've got a great laugh. Bet people say that all the time... Want to grab a drink?'

'Now?' Her face creases, unsure. Has he moved too fast?

'The Hamptons is open. I'll see if my mate's up for it. Back in a minute.'

Shit. Three's a crowd.

Will returns. 'Twin room,' he says, handing over the key. 'Room 22.'

'Great,' George says, nodding at the comedians heading out. 'Enjoy. See you in the morning.'

'You sure you don't want to come?'

'Absolutely. Go. Don't need to set off till midday tomorrow. Go crazy.'

George waits until the venue is almost empty, and the bar staff are cleaning up.

Jade appears, her drunk friend leaning on her shoulder. 'I'm sorry, I can't come. Maybe another time?'

The threat of loss hits him like a punch to the stomach. He takes a deep breath. He needs this.

'Tell you what,' he says, taking the drunken girl's arm. 'I'll give her a lift home, then we'll grab that drink.'

'Oh God, that would be great. Cheers.'

The bar staff barely notice as they leave. He supports the half-conscious friend upstairs, practically carrying her to the van.

He opens the back doors. 'Sorry, it's a two-seater. You'll need to put her in here.'

Jade looks unsure.

The drunken girl loses control of her legs and slumps onto the van floor.

'I need to get her home.'

Jade takes off her jacket and spreads it on the floor. 'Lisa, lie on that.'

Her friend grunts, swinging her legs into the van.

'We'll have you home in no time,' Jade says, turning to George. 'I can give you directions. It's not far.'

Chapter 17

'Just next to the post box,' Jade points as they pull up in a street of identical houses. George surveys the area—no lights, no cameras. Good.

He opens the van doors to find the girl passed out.

'You grab her bag, I'll carry her inside.' He scoops her up; heavier than expected.

Inside, she leads him to the bedroom. He lies her down. 'Home safe. I'll wait outside,' he whispers.

In the van, George adds Rohypnol to a bottle of coke, stroking the red tie with excitement. This is it!

Jade sits in the passenger seat. 'I doubt we'll make the Hamptons now,' she says, checking her watch.

'I came prepared,' he says, holding up the vodka and cups. 'How about a drink at Stonehenge?'

'I've always wanted to go there,' Jade coos.

'Perfect! You pour, I'll drive.'

Jade pours and hands him a drink.

'I can't juggle a drink and the steering wheel.'

Jade knocks both back. 'Cheers... You were really good on stage tonight.'

It's quiet and barren on the way to Stonehenge, illuminated by a bright full moon. George hops out, lays his jacket on the grass, and pours two drinks—his neat.

Jade chatters on while George caresses the silk ties in his pocket, his gaze fixed on her neck.

Just after midnight, her chatter slows, becoming a sluggish drawl.

She lies down. 'Look at all the stars... so many,' she slurs, eyes fluttering shut mid-sentence.

George stays still until she does too, then scoops her up and lays her in the back of the van. He strips her, gags her with silk, ties her arms and feet, and secures a final tie around her neck.

Jade's sound asleep. George hopes the dose is right and he won't have to wait long. He turns on the camcorder, the screen flickering to life, showing Philips introducing him. He fast-forwards.

A beautiful entrance, full of confidence—amazing mic control. Shame the thick fuckers in the audience didn't appreciate it. His humour's too sophisticated for them. He laughs loudly at his own material.

Jade twitches in her sleep. Is it time for his second performance?

He waves smelling salts under her nose. She flinches.

'Time for more comedy, Jade. Wake up,' he sings into her ear.

She stirs. He holds the salts until she coughs. Setting the camera on her face, he kneels in front of her. 'Wakey, wakey,' he croons.

He wants to capture her first reaction. Her head moves, but her eyes stay shut.

'Jaaaaddddeee, it's showtime.' He blows on her face, holding the camera steady. Her eyes fly open.

'Remember me?' George says, smiling, imagining himself as the Tin Man welcoming Dorothy back to consciousness.

Confusion, then bam… fear. Bingo! Her eyes widen as she looks down at her body.

'Smile, Jade, you're on *Candid Camera.*' George laughs, delighted, letting the camera—and his hand—travel down her body.

'We're going to have some fun now. Listen carefully or there'll be consequences. You've been selected for my private show because of your fantastic laugh. I'm going to remove the gag. When I do, you won't scream, or I'll kill you. I don't want to,' he lies, 'but I will. Nod if you understand.'

Jade nods. George rips the tape from her mouth.

'Please… please don't hurt me.'

'Of course not. Ready for the show?' He claps.

The performance begins. He belongs on a bigger screen. Sean Phillips appears.

'Did you think he was good, Jade?'

'Erm,' she hesitates. 'No.'

'Right answer. Now, the main event, the hilarious, the amazing Geeeeeooooorrrrrgggeeee Mailer,' he announces, circus-style. He sits inches in front of her, watching her reactions. He delivers his opening line. Jade doesn't laugh.

He pauses the film. 'Not funny?' Anger bubbles inside him.

'Yes, yes,' she chokes out, her smile strained, tears welling.

He tugs on the necktie. 'Don't tell me it's funny. Show me.'

The film resumes, and Jade laughs heartily at the next joke.

'I knew that joke would smash it. It's just so fucking funny! It's all in the delivery!'

Jade's eyes stay fixed on the screen as he replays it, squeezing her shoulder for bigger laughs. If he had two cameras, he'd record her watching the show. Her laughter becomes more manic, grating on him. He doesn't need sympathy laughs. He gags her, flings open the back doors, and lets the moonlight flood in.

'Disappointing, Jade!'

He lays her down, positions the camera for a different kind of show, and straddles her. As he tightens the tie around her neck, her eyes fill with fear. He tightens it further.

'I've been George Mailer, and you've been a shit audience. Good night.'

Squeezing the knot tighter, Jade's face flushes, her eyes bulging. The euphoria sweeps through George, laughter exploding as her life fades. With a sly wink at the camera, he takes a moment to admire her lifeless form, the moon illuminating every inch of her skin.

'And cut,' he yells.

Stuffing her into the large holdall, her body fits perfectly inside, the zips close with ease.

George follows the signs back to Salisbury, the buzz of having her in the back of the van electric—like carrying a trophy. The route to the hotel is easy to retrace. A fleeting thought crosses his mind: how long before her body starts to smell? He'll leave first thing.

He pulls into the empty hotel car park and parks discreetly in a corner. The urge to peek at Jade is irresistible. He opens the van's rear doors, unzips the bag. Her wide, shocked eyes stare blankly, frozen in fear. A quick pinch to her cheek, then he zips the bag up again. Moving quickly, he crosses the car park and enters the hotel.

Inside, the reception desk is unmanned, the garish carpets and matching wallpaper creating a tacky atmosphere. Thoughts drift to Will—whether he's back yet and what to say if he's awake. Better for his alibi if Will is sound asleep. Room 22 appears at the end of the hall. The key slides into the lock, and the door creaks open.

Darkness greets him as his eyes adjust to the room's shadowy interior. He glances at Will's bed. It's empty. *Shit—where is he?* If an alibi is needed, it would be stronger if he could've claimed he got in earlier while Will was still in bed. Fuck it—he won't need an alibi; he's been meticulous, professional. His plan is solid. Clothes come off quickly, leaving him in boxer shorts as he slips into the bed nearest the door. The phone alarm is set for 6:00 a.m. Early bird catches the worm.

The alarm startles him awake. Still no sign of Will. What if something's happened? Sean Phillips isn't trustworthy. George calls Will's mobile, but the answer machine picks up. He rubs his face as the room door swings open.

'Where the fuck have you been?'

Will sways slightly on his feet, still drunk with bloodshot eyes and crumpled clothes.

'Fell asleep in Sean's room. Few of us went back there when the bar closed. Smoked a few spliffs and crashed out. I'm fucked. I'm going to bed.' He sways on his feet, still drunk, eyes bloodshot and clothes crumpled.

'No, no, no,' George springs up, blocking the bed. 'Sleep in the van.'

'What? I thought we weren't leaving till midday?'

'Traffic will be crazy then. Let's go. You can sleep all the way.'

'Fuck, G. This isn't good,' Will says, desperation in his voice.

'You'll be fine.' George throws him his bag and holds the door open. Will caves with mumbled curses, dragging his feet down the hallway, shoulders slumped, head down, bag scraping behind him.

George opens the van door, relieved it doesn't smell. He sprays deodorant for good measure.

Will drops his bag beside him. 'Fuck, it's minging! What's that smell?'

'Lynx. Drives the women crazy. Buckle up, we'll get you home.'

'Can't I sleep in the back?'

'No, it's too dangerous,' George says quickly. 'Nothing to hold you down.'

'Since when did you become safety conscious?' Will grumbles.

'Safety's my number one priority for my best buddy. Hop in.'

Will collapses in the front passenger seat. George fastens his seatbelt. 'Clunk, click, every trip. Seatbelt, please.'

'God, you're annoyingly cheerful today. Get some action last night?'

'I didn't, my friend. What I got was a sound night's sleep.'

'Smug fucker,' Will mumbles, shifting for a comfortable position.

George hums along with the radio, drowning out Will's snoring, until he nudges him awake outside his flat. 'Wakey wakey, mate.'

'We home? Fuck, cheers, G, I'm off to bed,' Will mumbles, stumbling out of the van.

The smell is stronger when George opens the van door. He grabs Will's bag and quickly shuts it. 'See you later, bud.'

George reaches the lock-up in less than twenty minutes. It's deserted, the only noise is the hum of the freezer through the shutters.

'Welcome home, Jade,' he whispers, lifting the bag from the back of the van.

The smell is pungent now, stinging the eyes. The chest freezer swings open, ready to receive its guest. Jade is gently laid down, eyes staring up, frozen in her grey face. Arms are arranged like a resting angel, crossed in front. *Nice.* The blood-red tie looks great. The whole scene—beautiful!

The light starts to fade, and he forces himself to say goodbye. Driving through early evening traffic, a jaunty tune escapes in a whistle. The world takes on a rosy tint; he feels optimistic, indestructible.

At home, George checks the money and the coke—still there. It's time to get rid of the coke; keeping it in the house is too risky, and he doesn't want anything to interfere with what he's building. Finding a buyer for the coke could be tricky. He stands for a moment, fingers drumming on the counter, eyes flicking over the room as he mentally runs through the few people he knows who could help. None of them fit. He's not in those kinds of circles.

He rummages behind the deep fat fryer and finds shiny electronic scales, weighs the bag—exactly 1kg. He has it. *Gary*, his old raving pal. He digs out an old *Fantasia* flyer with Gary's number, holding his breath as he dials.

Chapter 18

It's early afternoon, and George knows Gary's not an early riser. Eventually, a breathless Gary answers.

'Gary, it's George. How you doing?'

'Scottish George?'

'The very one.'

'Fuck, mate, not seen you since Leicester. Still in London?'

'South London.'

'Thought you moved back to Scotland.'

'Nah, still here. Want to come round for beers tonight?'

'Where?'

'Tooting.'

'Bit of a mission, I'm in Manor House.'

'Come on, you won't regret it. I've got some nose candy.'

'Now you're talking. I'll be there at eight.'

A generous amount of coke is scooped onto the paper, folded into a neat wrap. A healthy sample, though the hope is Gary knows someone who'll buy the full kilo.

Checking the TV news, there's no word on missing persons. Maybe the *Evening Standard* will have something.

Shuffling into his jacket in the hallway, a door bangs open, pausing him. He creeps along the landing for a better view. The old guy, the last remaining tenant, hobbles down the hall.

George has never seen him before. He waits until the bedsit door shuts, then slips out. Not a recluse after all. He'll have to be careful coming and going.

He picks up a newspaper and a ten-pack of Stella. While the beers chill in the fridge, he scans the paper for news on Shelly—maybe even Jade. So many missing people! George chuckles. People should remember where they put them.

On page twelve, the headline screams *Ten Days Missing*. An unflattering picture of Shelly stares back—her hair badly cut; skin marked by teenage acne. He replays the walk to meet her at the station. The cap and plain, dark clothes kept him under the radar. No worries—no one's catching him out.

His mobile rings, flashing Will's name.

'Hello, Will, back in the land of the living?'

Will laughs. 'Just got up—phone rang. Guess who it was.'

'Who?' George plays along.

'Steve Trent. Apparently, he's tight with Sean Philips.'

George hears the excitement in Will's voice. 'And?'

'He wants to book me for a bloody tour.'

'A tour? What kind?'

'A singing tour. What do you think, G—a fucking comedy tour! Scotland's best and guests. It's small but a brilliant way to get my name out there. Guess who's headlining?'

'Who?' George asks, struggling to hide the envy.

'Ade Charmers from Comedy Central. I can't fucking believe it.'

The words stick in George's throat. 'Amazing, mate.'

'I'm meeting Trent at the Phoenix bar tomorrow night. Come with me... see if we can get you on too. You *are* Scottish after all.'

'And fucking hilarious.'

'Of course. I'll swing by yours—if you grab the wood, I'll sort out the platform bed in your van.'

Hidden storage space is badly needed. 'That would be ace, mate. What would I do without you?'

'Nothing, absolutely nothing,' Will jokes.

George bristles. 'Alright, come round about four. I'll see you then.'

Will is making a name for himself, he's on his way up. He needs to be there too. Touring would open doors to bigger opportunities for both work and play—giving him the chance to perfect his ritual.

After toast and beans in front of the TV, George has a nap and wakes up to his phone ringing.

'Alright, mate,' Gary says. 'Think I'm just outside your place. I can't see a buzzer.'

He glances at the clock: 8:00 p.m. God, he's napping like an OAP. 'We don't have one. I'll come let you in.'

Gary stands dripping at the door, shaking an umbrella. 'Lovely weather this side of town!'

'Come in! You're soaking. Give me your jacket.'

Gary looks around appraisingly. 'Nice place. Who did you rob to get this?'

George throws him a towel. 'My granny died a few months ago and left me some money.'

'Lucky bastard. My granny left me a clapped-out Skoda. £70 scrap.'

'Beer?'

'Lovely,' Gary says, pulling a bottle of vodka from his bag. 'Home warming gift.'

'Brilliant.' George grabs two beers from the fridge, passes one to Gary. 'Take a seat. I'll put some tunes on.'

He searches for a pirate radio station—London's got the best—and settles on one playing happy house.

'Looks like things are going well for you, George, while I'm unemployed and skint!'

George neatly puts out four lines of coke, snorting two back greedily and hands Gary the note.

Blood rushes to his head. It's been a while. Leaning back, he lets the drugs work their way through his system, barely registering Garry's chatter. God, it feels good. Different from before—cleaner, stronger. He straightens, feeling sharp and in control, and takes a long swig of beer.

'What do you think of the nose candy?' George asks.

'Fucking quality, mate. Where did you get it?'

'My granny left me it,' George says, laughing.

Gary joins in. 'Your granny's a legend man. That's all I'm saying.'

George plonks the bag of coke on the table, savouring Gary's shocked look. Gary weighs the bag in his hands, and finally recovers, 'Fucking hell mate, how much is here?'

'Just a kilo,' George says, casually. 'You know any big boys who'd buy the lot?'

'I know someone who might know someone. How much do you want for it?' Gary asks, staring at the bag with greedy eyes.

'How much is it for a gram these days?'

'About forty quid,' Gary replies.

'There's a thousand grams in a kilo. I'd say forty grand.'

Gary licks his lips—a sly look fleeting across his face. 'It's a dangerous amount of shit to be caught with. Serious risks involved. Give me a sample, I'll see what I can do. No promises though.'

To keep Gary from skimming the sample, George scoops a generous spoonful, folds it into a wrap, and hands it over before racking up more lines on the table. The night drags into early morning, and by 4:00 a.m., George is thoroughly bored of Gary's endless chatter.

'Shit, it's four. I've got a big meeting tomorrow. I need to call it a night, mate.'

'I've missed the last tube home,' Gary pouts.

George gives Gary £40 for a taxi and is rewarded with a tight hug and promises of a coke deal.

George wakes up with his tongue stuck to the roof of his mouth. He stumbles to get to the toilet but has to sit down, body dry heaving before barely making it to vomit. Hovering over the bowl, his eyes stream, spasms following. The crawl to the sink is tough, but the cold water gives him hope. The mirror confirms he looks like shit—bloodshot eyes like Will's yesterday.

Shit, Will.

He rushes into the living room. *Half fucking three! How did that happen?*

The room's a bombsite—traces of powder, rolled-up notes, beer cans, and an empty vodka bottle. The urge to vomit rises again. His mobile rings, Will's name flashing on the screen. *Shit.*

'Alright mate. I'm downstairs.'

'You're early,' George splutters.

'And helping your arse out… do you want to let me in?'

'Be down in a minute.'

George grabs a carrier bag, sweeping everything into it, and wipes the traces of coke from the table with a dishtowel.

Unbelievable, the place looks rough on Will's first visit. He throws on yesterday's jeans and a t-shirt before bounding downstairs to an empty doorstep. Stepping outside in his bare feet, he spots Will a few doors down, looking at his phone.

'You looking for me?' George shouts.

Will grabs his bag. 'You said next to the kebab shop,' he shouts back, walking toward George.

'Aye this side. Your left.'

'This is my left,' Will says, doing a half turn.

George is in no mood to explain. 'Come in, it's freezing.'

'Fuck, G, you look like me yesterday. Big night?'

'Nah, just coming down with something. You look smart,' George eyes Will's suit and tie.

'Came from work.'

'I haven't bought the wood.'

'Don't worry. I'll grab it after measuring up. Where's the van?'

'Two minutes away, behind the graveyard.'

The walk upstairs is exhausting, though the five-minute cleanup has been effective.

Will takes in the surroundings. 'Very nice. How do you afford this?'

'Same way you do,' George replies shortly. 'Working.'

Will flinches. 'Sorry, mate, no offence meant.'

'It's me, sorry. Just feel like crap.'

'Sit down, let's get some air.' Will opens a window.

The cool breeze makes George shiver.

'You look rough. You gonna be alright to meet Trent tonight?'

'I'll be fine. Just need a few hours rest and some paracetamol.'

'You chill. I'll grab the wood and use the tools and nails I've got,' Will says, holding up his bag.

George's mind races. Is there anything in the van that shouldn't be? He's sure it's clean. 'You're a fucking star, mate,' George says, passing him the keys.

'We don't need to be at The Phoenix till eight. Have a bath, try to sort yourself out.'

The hot shower helps, and, wrapped in a quilt, he closes his eyes for a power nap.

He wakes to darkness, no missed calls—just after 7:00 p.m. He calls Gary for an update, but it rings out. George leaves a message.

Still feeling rough, he finds the bag of coke, licks his finger, and dips it in. A top-up. It tastes vile, but a cold beer helps—it tastes amazing. Dressing takes a little effort, but he's ready when Will arrives.

'Feeling better?'

'Yes. How did you get on?'

'Looks great. A bit of foam on the bench, and it'll be comfy. That graveyard next door's creepy as fuck.'

'Doesn't bother me,' George says, handing over a beer.

'No time for that. We need to go, don't want to be late.'

George pulls on his trainers and grabs his jacket. The coke hits his system, giving him a rush. He can do this. Invincible George can do anything.

'Let's go and get our tour booked.'

George and Will arrive at the Phoenix right on eight. The Phoenix sign is lit up in light bulbs—very showbiz. The queue snakes around the corner.

'You need an equity card or guest list to get in,' Will says.

Every time the doors swing open, a blast of music hits, and George fights the urge to dance.

At the front, Will tells the bouncer he's a guest of Steve Trent.

The stocky bouncer checks his list. 'Yeah, on you go.'

George steps forward, but the bouncer blocks him.

'I'm with him.'

'Not how it works. You're not on the guestlist.'

'I'll sort it out, G, give me a minute,' Will says, opening the club door.

'Please stand over there,' Stocky growls at George.

'Arseholes,' George snarls at the people casting looks his way. A young girl flashes her equity card, winks at Stocky, and walks right in.

Eventually, Will returns. 'Steve says put his plus one on the list, he'll sort it later.'

'Suppose it clears my entrance. On you go.'

'Thanks,' George smirks, sarcasm thick in his voice.

He follows Will inside. A sparkling chandelier lights a large room with velvet sofas, chaise longues, and ornate brass-framed mirrors. Candlelight flickers on small groups chatting intimately, hair flicking, and theatrical laughter.

'You good?' Will asks.

'Fucking great,' George scowls.

'Look, G, sort your face out. Pain waiting at the door, I know, but you're in. Trent's over there,' Will points to the corner. 'With Hattie from Amusement House. Ready?'

George rolls his shoulders, takes a deep breath. 'Born ready. Just give me a minute.'

The toilets are decadent, with plush carpets and mosaic tiles. A bright orange chaise longue sits at the entrance. In the cubicle, George snorts line after line, checking his nose in the mirror on the way out. *Looking good—be cool.*

He joins Will at the bar. 'Let's do this. Destiny awaits.'

Will makes the introductions. Trent, is an attractive man in his sixties, looks like he's been around the block and may have seen his fair share of success.

'Pleasure to meet you,' George says, shaking Trent's cold, reptilian hand.

'The pleasure's all yours,' Trent replies, deadpan, a smile playing on his lips.

'Lovely to see you, Hattie,' George purrs, kissing her cheek.

'Take a seat, boys,' Trent says. 'Will... let's get to it. Scotland's best and guests—three cities, five nights. First stop Liverpool, then Leeds, finishing with two nights in Manchester, with Ade Charmers headlining. Any conflicts with those dates?'

'None at all. Sounds great,' Will says.

'I'm keen to come on board,' George blurts. Will gives him a look—so much for subtly.

Trent turns to George. 'This guy? I don't mean to be rude, but I've never heard of you.'

Prick. 'I've worked the Scottish circuit and gigged at the Melbourne festival last year. I'm pretty booked, but the dates are free. Will can vouch for me, can't you, Will?'

'Yeah. He's definitely on his way up, Mister Trent.'

'What do you think, Hattie?'

'He did ok last week. Both Will and George are on the bill next week. Why don't you come to the show… It would be great to have you there.' Hattie pouts.

'Alright. I'm not making any promises. If I like what I see, I may be able to squeeze you in for a short spot and obviously there'd be no money in it for you, just expenses.'

'I can work with that,' George says.

They say their goodbyes and head for the bar. Will's phone buzzes.

'Jemma's coming to join us.'

'Good luck getting past beefcake.'

'She has an equity card.'

'Great,' George mutters.

Jemma breezes in, planting a kiss on Will's mouth before pulling away to catch her breath.

'Sorry I'm late. Had to stay behind at work. They just found a body.'

'Really? Where?' Will asks, intrigued.

'You won't believe it,' she pauses for effect. 'In a graveyard. A bloody graveyard. Apparently, they were exhuming a body for an insurance claim—and they found two bodies in the same plot. Somewhere in Tooting.'

'George lives in Tooting. Right next to a graveyard, actually.'

'It was Garrett Lane.'

'God,' George exclaims, feigning shock. 'Have they arrested anyone?'

'Not yet. You'll probably get a visit soon. The police will be everywhere, going house to house,' Jemma says.

His mind races. *Has he been thorough in covering his tracks?*

George forces himself to stay for another hour. On the tube home, he replays his moves, scrutinizing every detail. Is there anything linking him to the dead girl? Two meeting places: the Amusement House and the tube station. The conversation at the Amusement House was brief, and the tube was quiet—no

CCTV, no Nosey Nora's. Garrett Lane residents keep their heads down.

The coke needs to be out of the flat. A routine door-to-door call could land him in trouble, especially with sniffer dogs. Gary's phone rings out again.

In bed, George's mind races, trying to figure out where to stash the drugs. The unit is too risky. The cocaine and the looming police investigation dull the excitement of the upcoming tour. Exhaustion takes over, and he eventually drifts into fitful sleep.

Chapter 19

George calls Gary every day. The phone rings out, then goes to voicemail. Twice now, there's been a knock at the door, sounding like a cop's knock. The cocaine needs to be gone. The unit could work temporarily, but it's too close to his trophy cabinet and too risky.

On his return from the shops, two policemen are at the front door. He keeps his head down and heads to the café on the High Street. Ordering a tea and bacon roll, he wipes the sweat from his brow and takes a seat by the window. The effect of the cocaine is wearing off. Daily use no longer blocks out his problems—police, the tour, the coke deal, or the recovered body.

Writing has become impossible. Why won't Gary answer his fucking phone? Will's birthday party is tonight—offloading some coke there and finding a good hiding place for the rest of it might work. He nurses the cup of tea for an hour before heading back home. No sign of the police. He walks straight in, gets dressed, and makes some wraps of coke for the party.

He arrives at Will's just before eight, bottle of tequila in hand and plenty of party powder. The music blares from the end of the street.

Jemma answers the door. Lady of the manor now. 'George,' she nods.

A tight smile is all George can manage. Will's in the sitting room with Nick and another guy from work.

'Alright buddy, happy birthday,' George says, shaking the bottle of tequila.

'Cheers, mate. Let's grab a beer.'

Jemma joins them in the kitchen. 'What've you been up to, George?'

'This and that, mostly writing. Let's have a birthday shot,' George says, setting them up.

'Arm up back,' Will chuckles. 'To my two favourite people.'

George knocks back the shot, then heads to the toilet. Jemma annoys him. Her expression, like she knows something no one else does, especially since Will's elevated her so quickly. My two favourite people. They only met two minutes ago.

Will's bathroom is surprisingly tidy for two blokes living together. No hiding places, cupboards full and clearly well-used. The window overlooks a tidy garden with a small shed at the end. *Perfect.*

Downstairs, the party is packed, the lounge feeling even smaller with all the bodies. In the kitchen, Will wears a polite smile while George tilts his head to get a better look at his friend's conversation partner—Dan the Man.

'Hello, Dan,' George says, forcing a smile. 'How are you?'

'Good, thanks. You?' Dan replies, his smile tight and awkward.

George suppresses a laugh, finding the mechanical politeness amusing. 'Fantastic, thanks for asking.'

Will raises an eyebrow. Dan casts a quick, uneasy smile at George before slipping out of the kitchen.

'What? Looks like he's had a change of heart.'

'Mmm. He's now my right-hand man at work, backing everything I suggest. Know anything about this?'

'Maybe he found God!'

Jemma swans into the kitchen. George seizes the chance to slip into the garden.

'How's it going, Nick? Nice shed,' he says, nodding at it.

'Erm, we never use it,' Nick replies.

George feels the rush as the coke mixes with the alcohol. 'You like coke, Nick?'

'Not my thing.'

'Not mine either, just a mate who needs some for his stag do.'

'Can't help,' Nick says, stubbing out his roll-up. 'Off for a drink.'

George waits for the garden to empty, then slips into the shed, feeling beneath a stack of wood for a good hiding spot.

'What are you up to?' Jemma's voice cuts through the quiet.

George jumps. 'Just checking out the shed.'

'Right?' She eyes him suspiciously. 'You spoken to the police? There's a huge task force.'

'Police haven't been round yet.'

'There you are!' Will appears at the perfect moment. 'Get out of the shed, weirdos, and come inside.' He laughs, throwing an arm around them and steering them toward the house.

He ducks to the toilet, tucking the bag of coke into his waistband. When he returns, a group of smokers clusters outside the shed. He waits for them to leave.

George peers through the window to check the shed's clear before stepping in, heart pounding, to hide the coke in a small crevice. It fits perfectly. It should be fine for now, but he needs the deal. Time to try Gary again.

The phone rings out. Just as he's about to hang up, Gary answers.

'Alright, G,' Gary says, like everything's fine.

'Where the fuck have you been?' George hisses. 'I've been calling you all week.'

'Lost my phone, found it under the sofa. Dead as a dodo. Wouldn't you believe it,' Gary laughs.

George takes a deep breath. 'You find a buyer? I've got a kilo sitting here, need to get it out.'

'Yeah, buyer's good. He'll give you twenty grand for the lot.'

'Twenty grand? It's worth forty!'

'Don't shoot the messenger, mate!'

'Get back to him with thirty. I'll call you tomorrow. Don't lose your fucking phone again, Gary.'

George pockets his phone and steps out of the shed. Jemma's there, smoking. Fuck. He forces a smile as he passes. Did she hear? Her face is unreadable—she'd make a great poker player. Time to leave.

'Hey, Will, I'm off. Gotta impress Trent tomorrow. Can't be hungover.'

'It's not even midnight, G,' Will slurs.

George hugs him tight. 'Need to catch the last tube. Happy birthday, buddy.'

'No hug for me?' Jemma pouts, stepping into his path. She pulls him into an embrace. 'Bye, George,' she whispers, her voice low and smooth, 'Your secret's safe with me.'

There's no mention of Shelly on the news the next day. Maybe they've hit a wall. Dinner is just heavily buttered toast, washed down with a can of lager. Gary's call interrupts.

'G, I told him you want thirty grand. He's getting back to me. I'll call you as soon as I hear.'

George ends the call feeling a surge of optimism. Inspired, he unpacks his kit, running the silk binds through his hands—their smoothness somehow amplifies their strength. The neckties work well for intricate knots, and a slender neck will sit snugly in the loop. Reviewing the footage of Jade, he decides he's pleased, though it would be even better if he could capture his next subject watching the footage during the private performance—taking in her laughter and joy. A portable computer would make things much more professional—he resolves to buy one once the coke deal goes through.

The urge to visit his trophy at the unit is strong, but, with the police sniffing about, it's too dangerous. At least the coke's out of the flat. That's a load off. The new material is coming along great—Trent's going to be floored tonight. Easy to picture a different girl in every city. Jemma's words interrupt his excitement: 'Your secret's safe with me.' His chest tightens at the thought of her telling Will or worse, finding the coke and giving it to the police.

There's heavy knocking at the front door—a cop knock. *Showtime.* There's an odd smell in the hallway coming from the old man's flat; burnt condensed milk? Taking a deep breath before pulling open the door, he's shocked to find his sister standing there.

He takes a step back. 'Sammy. Wh—what the fuck are you doing here?'

'That's a nice bloody welcome. You going to invite me in?' she asks rhetorically, marching past him, pausing momentarily to drop a huge bag at his feet. 'Be a dear,' she smiles, confidently ploughing ahead.

George is stunned, a million questions racing through his mind. What's she doing here? How did she find him? Has the family secret come out? No! Shaking it off, he jogs up the stairs behind her.

She floats around, moving things aimlessly. 'Nice place. IKEA too, classy.' She flops on the sofa, picking up the newspaper and nodding to the kettle.

George sets the mugs out, buying himself time to think. She can't be here—he needs her gone. 'Milk, sugar?'

'Just milk. Where's the girlfriend?'

'Eh— she's home, in Romania, visiting her dad. He's ill.'

'Oh, right,' she says, a smirk playing on her lips.

'How did you find out my address?'

'Through Kathy. I told her I was going to send a letter—she bought it! I wanted to see where my little brother lives. Is that so wrong?' she pouts.

'Where are you staying?'

'Here I hope?'

'What? Sorry you can't. I don't have the room.'

'No room at the penthouse for your little sis? Tell you what… the sofa's fine. It's actually quite comfy.' Sammy chuckles, spreading out.

'How long are you thinking?'

'Not sure actually… Got an open-ended ticket.'

George's heart sinks. 'Erm… I suppose you can stay a few nights but that's it. I'm off on tour next week… I won't be here.'

'Perfect,' Sammy screams. 'I'll flat sit, look after the place.'

'No— Anka will need her own space when she gets back.'

'George, I need to talk. I'm still worried about my ma. She's getting worse!'

Why can't she just leave it alone? 'She's getting on, Sammy. Old age isn't kind.'

'There's more to it, I think.'

'You can stay. Two nights max.'

His phone rings—Gary. 'I need to take this,' George says, heading to the bedroom.

'Good news, G! Thirty grand's locked in... Now, about my fee.'

George's heart races. Thirty grand!

'Of course, £300 seems fair.'

'I was thinking a thousand,' Gary counters. 'This took work.'

'Five hundred. Final offer.'

'Seven hundred.'

'Fine.'

'He's in Mitcham, wants it today.'

'Tell him 5:00 p.m. at Penville industrial estate, Morden, unit one.'

'Got it. When do I get my fee? I can swing by now.'

The music blares from the living room. 'I'll meet you in town. I've got a gig at eight, but I'll see you before.'

'Nah, man. I'll come to the gig. Want to see you in action, funny man.'

That's all he needs, more pressure. 'Fine. Amusement House on Oxford Street.'

Sammy is spreadeagled on the sofa, shoes off, half the pillows scattered on the floor.

'Make yourself comfortable!'

'Thanks. So, what's the plans for tonight?'

'I've got a gig.' George doesn't want her there but what's the alternative? Leave her here alone, nosing about the flat, answering the door to the police? He picks up her jacket and throws it at her. 'Let's go for lunch.'

'Great. I'm starving,' Sammy says, bouncing to her feet.

She's upbeat and friendly, not the Sammy of old—devious, nasty, vindictive, and cunning. She talks non-stop all the way to the old man's pub on the corner of Tooting High Street.

Sammy picks up the menu from the bar. 'Ploughman's for me,' she beams.

'Jeez, you don't mess about. What do you want to drink—whisky?'

'George, it's not even two o'clock,' Sammy says, feigning shock. 'Aye, that would be lovely, with ice please.'

A skinny, middle-aged, man serves the drinks with a minimum of words. George places the drinks on the table.

Sammy launches into a monologue about her new love, Eric. George struggles to pay attention, but his mind is racing. Should he be worried about meeting up with a drugs dealer in a deserted industrial estate? What if the guy doesn't give him the money, and takes the drugs? What if he's got a gun?

The food arrives. Sammy wolfs it down. George pushes his around the plate.

'Where we going tonight?'

'A gig in town,' he says, taking a sip of his shandy.

'I've no been to see any comedy since I saw you last. Is Will on too?'

'Yes. I'll just give him a bell now. Two minutes.'

He steps into the busy street and dials. Will picks up right away.

'Alright, mate, how you feeling? Hung-over?' George asks, observing two chav mothers in matching tracksuits and matching prams walk past, shouting and swearing at the top of their voices.

'Drank a pint of water before bed so I'm not too shabby.'

'Guess who's turned up on my doorstep?'

'Who?'

'Sammy. Your sister gave her my address.'

'Fuck. Sorry G.'

'It's fine, don't sweat it. Look, I've got to meet someone at five and I'm passing yours on the way. Sammy wants to come say hello.'

'Yeah, no bother. See you then.'

George finds Sammy texting on her phone.

'How do you do that?' George asks, pointing at her phone.

'What? You don't know how to text?' she sneers.

This is more like the Sammy of old. Always laughing at him, and never with him.

'Forget it. Let's go see Will.'

Chapter 20

Will swings the door open. 'There she is, the lovely Sammy,' he says, stepping past George for a hug.

'How are you, handsome? Kathy said you've got a girlfriend. How's it going?'

'Yeah, Jemma. Come in,' Will replies, ushering them inside.

'Watch out, the interrogation has started,' George mutters.

'Interrogation? Such an exaggerator, Georgie Porgie.'

The nickname stings—he hasn't heard that in years.

Will leads them to the kitchen. 'Tea?'

George takes a breath. Keep it together.

'I'd prefer whiskey,' Sammy says, looking around. 'Nice place.'

'No whiskey. Wine or beer?'

'Wine's fine. Oh, I'm a poet and didn't know it,' she laughs, plopping herself down.

'Tea for me, Will. Be back in a sec,' George says, heading to the garden.

He moves quickly to the shed, glancing over his shoulder. Kneeling, he checks his hiding spot. The hole is empty. Panic surges. He checks again, pushing shelves aside. Nothing. Frantic, he tries once more. Then—there it is. He reaches for the bag but it's just out of grasp. Jacket off, sleeves rolled up, he dives back down. Grabbing the bag, he stuffs it into his waistband just as Will calls from behind him.

'What…?' George jumps, standing quickly, pulling his shirt over the bulge.

'Thought I dropped my watch in here the other night,' he mutters, masking his panic.

'Your tea's on the table,' Will calls, oblivious.

George dashes upstairs, stashing the coke inside his bag and checking the time. Four o'clock. Time to go.

He finds Sammy and Will laughing in the garden.

'Will, could you do me a favour?'

'Yeah, what?'

'You two are so Englified,' Sammy mocks.

Will chuckles, giving her a playful punch. 'It's the Queen's English, love. Deal.'

'Can you entertain Sammy for a bit? Something's come up. I'll only be an hour.'

'Fine, mate,' Will agrees.

'Palming me off, cheeky shite!' Sammy laughs. 'I'll get the lowdown on the new bird. Take your time, Georgie Porgie.'

George bristles, muttering under his breath as he heads to the car.

The traffic's heavy, rain pelts down. Wipers on full, still hard to see. He winds down the window for air, sweating. Finally, at a quarter to five, he parks on the estate, facing outward. The rain bounces off the roof. Hood up, he waits.

At 5:15 p.m., a black BMW pulls up next to George. Wiping the condensation from the window, he wonders about the etiquette of a drug deal. Do you go to them, or do they come to you?

Wanting to get it over with, he exits the car and knocks on the driver's side window. It rolls down, revealing a grimacing, scarred face.

'Tony?'

'That's me. Get in,' Tony orders.

The car smells of fresh leather and cheap aftershave.

'You got the stuff?' Tony growls.

George pulls the coke from his bag. Tony reaches inside his jacket, pulls out a scooping instrument, dips it into the bag, and snorts. He grabs scales from under the seat and weighs the coke.

'This isn't a kilo,' Tony spits, glaring at George.

George freezes. He hadn't thought about the grams he'd snorted.

'It's ten grams short,' Tony snarls.

'Sorry, I…' George stammers.

Tony pulls out a stack of money, counting the crisp notes. 'You're light... I'm giving you twenty-nine thousand. Don't get caught short next time,' he warns in his thick cockney accent. 'That shit can get you killed. Lucky I'm a reasonable man,' he says menacingly, starting the engine.

George steps out of the car, clutching the money. In the van, he counts it—twenty-eight, twenty-nine. Just as promised. He lets out a sigh of relief.

Time for a celebration. He heads to the unit, quickly scanning the area to ensure it's deserted, and pulls up the shutter. Unlocking the padlock, he opens the freezer. Jade lies peacefully, frozen. George touches her face and tugs the tie. 'Perfection,' he whispers, stroking her cheek. 'I wish you could come home with me.' He kisses her forehead, lingering.

George arrives at the venue with Sammy and Will. Sammy's drunk, giggly, and George finds a table near the back, hoping it'll keep her less of a distraction during his set. Sammy almost topples off her stool.

'Whoa, steady there, Sammy. A water for you, I think!'

Sammy demands whiskey. At the bar, George watches Hattie flirt with a young comedian.

'We're both on in the first half, G,' Will says, nodding to Trent at the back of the room.

This is George's big chance. Will's on the tour for sure, but his spot isn't guaranteed. Deep breath. He's got this.

Jemma walks in, her confidence filling the room. Will jumps up to greet her, kissing her long and passionately.

'Get a room,' George grumbles quietly, annoyed.

When they finally pull apart, Will introduces her to Sammy.

'Great to meet you,' Sammy says. 'Will's sister gave me a list of questions… hope that's alright and you don't mind'

'Not at all,' Jemma laughs. 'Lovely to meet you too. I didn't even know George had a sister. So many secrets, George. I might have a few questions of my own—your brother's a dark horse.'

'Let's get you a drink first,' Will chuckles, taking her hand and leading her to the bar.

'God, your face!' Sammy laughs. 'You look like you're chewing a lemon. Not a fan?'

'What makes you say that? We're so close,' George says sarcastically, glancing at the door again.

Gary arrives late, wearing a bright orange baseball cap, almost colliding with Trent as he darts towards George. Trent gives him a filthy look before returning to his seat. George sinks lower in his seat, trying to hide. Gary spots him and waves, quickly reaching the table. He seems hyper, maybe even high.

'Hello, G. How'd the deal go? All good?' he booms.

'Fuck's sake, Gary. Shhh,' George hisses. 'Keep it down. It went fine.' He hands over the envelope with Gary's money. 'Here you go. Cheers. I'll give you a buzz for a drink in the week.'

'I'm gonna stay and watch your gig. Moral support and all that. I'll get the pints in.'

George watches him make his way to the bar, desperately hoping he won't speak to anyone. *How many more obstacles can there be tonight?*

He should go over his material, but instead, George seizes the opportunity to approach Trent, best fake smile in place. Trent's on the phone, so George awkwardly waits.

'Hello there. Glad you could make it. Fancy a drink?' he asks, his voice carrying the tone of a storybook urchin, 'Please sir, can I have some more?'

'A dry martini, thanks,' Trent replies. Hattie brushes past him, almost pushing him aside. 'Hello there, handsome,' she purrs.

'My favourite redhead,' Trent retorts. 'George is just going to the bar. Can we get you anything?'

'Sweet George,' Hattie acknowledges him at last. 'A large chardonnay, thank you. Such a dear.'

George forces a gracious smile before heading to the bar.

'How's things?' Jemma asks, startling him with her silent approach.

'Good. You?'

'I'm starting to get the impression you don't like me.'

He can't tell if she's sincere but decides to be diplomatic. 'That's just my gruff demeanour.'

'That's a relief,' she says, no trace of sarcasm.

'Work okay?' he asks, fishing for information.

'The graveyard victim's friend came in today... just back from a work trip. She's not happy. Raging about how poorly the investigation's been handled.'

'Right,' George replies, keeping his reactions in check.

'She told the police about a guy, a comedian, who was staring at Shelly the night before she went missing. She saw him get her number and can't believe they haven't questioned him.'

George feels a wave of fear creep through him.

'The police have forty-eight hours to find this guy before we release the info and point out their negligence. I'll be writing the piece, so part of me kind of hopes they don't find him.'

George feels a bead of sweat slide down his back as the scruffy barman finally arrives to take his order.

'You know, it was here that Shelly met the comedian. Wasn't you, was it?' she asks, laughing but scrutinising him with sharp eyes.

He digs deep to match her joviality. 'No, afraid not, Jem. I only kill people with laughter,' he replies.

In the toilet cubicle, George sits on the pan, trying to calm down, taking deep breaths to relieve the tension behind his eyes. He slaps his face a few times, focusing on the task ahead. Impress Trent. That's the priority. He splashes water on his face, gives himself a pep talk. 'Come on, G, you've got this. You were made for the big time.' He winks at his reflection when Gary enters.

'Alright mate. Thanks for sorting things.'

'No problemo, G. Glad to help.'

'No need to hang about. I know you're busy.'

'Wouldn't miss it for the world, G. Break a leg.'

Jemma and Sammy are deep in conversation. Not good.

George finds Will in the wings. 'I'm shitting it tonight,' he confides, eyeing Trent at the bar.

'Don't worry, Trent will book you, trust me. I'll make sure of it. Erm, not that I'll have to—because you're gonna smash it!'

The tour will be the making of him, with plenty of opportunities for private performances. He CAN do this.

The lights dim, the spotlight hits the stage, and the MC bounds on.

'Ladies and gentlemen, welcome to the Amusement House. A great line-up tonight.'

George watches Trent check his watch and talk to Hattie, who signals to the MC.

'Let's bring on the first act—Mr George Mailer.'

Great introduction, George thinks, simmering. He steps on stage, plastering on a smile. Invincible George. His jokes land—one after another. He wraps up his set with a quick praise for the audience, who reward him with applause.

He heads to the bar, head held high, making eye contact with anyone who might be watching. Will approaches Trent, all charm, before joining George at the bar. 'So, what did he say?'

'Who?' Will asks, looking confused.

'Mate. Come on.'

'Oh, you mean Trent. He loved your gig. You're on the tour, G!'

George fights the urge to jump for joy. This is exactly what he needed. They share the news, and Sammy hugs him, congratulating him. Then she says how brave he is—basically the worst thing to say to a comedian. It's code for 'more brave than talented,' but he's too relieved to care. His first tour is coming, and success is close—he can feel it.

His elation dips briefly when he sees Jemma in deep conversation with Will. Is she asking him about the night Shelly gave her number? Will might remember that.

'You hungry, Sammy? I'm starving,' George says, recalling he hasn't eaten all day except for a bit of cheese. 'Fancy a curry? My treat.'

'That sounds good,' Sammy replies, knocking back the last of her drink. 'Shall we invite them?' she nods toward Will and Jemma.

'You mean Jemma? "I'm fantastic, the best journalist in the world"?' George mocks. 'And a top sleuth,' he adds, raising his voice and putting his hands on his hips. 'Jessica Fletcher's got nothing on me.' He's clearly enjoying himself.

Sammy stops laughing and looks over his shoulder. He knows. He turns around to find Jemma standing there, her face dark with fury.

'Erm, hi, Jemma. Just telling Sammy about a woman I used to work with,' George stammers.

'Were you?' Jemma snarls.

Will joins them, sensing the tension. George quickly distracts him.

'We're grabbing a curry. Got a lot to catch up on. See you on tour!'

On Oxford Street, Sammy giggles uncontrollably. 'You idiot, did you not see my eyes?'

'Not till it was too late. Shit.'

'Fuck it. She's a bit up her own arse.'

'She is, isn't she? Nice to see we agree on something.'

'A first for everything,' she replies.

They find an Indian restaurant nearby and order starters, mains, and sides, eating and drinking excessively. A few curious glances from other diners don't pass unnoticed.

'You think we're being too loud?' George whispers.

'Frankly, I don't give a shit,' Sammy slurs, ordering more drinks. What am I going to do about my ma? She burst into tears last week…' Sammy covers her eyes with her hands. 'She said it was her darkest day, the day I went to Aunty Anne's. I asked her what she meant.'

George steadies his hands underneath him, 'What did she say?'

'First, she said the monster had returned.' She brushes away a tear with the back of her hand. 'I pressed her,' Sammy's face pales and she struggles to speak. 'She said our dad came back home that night. I mean, that just isn't possible. Why would he come back? He did a runner years ago.'

'She's ill.'

He shuts his eyes tightly, trying to push away the awful images. The waiter brings over their drinks and places them on the table. George uses the moment to take a few deep breaths.

'You should've seen her! Rocking in her seat. She was so upset.' Sammy's eyes well up. 'I don't know what to do with her.' Her voice cracks with frustration. 'She keeps muttering about "the monster" like it's some ghost from her past. The other day she said she saw him in the garden, standing outside the window. It's *not normal*.'

George shovels the curry into his mouth, his movements deliberate. Nothing to see here.

The dinner conversation sours the mood and the food, and they finish their meals in silence, each lost in their own thoughts.

George can't shake the image of his mother, desperate, terrified, his dad looming over her. Then the idea of the blue-eyed monster standing right outside her window. Surely he can't be free—she must have imagined that.

He pushes his plate aside, a knot of unease tightening in his stomach. So much he's not ready to face. And the question lingers—how much longer can he keep Sammy in the dark?

Chapter 21

George tiptoes into the living room, where Sammy lies curled up on the couch, still asleep. He'd slept surprisingly well, after putting everything back in its place, burying it all in the past where it belongs—something he's become good at over the years.

He takes a quiet shower, gets dressed, and slips out of the flat, careful not to make a sound.

Outside, the cold, cloudy morning air bites at his skin. He buys bacon, bread, milk, and a Twix for Sammy. As he approaches his front door, he spots two policemen waiting. His palms sweat. They can't have any evidence, so he decides to face them.

'Hello. Can I help you?'

The taller officer, PC Johnson, introduces himself and his colleague, PC Green. 'We're carrying out routine enquiries. Could you spare us ten minutes?' Johnson asks.

'Yes, certainly,' George replies. 'Come in.'

The bedsit looks as he left it—tidy, musty. He opens a window. 'Sorry, it gets a bit damp in here. Tea?' he offers, placing his shopping down.

'No, you're alright,' Johnson says, eyeing the place with disdain. 'We've knocked a few times but didn't get an answer.'

'There's just me and one other tenant. An old fella, hard of hearing. I'm a comedian—gig around the country.'

'A comedian?' Green sounds impressed. 'That must be tough.'

'It has its moments,' George says, trying to keep it light.

Johnson clears his throat, unimpressed. 'A body was found in the graveyard next door. We suspect she died in the early hours of Monday, the 5th of March. We're asking around to see if anyone heard or saw anything on that date.'

George looks up, thinking. 'I didn't see anything unusual around that time. My schedule's hectic, though. Could've been out of town.'

'It would help if you could tell us where you were on the 5th of March,' Johnson presses.

George taps his chin. 'I wasn't away. I was here, but nothing stands out. Didn't see or hear anything strange.'

'Can you recall your movements that day?'

'Watched TV, wrote some material. Nothing special.'

'Was anyone with you?'

'No, I was alone. Didn't go out. Sorry I can't be of more help.'

'If you remember anything, give me a ring,' Johnson says, handing over a card.

'I certainly will,' George says, showing them out. He locks up, congratulating himself on his performance. Sammy would've blown it.

Sammy is snoring heavily on the couch. George throws bacon in the frying pan and boils the kettle.

'That's how I like to wake up— to bacon crackling,' Sammy says, sitting up. Her hair's a mess. She stands, folding the blanket.

'Sleep alright?' he asks.

'Yeah, not bad. Is that a Twix for me?' she asks, hopeful.

He hands it over. 'Got any plans for today?'

'Heard the markets in Camden are good. Might check it out. You up for it?'

'I can't. Got tons of material to write for the tour. Sorry,' George says, piling bacon onto bread.

'No bother. Off for a shower,' she says, grabbing her sandwich.

He eats while mentally planning his day. First, find a compact screen to record his private performances on tour. His stomach flutters at the thought of the lucky ladies, as well as the agents and TV opportunities. He grabs his notebook, writing furiously as ideas flow.

Sammy appears, dressed in a long flowing dress, her hair in a scruffy bun.

'Right, I'm off,' she says. 'Can I have a key?'

'No spare, but call me when you're back, and we'll sort it out.' He writes down his number.

'Alright. Laters,' she says, bouncing down the stairs like an elephant.

George doesn't mind having her there, surprisingly. She's not as bad as he remembers. He grabs £500 from his stash and heads out to Oxford Street. As he slips on his jacket and heads down the stairs, the doorbell rings. What now? He opens the door to find DI Tanner and DC Stone.

'Hello, Mr Mailer,' Tanner says. 'Can we have a word? Just a few questions. Won't take too long.'

George screws up his face. 'I already spoke to your lot this morning.'

'This is a follow-up,' Tanner explains.

'Erm… of course. Anything I can do to help.'

He locks up and follows the officers to the car, running his rehearsed responses through his mind. At the station, he's led into the reception area, where other comedians from the Amusement House sit. One gives him a nod, but there's no upbeat chatter. A policewoman keeps watch. Will enters with a police officer, looking confused and stressed.

'What's going on?' George asks.

The officer intervenes. 'Please do not speak to each other. We'll be assigning you to individual interview rooms in a few minutes.'

George sits down heavily. *This is not good.* Have they found something?

The policewoman leads each comedian away, one by one, leaving George alone in reception. Every time the door swings open, he glances at the narrow hallway stretching out with numbered interview rooms. A wave of panic washes over him, like an electric shock.

If they search him, how will he explain the £500 in his pocket? He's relieved the drugs are gone. All he knows is that the friend saw a comedian staring at Shelly, thinking she gave him her number. But did she see him well enough to identify or describe him? He's not sure. Fuck!

He's led to a room where Tanner and Stone sit in silence. George does his best bewildered look as he's shown to take the seat opposite them.

'Thank you, Mr. Mailer, for helping us with our enquiries. Can you tell us where you were on Monday, the 5th of March?'

'At home, I think. Pretty sure.'

'Anyone else with you?' Stone asks.

'No. I was alone. Watching TV.'

Tanner gives George an encouraging smile. 'What did you watch?'

George senses a good cop, bad cop setup at play.

George scratches his head. 'Er, I can't remember,' completely unable to think of a single programme.

'You performed stand-up comedy at the Amusement House the night before, on Sunday, the 4th of March. Is that correct?' Tanner asks, checking his notes.

'Yes.'

'Did you see this girl there?' Tanner slides a photo of Shelly over to him.

George studies the photo, picking it up off the table to have a better look. 'She doesn't look familiar.' He pushes the photo back to Tanner.

'You didn't talk to this lady that evening?' Stone asks, pointing at the photo.

'No, definitely not.'

Tanner writes something down. 'Okay, we don't have any more questions for the moment, Mr. Mailer.'

'Call me George, please,' he says, breathing a sigh of relief. That was easy enough.

'George, we would appreciate a little more of your time today. If you consent to five more minutes to clear up this enquiry.'

'Okay,' George says cautiously.

'Will you take part in an identification parade?' Tanner asks.

'An ID parade?'

'Yes. All the comedians from that night are taking part. It will help us eliminate several lines of enquiry.'

George thinks back to the night again. Even if the friend did get a glance at him, it would have been from a distance in a dimly lit room.

'If you think it will help, I'll do it.'

'Okay, please follow me.' Tanner stands and opens the door for him.

George heads along the corridor, wondering if he'll be in the same lineup as Will and the other comedians or with strangers. He's ushered into a room with a large, tinted glass window. There are several strangers who have similar height, hair colour, and build to him. George stands at the end, nearest the door and furthest away from where he imagines the scrutiniser to be.

Tanner's voice pierces through the intercom, 'Please face the front.'

George is sweating profusely. He battles to slow down his breathing as sweat drips down his neck.

Tanner barks more instructions. 'Turn right, turn left.' The man next to George steps forward. George braces himself. He should have asked for a lawyer. Would it make him look more suspicious though?

Eventually, the door opens, and a woman instructs them to file back out to the corridor. George is taken back to an interview room and left alone for ten minutes, maybe longer. He wills himself to stay strong, once again considering requesting a lawyer. He drums his fingers on the desk, checking his phone for a message from Sammy. Nothing. Just as he's about to text Will, Tanner enters.

'Mr. Mailer, thank you for your cooperation. You are free to go.'

'Happy to help,' George stammers, relief sweeping through him.

He finds Will sitting alone in the reception area. 'Fucking hell. This is mental.'

'Let's get out of here,' Will says briskly, walking towards the exit.

'Why would they interview the comedians? I hope they're interviewing the audience too. Rounding us all up like a bunch of crims,' George spits, indignantly.

'Didn't you recognise the girl in the photo?' Will asks, turning to face him.

'No, I didn't. Do you?'

'Fuck, yeah. Thought she looked familiar when I saw the picture in the paper. She was at the Amusement House that night, sitting at the front with another chick.'

'I can't recall her. Look, I need to go meet Sammy. She doesn't have keys,' George says curtly, flagging down a cab. 'You want a lift?'

'No. I'll get the tube.'

George gives the driver his address and leans back, wondering if it's over. Will seemed pissed. At home, the TV and beer distract him. Three beers later, the doorbell rings.

Sammy hands him a carrier bag. 'Chips and chilli sauce with raw onion for you.'

He takes the chips. 'How was Camden?'

'Great. Bought a scarf, went for a drink with the guy I bought it from.'

'You had a good day?'

'Uneventful,' George says, tossing the remnants of his chips in the bin. I'm off to bed, night.'

In the morning, Sammy says her goodbyes. George is sad but relieved to see her go. He doesn't need ties to his childhood. After buying a computer in town, he spends the day figuring out how to play the camcorder footage. When he cracks it, he watches Jade on screen, feeling a huge sense of achievement. He knows now how to get the best out of the private shows too.

At seven o'clock, he calls Will. 'Alright, mate. What time are we leaving tomorrow?'

'Leave at one, should get us to Liverpool in time for the gig.'

'Good. You alright?'

'Yeah, fine, just about to order dinner with Jemma. See you tomorrow.'

'Okay. Bye,' he says as Will hangs up abruptly.

George pushes Will out of his mind and focuses on his new material, laughing to himself now and then. He watches the Jade footage again, eager for his next private audience. The new equipment opens up a whole new world of possibilities. *Exciting times.*

Chapter 22

George and Will set off for Liverpool, the van's atmosphere colder than the brisk weather outside.

'How was your meal last night?' George asks. 'Chinese or Indian?'

'Sushi. Jem loves it.'

'Rice and raw fish? Doesn't sound like much of a treat to me.'

'It's great,' Will responds, his tone sharp.

George switches on the radio, trying to lighten the mood. They arrive in Liverpool early evening and drive through the busy city centre. The high street is vibrant with animated shoppers. Some women wear hair rollers and pyjamas. Odd! It's like the female population is divided into makeover BEFORE and AFTER. The men too—half in jogging bottoms and sports gear, the other half tanned with jelled hair, tight jeans, and super-white teeth.

George nudges Will awake. 'Look, the women are in their jammies. Makes bedtimes easy I imagine. Can you look at the map to see where the hotel is. I've circled the road.'

Will gives directions, and they arrive at the hotel without a hitch. The receptionist, a model-like figure, checks them in with indifferent professionalism, handing over key cards and muttering 'second floor'. They head up in the lift in silence, reaching a twin room that's basic but clean. George flops onto one of the beds, switching on the TV.

Sharing a room should provide a solid alibi. Too bad the atmosphere is so strained. This is their first tour—they should be thrilled, best pals, yet something's off.

'I'm going to grab a quick shower before we go,' Will mumbles, shutting the bathroom door behind him.

George jumps up, pulling the camcorder from his bag. He takes the Jade footage tape out and slips it into his pocket, inserting a fresh cassette before stashing the camcorder and Rohypnol back in his bag. *Ready.*

On the walk to The Rawhide Club, Will is in a better mood. They're early, but a queue forms at the door as they arrive.

'Fuck, they're keen,' George says, walking smugly to the front. 'We're on tonight,' he announces to the female bouncer.

'On what? Crack?' she retorts, enjoying the sniggers from the punters.

Everyone's a comedian.

'Sorry, it's Will Devon and George Mailer.' Will points to the poster on the door.

She ignores him, focusing on her tiny list. Maybe she can't even read, the stupid bitch. George eyes the poster, frustration growing. Ade Charmers' face takes up most of the space, Will's is smaller and lower, and George's name? In miniature font at the very bottom—no photo. Cheeky bastards! His picture should be up there; it'd pull the ladies in, no doubt.

The queue of punters watches on, some amused, others uninterested. Then a commotion breaks out. Ade Charmers steps out of a tinted Mercedes. What a prick. He strolls to the front, and the bouncer opens the door immediately, all smiles. George steps up, ready to follow, but she stops him.

'Hold on a sec,' she smirks, still scanning the list. After a beat, she looks up. 'Oh, yes, I see you now. You can go in.'

'Female or male bouncer, makes no difference,' George mutters, 'they're all arseholes, mad on the power.'

Will strides ahead into the club. The main room is impressive—huge stage, around 300 seats. George feels the excitement surge. 'Nice venue, eh?'

'Impressive,' Will agrees.

In the green room, Ade Charmers is sitting on a stool, looking over his notes. He looks up and smiles. 'You must be Will. I recognise you from the poster. How's it going?' He stands to shake Will's hand.

George steps in, sticking out his own hand. 'I'm George Mailer.' Ade shakes it with barely a glance.

'It's going to be packed tonight. The scousers are lively,' Ade chuckles.

'You've gigged here before?' Will asks.

'Loads,' Ade replies smugly. 'Great gig. If they don't like you, they'll let you know. But I've always smashed it.'

Sean Philips walks in. 'Ade, how's it going, mate?' They hug and start exchanging pleasantries. George nudges Will, rolling his eyes. Will smiles politely.

Sean brags about his recent success, then slaps Will on the back. 'Glad to have you on the tour.'

Will thanks him, clearly pleased. George heads to the bar, trying to calm his nerves. The large crowd buzzes with anticipation, and the butterflies hit him hard. He quickly detours for a line of coke.

Will, Ade, and Sean are deep in laughter in the green room. George takes Will's drink over, but they continue joking and laughing.

'Can you stick it on the table?' Will asks.

Do I look like your fucking servant? George bristles, but he stalks to the back of the room and starts going over his lines.

Sean Philips announces the line-up. George is on first again. The sacrificial lamb. Surprise, surprise. His heart pounds as Ade's words echo in his head: *'Crowd can be vicious.'* George paces back and forth.

'You nervous?' Ade asks, smirking.

'Not at all, it just helps me focus. Is that alright with you?'

Everyone turns to look at him. Ade laughs, and Sean joins in.

Will walks over, lowering his voice. 'What's up with you?'

'Fine,' George mumbles, throwing a harsh look at Ade.

'You're irritable,' Will says, studying George closely. 'Have you had something? Coke?'

'No, don't be daft,' George replies, rubbing his nose.

'Your pupils are massive.'

'Could do without the third degree. About to go perform to a packed room for fuck's sake!'

The stage music stops, and Sean Philips exits the green room to start the show. George gulps down his pint and stands behind the curtain, ready to go on.

'Can we welcome to the stage, George Mailer,' Philips announces. Not much of an intro.

George grabs the mic. 'Hello, Liverpool!' he shouts.

Blank stares.

'Before we left this morning, I took all the cards out of my wallet, my money, then thought, fuck it, be extra careful, and removed the condoms too. So, Liverpool, I've officially got nothing to steal.'

'Not your fucking material, anyway, mate. That's for sure,' a thick-accented voice shouts from the back. The room bursts into laughter.

George's taken aback by the venom but ploughs on with his reliable material. Five minutes feels like five hours. He's supposed to be on for ten to fifteen. The audience stays mostly silent, with the occasional angry heckle cutting through. He tries a scouse accent to lighten the mood. It's a disaster. Fuck it—he's not getting paid anyway. He cuts it short.

'I'd love to say you've been a great audience, but frankly, you've been shit,' George growls, pushing the mic back into the stand. A plastic bottle flies past his head.

'You're shit, mate, fuck off!'

George locates the gobshite and gives him a two-fingered salute. The guy stands, taller than he expected. Sean Philips strides on with a grimace, scowls, and gestures for George to leave, then tries to calm the crowd. George storms off into the green room.

Ade Charmers stares, speechless.

'What the fuck?' Will stammers. 'What did you do that for?'

'I'm off. See you back at the hotel,' George spits, grabbing his backpack and storming out, giving the female bouncer the finger as he goes.

He storms through the city centre, burning with humiliation. Back in the hotel room, he racks up two thick lines of coke. Will didn't help, asking if he'd taken coke. George snorts the lines, one after the other. Catching his reflection in the mirror, he shouts, 'Fuck you all.' He throws on his jacket and heads out, looking for the nearest pub.

He doesn't walk far before finding the Wetherall Arms. The sound of someone murdering a song greets him. Karaoke? Jesus. The heat and noise hit him like a tidal wave. The pub is packed. People are five deep at the bar, waving notes to grab the attention of a flustered barwoman. The current slaughter of 'Simply the Best' is being belted out by a woman who reminds him of his mum—small, brassy, with a face that looks unhappy with her lot. Unlike the women he's seen since arriving in Liverpool, this one's peroxide blonde, no teeth whitening or perfect curls—just a real woman giving it her all.

He waits ages at the bar, jutting his chin out, hoping to be served. A young guy with heavy eyeliner and plenty of sass arrives. After a quick scan, he stands directly in front of George, asking him what he wants with a strong Liverpudlian accent and a cheeky wink. George orders a pint and a shot before moving away.

His phone buzzes, and Will's name flashes up. He turns it off, knocking back a chaser and a pint, scanning the room for potential fun. Nothing piques his interest.

By 10:00 p.m., the women are heavily drunk, laughing too loudly and dancing in tight spaces. A small brunette steps out from a circle of older women. Bingo. She has a fuller figure than he expected, but her swan-like neck is delicate. She grabs the mic and belts out 'I Will Survive' with power and conviction, earning a massive round of applause. She joins her friend and knocks back a celebratory drink.

George keeps his eyes on them while the next act—a crooner belting out 'New York, New York'—sings in a way that would make Frank Sinatra cringe.

George sizes her up for the new sofa bench in the van. Will she fit? Ideally, the van would be refrigerated. A body will stink after five days of touring. He'll need to dump it locally. It could be challenging, but he needs something tonight. If a body is found in Liverpool, the police will assume it's a local. No one's going to think someone travelled from London to kill.

A group of loud, drunk young guys enters and orders shots at the bar. George sidles up behind them, listening in. They mention a club called The State, one of the top spots in town. The loudest one pops a red Liverpool football cap on the bar. Twelve shots are lined up; they cheer and knock them back before ordering another round. George moves closer, swipes the cap, and slips it into his jacket pocket.

In the toilet, George takes another generous line. The club will be the best place for prey, especially if they're drugged out of their minds.

'Same again?' the barman asks, smiling cheekily and flirting.

The group leaves as rowdily as they came in.

'Yes, please,' George replies, checking to see if the girl is still there. She is.

'I love your accent. Is it Scottish?' the barman asks.

'No, Irish,' George lies. He heads back to his spot.

The girl's friend has the bladder of a cow, though she eventually goes to the ladies' toilet.

He does a subtle 360 inspection around the room, plonks the baseball cap on and makes his move. 'Hi there, how you doing? Amazing song earlier. You've got a right voice on you.'

She looks pleased. 'Yeah, I'm ok. Nearly got on *Stars in Their Eyes* last year but my throat was sore so didn't get through.'

'My name's Bill. What's yours?' George asks, aware of time.

'Shirley.'

'That's a lovely name. Look, I hope you don't think me cheeky, but I've a plus one for The State club tonight. My mate had to pull out last minute, so I've got one spare ticket. Do you want to come with me?'

'Erm. Yeah, that would be boss,' she chirps.

'Ok. I need to go sort something out, but I can meet you in half an hour? Outside McDonald's on the High Street?'

'Yeah, boss,' she gushes, revealing a mouthful of uneven teeth. 'I've always wanted to go there.'

'Great. Look forward to it, Shirley,' George says.

He ducks out of the pub, keeping his head down. Outside, he snatches off the cap and tucks it in his pocket. He turns on his phone; two missed calls from Will. He can fuck off, with his bird and his comedy career. He walks to McDonald's and checks out the area for cameras. None. The bigger question of where he can dump the body can wait. It's a shame he can't just tap someone on the shoulder and ask, 'Where's a good place to hide a dead body?' It would be much easier. How helpful would the people of Liverpool be then?

He buys two small bottles of alcopop, parks a road back from McDonald's, and pours Rohypnol into one of them. Excitement courses through him. Tonight will have a happy ending.

Hiding in the entrance of a closed-down travel agent, he waits. By eleven, there's still no Shirley. He waits another half hour, before pulling the baseball cap on and heading to the bus stop across the road from the pub. The pub doors swing open and Shirley stumbles out, followed by her mate. George steps back into the shadows, pulling up his collar.

'I know, it'll be fucking boss,' Shirley shouts. 'He's got money, and guest passes for The State. He's probably got drugs too,' she says, grabbing her friend's arm as they head toward McDonald's.

George clenches his fists, keeping his distance. What is it with these stupid fucking girls, dragging their mates everywhere? He takes a sharp left into a side street, stomping back to the van. Night's fucking scuppered, again.

Back at the hotel, Will's watching TV. 'Where the fuck have you been? I've been calling you.'

'You're not my keeper, Will. Back off.' George tosses his jacket on the bed.

'Why are you being arsey? Is it the coke? Nick mentioned your little chat about it at my party.'

'You're full of shit, Will. Where are your new best mates?'

'You're acting like a kid. You've probably blown your chances of staying on the tour. Get it together.' Will climbs into bed, switches off his lamp, and turns his back.

George slams the bottle of spiked alcopop back, craving oblivion.

Chapter 23

He wakes up with a groggy, hot head. The bed beside him is empty. The events of last night flood back—the terrible gig, the failed attempt at finding a victim, and the argument with Will. In the bathroom mirror, his pasty face stares back at him. He stumbles back to bed, watching awful daytime TV.

Will walks in, looking fresh. He sweeps past George, opening the curtains and a window.

'Alright, Will?'

'Yeah, fine,' Will replies, rummaging through his bag.

'I'm sorry about last night. I was out of order, the gig fucked me up.'

'The coke didn't help.'

George stays quiet, trying a pleading look.

'I put you on this tour. How does that make me look?'

'I know, sorry. I fucking hate Sean Philips. He's a wind-up merchant.'

'He's not that bad. He could've told Trent what happened, but he didn't.'

'Maybe you're right,' George mutters.

'Forget it,' Will says, a hint of a smile breaking through. 'Try not to be a prick for the rest of the tour. Can you manage that?'

'I'll try,' George replies sheepishly. 'Thank God it's not the same club tonight. That would be a nightmare.'

'A lynch mob would be waiting for you,' Will laughs, sitting on the bed. 'Honestly, G, I thought you were going to get battered.'

'I would've if I hadn't made a sharp exit. "Comedian battered for insulting angry audience,"' George chuckles.

'They could sue you for defamation. On a no-win, no-fee basis, of course.'

'Not a court in the land would rule against me,' George replies, sitting on the bed.

'Let's smash it tonight. Get this back on track, G. We should explore the town and see if there's anything useful for the gig. I've got a warm-up before.'

'Warm-up gig?'

'Sean mentioned it. Open mic to try new stuff. Fancy it?'

It's beneath George, but he's got bridges to build. 'Sounds great, or boss, as they say up here.'

'Good. Grab your jacket. It's pissing it down,' Will says, picking up his wallet and switching off the TV.

George feels lighter now the air's been cleared. Tonight will go better, and the audience will love him.

Saturday shoppers weave between umbrellas, ducking in and out of shops. The rain keeps coming, as his mum would say, it's 'a day for the house'. George scoffs a cheeseburger and chips in a busy café, people-watching. He puts up his collar and steps into a large puddle, soaking his feet and jeans.

'Fuckin hell,' George yells, then checks himself and smiles at Will.

By the time they get back to the hotel, George is sneezing, flu symptoms start kicking in—headache, runny nose. Not great timing. He showers, feeling a bit better under the hot water.

'You better get a move on. Leaving in ten minutes,' Will says, changing into a fresh shirt.

George would rather curl up under the duvet. He resists the temptation for a little pick me up. Will's onto him, and he doesn't want to rock the boat.

The front doors of the venue are flaking, and the mismatched seats outside are broken—a dump. Inside, the carpet's stuck with so much chewing gum, it feels like part of the decor. At the far corner, a banner reads 'Comedy Night' with a mic stand in front of it. A group of twenty-somethings knock back pints of snakebite—the student's nectar. George counts thirty people. Big crowd.

'Pint?' George asks, nodding to the bar.

'Yeah, cheers. I'll find this Liam guy and get our names down.'

George holds out a twenty to grab the barmaid's attention. After ten minutes, he's served by a surly woman who reminds him of someone from *Brookside*.

Will introduces Liam, a lanky teenager in John Lennon glasses.

George sets the pints on the table and shakes Liam's hand. 'You expecting more punters?'

'I don't *expect* anything. Do you want a spot?' Liam asks sharply.

'If there's a spot needing filled,' George retorts, holding Liam's gaze.

'I don't need anything! Plenty of clowns around here to keep the mic company,' Liam says, his accent thickening with every word.

George catches Will's stony look. 'I'd love a spot, mate. Thanks. Can I get you a pint?'

'Snakebite,' Liam grunts. 'You're on first. You'll follow, Will.'

'Still in Pricksville, huh?' Will says, shaking his head. 'Get a grip.'

George knocks back his pint, watching as fresh students trickle in. The bar quickly fills. Liam grabs the mic, scans the paper, and calls George's name. George strides to the stage, smiling confidently.

'Hello, how's everyone doing? I see a few students in tonight,' he says, glancing at his watch. 'Bit early for you guys, isn't it?'

A few laughs. 'I love Liverpool. It's the only place where healers are banned for fear of folk losing their disability benefits.'

Big laughs. George turns the charm factor up and spends the rest of his set flattering Liverpudlians and slagging off the rest of the country. Every joke gets a good laugh, as he gathers momentum towards his closing joke which earns him a huge round of applause and he leaves the stage, buoyant. *Yes, he's back!*

Will has a great gig. George claps and whistles as he leaves the stage.

'I'm not being funny, mate, well I am, cos I can't help it, but we were brilliant tonight. Let's kill the next one,' George says, as they arrive at The Laugh Cafe.

The room is packed, alive with energy, around 400 seats. A pretty bartender leads them to a green room with a star on the door. She bats her eyelashes at Will before leaving them with a playful glance.

This is more like it! Complimentary water bottles—a first.

George takes a deep breath and approaches Sean Philips. 'Hey, I'm sorry about yesterday.'

'Trent would've sacked you.'

'Thanks for not telling him. I'll be on top form tonight.'

'Let's hope so,' Philips says, turning to his notes.

George gulps his pint, still nervous but more confident than last night. The music stops, and Philips leaves. George recalls the last round of applause as Philips introduces him with a warmer welcome. On stage, the first joke lands with less impact than expected.

'God, that went down like a lead balloon, but I know you're there. I can hear you breathing.'

That gets a slightly bigger laugh. He builds momentum and finishes strong. Proud of the set, he hands over the mic to Philips, giving him a look that says *told you so.*

Will hugs him on the way to the stage. 'Amazing, G. Well done.'

George drinks his pint, pride swelling at his own prowess but also at his friends as Will delivers a solid set.

'Your gig went well, eh?' the pretty bartender asks.

'Thanks very much,' George says, grinning.

'Your mate's smashing it,' she nods at Will.

'Yeah, he's great, and I think he fancies you.'

She lights up. 'Really?'

'Yeah, really. Come join us for a drink after?'

'Where to?'

'Any late bars around?'

'Rhino Bar, open till three. I'm done by midnight.'

Will exits the stage to bigger applause than George's, which he notes with a hint of envy.

'Brilliant. And if you want to bring a mate, do.'

'I'm Cheryl by the way.'

'Pleasure to meet you. See you later.'

Backstage, the mood is celebratory.

'Let's go celebrate, Will. There's a late bar nearby,' George says.

They head to the Rhino bar, all glass and chrome with coloured lights illuminating the bar and tabletops. Squeezing to the front, they order pints and tequila shots.

George raises his glass. 'To us, the funniest comedians in the world.'

They down the shots, and George immediately jumps up to get more. 'Drink up, mate, we're celebrating!'

They knock back the shots and gulp down their lagers. No sign of Cheryl. George is starting to think the women in Liverpool are unreliable.

Will slurs, 'I'm sorry I was a bit off with you after the police questioning the other day.'

George perks up. 'What do you mean?'

'It's just that...' Will pauses, confused. 'I thought that girl was the one you had your eye on at the Amusement House. I was sure of it. And it pissed me off when you lied to me about it.'

George nods. 'Will, I wouldn't lie to you. You're my best mate.'

'You told Jemma you never gigged at the Amusement House though. That's weird!'

George shrugs. 'She picked me up wrong. I thought she was asking about a paid gig there, which I haven't had.'

Will rubs his face. 'Right. Well, now she's convinced there's something suspicious about you.'

'She thinks I'm a murderer?' George asks.

'Maybe not a murderer. But you did speak to the girl, G.'

George puts his hands up. 'Alright, alright. I said hello. She had the most annoying voice I've ever heard, high and shrill, so I made a sharp exit. End of story. I didn't say anything to the police in case they tried to fit me up for it.'

'You should have told me,' Will says, relieved. 'I knew it would just be something daft. I told Jemma that. She wasn't having it.'

'She's had it in for me since we met. Says snide things when you're not around.'

'Why didn't you tell me?'

'Because you like her, and I didn't want to come between you two.'

'What did she say? I'm not having that,' Will says, angry for the first time.

George notices Cheryl and another girl entering the bar. Perfect timing. Cheryl waves at him.

'Is that the girl from the Laugh Cafe?' Will asks.

'Yep. Must be a popular place. More tequilas, I think,' George says, standing up.

Will puts his hand on George's arm. 'I'm sorry I ever doubted you. I don't know what I was thinking.'

'It's forgotten. A woman will never come between us, mate.'

'Here's to that,' Will says, lifting his drink and gulping it down in one.

George greets Cheryl and her friend, Kirsty, buying the drinks and inviting them to join them.

'We've got company,' George says as the girls sit next to him.

He keeps Kirsty entertained with small talk while Cheryl immediately starts flirting with Will. George watches, hoping Cheryl will turn Will's head. Will, very drunk, seems pleased with the attention. Kirsty mentions she's hungry.

'Let's go eat and leave these to it,' George says, grabbing her jacket.

'A gentleman, how refreshing,' Kirsty says, shaking into her jacket and waving Cheryl off with a wink.

'Won't be long, Will,' George says, moving quickly. He catches the brief, alarmed look on Will's face, but Cheryl whispers something, and Will's attention returns to her. George exits with Kirsty.

'Sorry, Kirsty, I'm not feeling great. Mind if I call it a night? I'll pay for your cab.' George pulls a twenty from his wallet.

'I can pay for my own,' she replies sharply, turning away.

He heads back to the bar, peeks inside. Will's being devoured by Cheryl.

'Sorry, am I interrupting?' George asks, smiling.

Will looks like he just remembered something.

'Shit, I have to go,' Will stutters, grabbing his jacket. Cheryl glares at George.

George shrugs. 'Sorry about that. He gets a bit emotional. Take care.'

After a few vomit stops, George gets Will back to the hotel. Will crashes fully clothed on the bed. George takes off his trainers, turns off the light, and stretches out with a satisfied grin. It's been a successful evening.

The first thing George hears in the morning is Will being sick. He knocks on the bathroom door. 'You alright, mate?'

'No, I'm dying. I need water and paracetamol.'

'I'll get some,' George says, heading out. He picks up juice, water, croissants, and paracetamol from a nearby shop. As he pays, he enjoys the assistant's impressed look. Yes, I'm minted, and a successful comedian. Get over it, he thinks with a chuckle.

Back at the hotel, Will's curled up on the bed. 'Give me the drugs,' he pleads weakly.

George opens the packet and hands Will two pills with a bottle of water. 'There you go, mate. You'll be good as new soon.'

Will swallows the pills and lies back. 'How much did we drink last night?'

'Quite a bit. We need to head to Leeds soon, but you can sleep on the way if you want.'

'Okay, just let the pills work first,' Will says.

George packs both bags, grabs toiletries from the bathroom, and settles down to watch a double bill of *E.R.* When it finishes, he wakes Will up.

'We need to go, bud. You good?'

'Not great, but I'll manage. I'll meet you at the van.'

George loads their luggage and finds a radio station for the drive. Will climbs in, clutching a pillow.

'That's stealing, mate.'

'I don't give a shit. Drive,' Will says, settling back with an eye mask.

'Where's Batman, Robin?' George laughs.

'Piss off,' Will mutters.

George wakes Will when they reach the hotel in Leeds.

'Another gig, another hotel,' Will complains. 'How long since home comforts?'

'Three days.'

'Shit, I'd be a terrible rock star.'

'Yeah, you can't sing and the recorder's your only instrument. Stick to comedy.'

Will's phone rings. 'It's Trent.'

George's heart races. Could Phillips have reported the disaster? Will says 'yes' a few times, his face lighting up.

'Guess what?' Will exclaims.

'What?' George asks, anxious.

'Trent got a call from a production company in Leeds. They want to film up-and-coming comedians. He asked if we want to do it.'

'And you said yes?'

'Hell yes! We're going to be on TV. They'll film the gig tonight in front of a live audience!'

George hugs Will. 'We're going all the way to the top, mate!'

They unload the van, check in at the hotel, and go over material. At 7:00 p.m., Will arrives with food. The smell of chips makes George's mouth water. He digs in while watching TV.

George is nervous but confident as they arrive at Jesters Comedy Club. The room is half the size of the last place, but it's packed. In the green room, Riley, the head of production, briefs them on timing and where the cameras will be. George's heart races—he needs this.

Ade and Philips chat casually. Ade turns to Will. 'First TV gig?'

'Yeah, I'm shitting it,' Will admits.

'It can be nerve-wracking. Forget the cameras,' Ade advises.

George almost wants to throw a football at his head. 'Pint, Will?'

'Yeah, best settle the nerves.'

Riley pops in. 'We're going in five.' George hurries to the bar, debating a pick-me-up. Fuck it, yes. He takes a quick line in the bathroom, then heads back.

At the side of the stage, he notices a laugh-o-meter with four sections: 'hee hee', 'ha ha', 'lol', and 'lmao'. He imagines the audience staying in the red 'lmao' zone when he performs.

As production runs through cards with the audience, George mentally prepares, confident he'll bring the laughs.

The gig goes off without a hitch—George nails it. After the show, the audience filters out slowly, and the production team packs up at midnight. George slips the laugh-o-meter under his jacket, heads back to the green room, stashes it in his backpack, and joins Will at the bar.

'Best gig ever,' George boasts, knocking back another drink.

'I know, you were great,' Will agrees, leaning on the bar. 'We had them.'

Philips, from his bar stool, interrupts, 'Nothing to do with the stage prompts, huh?'

George ignores him. 'We should celebrate somewhere else.'

'Not for me. Saving it for Manchester,' Will says.

George drains his drink. 'Yeah, probably best.'

Back at the hotel, Will crashes straight to bed. George takes out the laugh-o-meter, admiring it. He hides it back in his bag, lies down, and thinks of the future—interviews, autographs, money. Will snores lightly as George turns off the light.

Chapter 24

The drive to Manchester is a mess—two accidents, heavy traffic, and torrential rain. What should've been an hour-long journey takes nearly two and a half.

'About the other night,' Will begins.

George waits for him to step into the pew.

'I just can't believe I cheated on Jemma. What a fucking arsehole.'

'Don't beat yourself up, mate. What happens on tour, stays on tour,' George laughs.

'It was a shit thing to do.'

'You've not been dating that long, shit happens,' George says, fiddling with the radio.

'It's just not my style. I really like her.'

'Maybe you don't like her as much as you think?' George glances over, reading his face.

Will frowns. 'What the fuck do you mean by that?'

'Maybe you wouldn't have snogged Cheryl if you were mad about Jenna,' George shrugs.

'It was just the booze,' Will insists.

'Okay,' George says, leaving silence to settle.

They reach Manchester early evening, already dark, and check into another faceless hotel. Will heads for the shower.

'Just popping down to the van, mate, back in a minute,' George shouts.

He grabs the keys, drives the van out of the car park, and searches for a quiet street. After fifteen minutes, he finds a secluded road with one lamp post. He checks for cameras, finds none, parks up, and opens the back doors. He pulls out the laugh-o-meter and checks off his list—smart tie, silk ties, laptop—everything's set.

On the way back to the hotel, he grabs vodka and coke from an off-licence. The list is complete. He smiles, wallet in hand, and tolerates the shopkeeper's outstretched hand.

'Is there any free overnight parking nearby?'

'Not in town. You'll need to head out a bit,' the man replies, pointing to a spot on a map.

George thanks him, grabs his shopping, and heads back to the hotel. He picks up a cab card at reception and calls for a ride.

When he enters the room, Will's sitting with his notebook.

'Where the fuck have you been? It's nearly eight. We need to leave in half an hour.'

'Don't panic. I've got a taxi on the way,' George says, closing the door behind him.

A few minutes later, they hop in the cab, heading to the Frog and Bucket. They arrive before half past eight and find a queue inside and outside. They squeeze past, give their names, and are shown to the green room. It's basic: a few chairs, a lamp, and a table. No complimentary drinks.

On his next gig, probably another TV one, he'll have a rider—he's pleased he already knows the technical term—with Evian at room temperature, Carlsberg on tap, and roasted peanuts in a bowl.

Philips is in the green room, texting. He looks up. 'Someone's looking for you, Will.'

'Fans probably!' George jokes.

The door swings open. 'Hello there, stranger. Surprise!' Jemma says, throwing herself into Will's arms.

Will, though shocked, is ecstatic. He kisses her deeply. It's like a bad B-movie as they slobber all over each other, oblivious to anyone else. George clears his throat.

Jemma looks at him for the first time, disdain clear in her eyes.

'George,' she says.

'Nice to see you, Jemma. Sorry, this is a comedians-only area,' he says, offering an apologetic expression.

'How did you get in then?' she demands, giving him a cold look before turning back to Will and kissing him. 'I'm going to watch the show. Break a leg,' she says, sweeping past him and disappearing behind the curtain.

'Respect, Will, she's a fox,' Philips comments.

George ignores him and heads to the bar, surveying the audience, hungry and ready.

'A chardonnay would be lovely,' Jemma says, her talent for silent approaches undiminished.

'There's been some interesting developments in the police investigation. They've interviewed most of the audience from the Amusement House, and they've done a photofit of the guy who was talking to her that night. Do you want to see it?'

She opens her handbag and removes an A4 sheet of paper, handing it to George. 'Looks remarkably familiar, don't you think?'

George looks at the picture, and his stomach drops. It's not a mirror image, but it's a strong resemblance. How can this have happened? Why wasn't he picked out from the I.D. parade?

'They're releasing the photofit on tonight's news. It's only a matter of time. George?'

'What? Talking to someone and murdering them are very different things.'

'You admit talking to her then? Why lie?'

'You know, Jemma, you might want to concentrate your energies closer to home, possibly starting with your relationship,' George states with a smile. Leaving her with her mouth hanging open.

George carries two pints into the green room and finds Will looking awkward. Ade and Philips exchange a look—excitement, maybe?

Trent enters. 'Gentlemen.' Ade and Philips fall over themselves to shake hands and even hug. George and Will stick to firm handshakes.

'How did the TV gig go? They just emailed me with the final edit. Exciting, eh? Sean, can I have a quick word at the bar? Can I get anyone a drink?'

'A pint would be great,' George replies, despite having three-quarters of one left. He's surprised when the rest politely decline. Well, he's the only one not getting paid!

George steps out of the green room, debating whether to call DI Tanner and feel out the situation, mention he remembers something, maybe spoke to the girl. It was just a chat. He feels a tightness in his chest. It's like the nets are closing in around him. He needs to stay focused and remember there's no proof linking him to anything. The photofit could be a thousand guys.

The audience pours in, aiming for the safety of the middle row to avoid interaction with the comedians. He really needs a private performance tonight. He scans the room, looking for a likely lady, but his eyes land on Philips and Trent, deep in serious conversation at the bar. Tonight's gig is crucial; Trent needs to see him shine. He steps back into the green room.

Ade is blowing his own trumpet again, telling Will how TV appearances are second nature to him.

Trent and Philips enter.

Trent hands George a pint. 'I need a word with you, George.'

George's heart skips a beat. This doesn't sound good. 'When? Now?'

'No, after the show will be fine.'

He's reminded of Darren, the Mr. Jeans supervisor. Why can't people just say what they need to say right there and then? Why drag it out? *Because they enjoy the power.*

Fuck him. The success of his TV debut will be enough to catapult his career to the next level and secure management far better than Trent's. Philips catches his eye and overacts an innocent look. The fucker's told him about Liverpool.

George feels for the coke wrap in his pocket and heads to the toilet. Two thick lines and a pep talk in the mirror buoy him up. Back in the green room, George sets Will up with the camcorder to record what will be a spectacular performance.

The music stops, and George moves to the wings of the stage, waiting. Philips introduces him again as a new comedian. *This guy really is a tosser.* George gives him a vicious look as he grabs the mic and steps into the spotlight.

'Hello, Manchester,' George says, emphasising 'Manchester', raising his arms high like a football supporter missing a scarf.

The Mancs enjoy the sound of their city, and he gets a solid response. He delivers his material with effortless perfection. Spotting an interesting prospect in the front row, her laughter dirty and throaty, George moves closer, performing like a mating bird, delivering his favourite punchlines to her, keeping eye contact. Her laugh is hearty. She'll do nicely. He finishes the set with expert timing, no nerves, just confidence. The applause is off the scale. He heads back to the green room. Only Will congratulates him.

Trent enters. 'Let's have that catch-up now, in the back bar.'

George picks up his drink and follows Trent, taking a moment to catch the eye of his lucky lady as he passes. She smiles, definitely interested, and George returns a wink.

Trent sits at a table in the deserted bar. 'Take a seat,' he says, setting down his martini glass.

George sits opposite him, wondering if he's wrong—maybe Trent's keen to sign him up before he goes stratospheric. He'll need to get advice before making any big decisions.

'How've you been enjoying the tour, George?'

'It's been great. Had some cracking gigs, and the TV gig... that was the icing on the cake. It's all going so fast.'

'Right,' Trent says, looking uneasy. 'So, you're happy with how the gigs are going?'

'Yes, totally. Great audience responses.'

'And what about Liverpool, George? What happened there?'

Fucking Philips. 'You know how it is. You can't win over every audience,' George says, shrugging.

'Win them over?' Trent repeats, his eyes widening. 'You almost started a riot.'

'Bit of an exaggeration,' George says. 'Had a rough heckler. It's Liverpool, home of the thief. What do you expect? They spend more time inside than out in civilised society.'

Trent shakes his head. 'It wasn't the city, or the audience, it was you. You had a crap gig, your material was poor, your timing was off, and you were picking fights in the greenroom before you even went on.'

'Look, I don't know what you've heard, but Philips has had it in for me since we met.'

Trent looks exasperated. 'George, it's not just Philips. In fact, he did you a favour, because if he had told me what happened in Liverpool right away, I would've replaced you immediately.'

Who does this guy think he's fucking talking to?

George struggles to keep calm. There might still be a happy ending. 'And what about the gig I just did? That went brilliantly.'

A look of wonder passes Trent's face. 'One loud, drunk girl laughing doesn't make it a storming gig.'

'It wasn't just her. Loads of people were laughing.'

'George!' Trent says, raising his voice, 'Loads of people weren't. You had more silences than laughs. It wasn't a good gig by any stretch of the imagination.'

George wonders if Trent has lost the plot.

'I hate to break it to you, but your comedy isn't great. I didn't even want you on the tour, but Will begged me to give you a chance.'

'We'll see if you're still singing the same tune once my TV gig airs.'

'They cut your ten-minute set down to a minute and a half. I wouldn't count on that to launch you as the next Billy Connolly, mate.'

'It's not like you have an eye for talent. Who have you catapulted into superstardom?' George retorts, unable to hold back any longer.

'More than you would know,' Trent replies, looking resigned. 'Needless to say, you won't be doing the last couple of tour gigs. You're just not a comedian, son.'

'Don't patronise me, you poncey arsehole. I wasn't keen to do this tour. I only did it because Will asked me as a favour. I'll have a massive comedy career ahead, you mark my words.'

Chapter 25

George can't face the green room—he might end up decking Philips. He knows what he needs. Focus. He spots her in the audience. Taking a seat at the bar, he orders a pint and a rum and coke chaser, glancing between her and Will on stage. Will's working hard tonight, but George knows he's no better than him.

Will finishes to strong applause. Jemma whoops loudly, clapping like mad, then surprises him by putting her finger in her mouth to produce the loudest whistle, like she's at a football match. The photofit flashes in his mind again. He'll go to the cops when he gets back to London.

Philips announces a break. George stands at the bar, bracing for the usual 'Is it really you?' He doesn't have to wait long.

'Hi there. You were brilliant,' she says, practically vibrating with excitement. 'So funny!'

'Thanks. Drink?'

'A pint of cider and black, please.'

'What's your name?' George asks, studying her. Her hair's shiny but tangled, makeup too thick, mascara smudged like a panda's eyes.

'Sharon.'

The barman arrives, and George orders her drink. They chat at the bar, no one else coming near.

'Look, fancy getting out of here and going somewhere else?' George asks.

'I'm meant to meet someone, but he hasn't turned up.'

'His loss, my gain.'

'Yeah, I'll come for a drink.'

George ducks into the bathroom for another few lines. He's sweating like a nervous virgin. He stops by the green room to grab his bag.

'Jesus, G, what happened?' Will asks.

'Trent's an arsehole. Don't worry about it. I've had enough of these pricks,' George says loudly.

Will shakes his head. 'Here's your camcorder. I'm heading to Jemma's hotel. See you in the morning.'

'Maybe,' George replies, not in the mood for more shit tonight.

He bags the camcorder and gives Philips the finger on his way out. Philips and Trent laugh, and George fights the urge to turn back and cause a riot. She's waiting by the exit, her tight jeans accentuating every curve of her small body. What part of 'meet me outside' did she not understand? Luckily, the bar and exit are quiet; most people have already left.

'Shall we go, my love?'

'My love? God, you don't waste any time.'

'Sorry, just wishful thinking on my part. Can I help with your coat?'

George knows he's laying it on thick tonight, but it could be his last performance. He needs her in place, and fast. She shakily stands, hindered by several cider and blacks which have tinted her teeth purple. He helps with her coat and offers his arm. 'Shall we?'

He pulls on his baseball cap, and they leave the club arm in arm. The streetlights illuminate the light rain and the dark car park. There's no sign of CCTV cameras, which would have made tonight easier had he known—club to van. More planning, less haste.

'You know, I've never been with a comedian before.'

George catches the choice of words—'been', not shagged or snogged. 'Been', leaving it to the imagination. He likes that. 'The expression "you can laugh women into bed" isn't made up, you know.'

Instead of the anticipated cackling, she stops dead in her tracks. Silence. She looks at him, a flicker of something in her eyes. 'Is this what you do then? Use women, a girl in every port?'

George puts on his most sincere expression. 'No, not at all. Actually, I'd love to meet someone like you. It's tough, being a comedian. Always on the road, different city, different hotel every night. It's hard to find someone to settle down with.'

A flicker of suspicion crosses her face, but he pushes on.

'Honestly, all I've ever wanted to do is make people laugh. But it's impossible to stay in one place with one great woman when you're constantly travelling.'

He looks into her eyes, then gently takes her hand and kisses it. She relents a little.

'Is that where we're going now then? Your hotel?'

'Oh, yeah, right. I just need to drop my bag at my van and grab my pyjamas.' He winks.

'I'll tell you what, I'll come with you if you can tell me my name.'

'Why, have you forgotten it?' he laughs, but she doesn't.

Fuck, what's her name? Sarah, Sandy, Shandy…?

'You haven't a clue, have you?'

'Well, "my love" suits you more than any other name could,' he says smoothly.

'My name?' She glares at him. The cider and black mist is setting in, and she looks more ready for a fight than a laugh.

'Okay, Jesus. I'll tell you your name. It's Sandy.'

'Fraid not. You know, I thought you liked me. Guess I'm just another shag to you.'

'Shag? Who said we're shagging?' he says before he can stop himself.

The girl looks at him with disgust. 'Delightful meeting you, now fuck off!'

She turns and starts marching toward the high street. She wobbles on her high heels but still manages to move swiftly, not looking back. She's getting away. The show might be his grand finale.

George moves quickly, running after her and catching up. 'Now, come on, let's not be too hasty. You know, they have some top cider at my hotel, and the food's cracking too. If you're hungry, we can order room service, eat and drink whatever you want.'

She hesitates, unsure.

He knows when more pleading is required. 'I'll treat you like a queen and even drop you home when you want to go. Your own chauffeur, ma'am.'

She stifles a giggle behind her hand. 'My name is Sharon. Remember it now because I'll test you later.'

George wonders how she'll manage that gagged. 'Sharon, of course it is, and a beautiful name too. Shall we press on? Food to eat, cider to drink.'

'How far is it?'

'Oh, just the next street. I'll pop my things in the van first if that's okay?' he says, slipping his arm around her.

'Yeah, that's fine,' Sharon says, leaning her head on his shoulder.

As they walk along the dimly lit side streets, George keeps his eyes peeled. For a moment, he wonders what would happen if the van were stolen. That would be a disaster. He picks up the pace, eager to reach their destination. They turn onto Jury Road, and George breathes a sigh of relief when he sees the van, just where he left it.

'Here we are,' he says, as they reach it. 'This is my baby, like a second home. Want to see inside?'

'Yeah,' Sharon says, 'as long as we're quick, I'm bloody starving now.'

George looks around the street, double checking for security cameras. He puts the key in the lock and opens the back door. 'Ta da, what do you think?'

Sharon moves closer to have a look. George jumps inside and takes her hand to guide her in. She hesitates. 'I thought we were going to your hotel?'

'We are, but I have to give you the guided tour and actually I have some vodka here.' He takes out the camcorder from his bag. 'Plus, I really wouldn't mind seeing a teeny bit of my gig. I have it recorded it.'

'What, from tonight?'

'Yep, I bet we can hear you laughing on it. We might even see you.'

George brings out the vodka. He puts his hand out again and this time Sharon takes it and takes a seat on the small makeshift bed. He pours the vodka and coke into white plastic cups and, keeping his back to her, tips in a good dose of Rohypnol in one of them. He puts the lids on and passes her the drink.

'That's premium Russian vodka, Sharon. You'll like it.'

George drowns the whole lot from his cup. 'Drink up there's more where that came from.'

Sharon knocks it back and holds out the cup for George to fill. He tops it up, wondering how long it will be before he can take her on a little drive.

'Tell me all about you?' he says, closing the back doors. 'Let's get nice and cosy.'

She's happy to be asked. 'I work as a hairdresser, been doing it now for four years. I share a flat with this bitch that I just hate. She's jealous of me and, I swear, she borrows my clothes because the perfume on them certainly isn't mine.'

On and on she goes. Twenty minutes pass before her speech slows to a stop and her eyes close. She mumbles something he can't make out.

'Just relax, my love,' he says, stroking her leg.

Her eyes spring open and her body tenses under his touch. He could do without any more agro tonight. He squeezes her knee and moves closer till his face is almost touching hers. She draws back and tries to stand up but only levitates a few inches before falling back to a seated position. Her eyes open in an exaggerated way, like she has just realised something. *Too late*. Her shoulders slump and her eyes close.

He springs to action, laying her out flat on top of the makeshift bed. He opens his backpack and takes out two straps of fine silk. *Only the best.* He takes off her shoes, ties her feet together, and binds her hands tightly, checking both knots are secure. He takes the mobile phone out of her handbag and switches it off. He picks up his van keys and crouches to listen at the back doors. Nothing. He pushes open the door, looking as casual as he can. He goes round the front and gets in the driver's seat, putting the key in the ignition and switching the lights on. He looks around and pulls out. There's no traffic, it shouldn't take him long.

He drives just below the speed limit and finds the defunct industrial estate easily. It's large and dark. He parks and turns off the engine. It's quiet. The only light is from the moon. He takes a torch from the glove box and goes to the back of the van. He puts his ear to the door, silence. He opens it a little and looks inside. Sharon has rolled onto the floor and her head is bleeding a little. Shit, he didn't secure her. How could he make such a schoolboy error? Blood on his floor, this is not good. *Messy cow!* He hopes that she's not unconscious or she won't be able to enjoy the show. He struggles to pick her up and manages to sit her down on the bench. He takes a dirty cloth from the floor and wipes the blood from her head.

Movie time at last. He connects the camcorder to the laptop and transfers the night's performance, then puts a fresh tape in the camcorder. He props his bag against the van wall and sits the camcorder on it, facing Sharon. He places the laptop on the floor directly below it. She is the star of the show watching the real star of the show. He wants her to have the best view in the house. He hopes that she's going to be generous with that hearty chuckle of hers.

He inserts the cloth in her mouth, time for the wakeup call. He hates screamers, hysterical woman. The smelling salts are waved under Sharon's nose. She flinches and pulls away. He puts them nearer. Sharon groans and then opens her eyes. George's nose touches hers. She tries to focus and shakes her head in a comical way, like a cartoon drunk that's just seen double. She looks at him dead in the eye. He smiles.

Her eyes dart to her bound feet. There's confusion and then fear. Bingo. Sharon jerks her head back up to look at him, with wide pleading eyes, and tries to speak but only garbled sounds come from her gagged mouth. She stands up and bangs her head on the roof plonking her back into a seated position.

'Hey there, sleepy head. How are you? You look peaceful when you sleep.'

He lifts his hand and strokes her hair. She stays perfectly still, the only thing moving are her eyes darting around her surroundings. He suspects she's looking for an escape route—he wonders why it is that people just can't accept fate and relax. It's much more dignified. He takes the laugh-o-meter from the bag and bends down to her eye level.

'Right, Sharon, this is a laugh-o-meter,' he says, holding it up. 'You see we have four sections, 'hee hee', 'ha ha', 'lol', which I think means laugh out loud, and 'lmao'. Do you know what 'lmao' means?'

Sharon shakes her head.

'I didn't either, but I asked around; it means laugh my ass off. This is where you're aiming,' he says, pointing to the red section of 'lmao'. 'You really don't ever want to be below 'lol'. In a minute we're going to settle down to watch my performance from tonight. I know… it's exciting. You loved it so much the first time. That dirty laugh of yours is why you were lucky enough to have been chosen, and you can laugh your pretty little head off as loud as you want. And you do want, Sharon, believe me, you want. The laugh-o-meter will tell me how much you're enjoying my performance.'

George places it on the floor next to the laptop and pours more vodka into the two cups. He sees the fear in Sharon's eyes. 'Don't worry, Sharon, this is just vodka. There are no special ingredients in it. Trust me, I want you wide awake for the premier. Now, I'm going to remove the gag. If you scream, I will hurt you. Would you like to know how I'll hurt you?'

Sharon shakes her head, tears filling her eyes. George thinks back to Jade at this point in the proceedings. Like Jade, Sharon's wondering if there can still be a happy ending. There can't. He fixes her with a hard stare and slowly removes the gag. He pauses then puts the cup to her mouth. She opens it and drinks a little and mutters, 'Thanks.'

'That's a good girl. Now let's watch the show.' George giggles with excitement.

Chapter 26

'I was fucking brilliant tonight. This is going to be great. It's a shame that there weren't any agents in—they would have been falling over themselves to sign me up. Did you think I was the best of the night?'

Sharon nods.

'Really, did you?' he says, concentrating on her response. He is a master of body language as well as comedy. He'll know if she's lying. He leans forward, staring at her. She nods with more enthusiasm.

'If you were to sum it up in one word, what would it be?'

Sharon's eyes move about frantically before resting on George. 'Brilliant.'

'You're not just saying that are you?'

She shakes her head.

Satisfied, he drums rolls an introduction. 'Right, now for the comedy performance of the century. Can we welcome to the stage, the one, the only Geeeoooorrge Maillerrrr.'

He hits a key on the laptop, the show starts, and Philips comes on the screen.

'Next on we have a comedian all the way from London. He's a good friend of mine, no I'm kidding, he's not. I've never met the bugger before, he's probably crap, ha ha.'

'Fuck that bastard, Sean Philips. He's shit.'

George lunges for the laptop. He moves the cursor along to find the start of his act. 'Arsehole,' he shouts at the screen, he's angry now.

He picks up the vodka bottle and takes a swig then presses play. George bounds on with a tight smile on his face, snatching the mic off Philips. He does his first line on stage.

He looks at Sharon to see if she's laughing. She's not. He pauses the footage. 'Did you not think that was funny, Sharon?'

She doesn't respond. She's fighting back tears.

'I'm talking to you, my love.'

She mumbles, 'Yeah.'

'Yeah what?'

'It was funny.'

'Is that how we show something's funny? By just saying, "That's funny"? Don't tell me, show me. I shouldn't have to keep telling you lot this. We're not fucking Americans. In this country, we don't say "that's funny", we laugh.'

He picks up the camcorder and stops recording. 'I am not going to film you as a selected private audience member if you aren't going to give it your all.' He reaches into his bag and fishes out a tape, puts it in the camcorder and presses play. The laptop screen flashes to life with a naked, unconscious Jade. Sharon looks at him desperately.

'She's not dead,' he laughs. 'Not there, anyway. You decide your own destiny. Shall we try again?'

She nods enthusiastically. He taps a few keys on the keyboard and the show resumes.

George wonders if he's chosen badly. She seemed to have a better sense of humour earlier. That opening line is seriously funny, and she barely cracked a smile. He's pissed off but decides to let it go, she'll warm up soon and there's no way she'll get through the hedgehog material without wetting her pants. He slides his finger along the top of the laugh-o-meter as a gentle reminder. He watches a tear slide down her face, miserable cow. She looks at him and forces a smile. He doesn't want smiles. The punch line for the hedgehog joke is coming up. It's hilarious. He holds his breath in anticipation. Sharon laughs, a big laugh, a big false laugh. He looks at her and pauses the show.

'You're not putting it on, are you?'

She speaks up a little louder this time. 'No, it was really good. The laugh-o-meter moved didn't you see it?' she says, in a high-pitched voice. 'I especially liked the bit...'

'SSshhh.' George presses a finger to her lips 'No words, just laughter.'

Sharon laughs hard in regular intervals till the end.

'What did you think? Was I brilliant or what?' George says, standing up and grinning.

'Brilliant,' Sharon says.

'You know, you laughed much more, earlier. Why is that?'

'I don't know.'

'I think you do. Tell me?'

'I thought you were the best and I laughed and laughed,' she says, her voice rising. 'It's just that I'm scared now.'

'Scared of what? There's absolutely nothing to be scared of.'

He sees a flicker of hope in her eyes. There it goes. 'You mean you're going to let me go?'

'Look, Sharon, I'm not some kind of weirdo. All I wanted was for you to be my private audience.'

She smiles weakly, relief sweeping over her face, transforming her to someone much younger. Young and innocent. Bless her. *Stupid girl.*

'Unfortunately for you though, you didn't hit the laughing my ass off on the meter, that's a real shame.' He runs his finger along her temple to her cheek and keeps his hand there. He leans forward an inch from her face. 'You think you can laugh more than you just did?'

He trails his finger along her cheek. Sharon is completely still.

She starts to cry quietly, her eyes begging George to have mercy. 'Please just let me go. I won't tell anyone. I promise.'

'Ok, Shaz, can I call you Shaz? Seems a lot less formal than Sharon and we are friends now, aren't we?'

'Yes, we're friends,' Sharon whispers, between sobs.

'I'll tell you what I'm going to do then, Shaz. I'm going to give you another chance because guess what? You'll love this. I wasn't even recording you the first time.' George looks at her and laughs. 'Private audiences never laugh their best on first viewing. You get another chance. Isn't that great?' George smiles at her. 'I'll top us up and go for a quick piss then we're good to go again. Back in a minute.'

He opens the back door, flooding the van with moonlight, climbs out, and heads to the side. A smile spreads across his face as he pees, savouring the evening. The surroundings are peaceful. Finished, he moves toward the back of the van.

The full force of Sharon's body hits him, knocking him over. His head hits the ground with a thud. She rolls onto her front and slithers in halted caterpillar movements along the ground. Her bound hands and trussed feet make escape difficult but she's undeterred. She starts to jump forward. George watches her for a minute before snatching the camcorder from the van to zoom in on her progress. 'This is hilarious, honest! That bunny hop works for you. Bet you were champion at the sack race on sports day,' he says, striding towards her.

Sharon starts screaming. 'Help me, someone help me.'

He grabs a clump of her hair at the back of her head, halting her mid jump. He holds her still, until she stops screaming. 'Naughty girl, Sharon, very naughty indeed.'

He zooms into her face with the camera in his other hand. 'Smile now, you're on *Candid Camera*.'

Sharon's scream is high and shrill.

George slaps her in the face and sits her down, kicking her feet from under her. She flops like a bag of potatoes, crying bitterly. 'Sharon, Sharon, Sharon. What are we going to do with you?'

'Fuck off! Just fuck off and leave me alone,' she snarls.

George stops recording and puts the camcorder down. 'That's not very nice, is it? When all I've ever done is entertain you.'

'You didn't entertain me. You were shit. I wasn't laughing with you… I was laughing at you. You're a complete joke.'

She looks at George and tries to spit at him—it lands on her own leg.

'You sound as if you're sick of living, Shaz. Got a bit bored of it? Life can be like that sometimes, quite tedious.' He takes a tie from his pocket and puts it round her neck. 'Ready to meet your maker?'

Sharon changes tack. 'Maybe we should have sex?'

'Sex. Is that what you want?'

'Yes,' she whispers and smiles.

'Shame that, Sharon, because I don't fancy you. In fact, I'm having trouble now thinking what I ever saw in you.' George moves his hand to the back of his head and looks at it. There's blood. 'You cut my head. I think we're done here.'

'Please. I'll do whatever you want. Anything.'

George looks at the pitiful, snotty sight in front of him and remembers her laugh. 'Okay, this is your last chance to impress me now. Get in, and get ready!'

He trains the camera on her. 'Private audience member number three. Gig: The Frog and Bucket. Audience response: uproarious.'

He presses play, and points at the laugh-o-meter. Sharon laughs hard in all the wrong places.

George has had enough. He springs to his feet, picks up the cloth, stuffs it back in her mouth and films a hard close up of her face, her eyes, capturing the fear. She whimpers, making him unable to hold back anymore. He positions the tie around her neck and pulls it tight, then tighter still, staring intently into her face, watching her last moments.

He takes a minute to savour the experience before tidying up, putting her body in the little coffin-bed and driving back to the hotel.

He sleeps soundly in the room alone and checks out before Will's return. He leaves a note:

Hope the rest of the tour goes great for you. I'll see you at The Comedy Store next Saturday, where I'll be strutting my stuff.

Cheers mate

G

He takes a quick peek at Sharon before setting off. 'Morning,' he sings cheerfully. He closes the door, settles into the driver's seat. Home sweet home, he thinks. The radio hums to life as he drives, without stopping, all the way back to London. He's not hungry, not tired—he's on the brink of superstardom. When will the TV footage air? Maybe he should approach an agent once it's on screen. He drives to his unit, parking right up against the shuttered opening. Unlocking the padlock, he pushes the shutter up, then opens the freezer. Jade lies there, looking angelic.

'You have company, Jade.'

He struggles to lift Sharon out of the makeshift coffin-bed. Rigor mortis has set in but she's not yet completely cold. He drops her in on top of Jade.

'Sharon, meet Jade. You both have lots in common. I'm sure you'll get along famously.'

Sharon's arms are too stiff to fold over her chest in the angel pose, like Jade's. He could fit a few more ice angels in here. Anka and Shelly would have made the perfect set. He locks the freezer, locks the unit, and drives home.

George decides against speaking to the police, opting instead to spend the week glued to the TV news and scanning the newspapers. There's no photofit anywhere. Surely, if there's a picture that looks like him, he would've been questioned by now. DI Tanner knows what he looks like—he would have picked him out right away. Something doesn't add up. *Is that bitch Jemma lying?*

Will's message confirms he'll be back in time to support tonight. Excitement builds—the Comedy Store, home of legends. The day's spent fine-tuning material and watching previous gigs—owning the stage.

Stepping off the tube, George navigates through the early evening crowds in Leicester Square, ready. New material is phenomenal, though nervous energy hums. Agents and reviewers frequent this spot. Will the debut TV performance or tonight's gig catapult him into the big time?

A queue's already forming outside, over an hour before showtime. George loves a keen audience. He plans to have the hen group, dressed as devils, pissing their pants later. One of them would make a great private audience member, though private performances are on hold for now.

He walks to the front of the queue, drawing attention, making eye contact with potential fans. He knocks on the door, smugly surveying the crowd. Yes, it's me, he thinks, adopting his best modest look.

'Lost, mate?' someone shouts from the back. George spots the cocky young lad staring at him.

'Is that your idea of heckling, son? Looks like there's a village missing an idiot,' George retorts, addressing the crowd.

A few laugh, job done. The door opens, and George states his name to the security guard, who checks the list.

'Mailer… Mailer… got you. Bit early, but come on in.' The guard lets him in and closes the door. 'Straight through, green room to the right.'

George steps inside, scanning the room. Tables and chairs are crammed together, seating about four hundred. The bar staff are setting up. He heads over and orders a beer, but a harassed young woman tells him that the till's without a float, and he'll have to wait. Offended, he turns on his heel and heads backstage. *Do they know who I am? Probably not. They soon will.*

'Hey, you can get a drink now,' the girl calls from the bar.

George feels like a twat but holds his head up and places the mic back in the stand. He walks over to the bar, gets a drink, and studies the poster for tonight's show. *Fuck, Ade Charmers is here!* That bastard turns up everywhere. Big Paddy's listed as Big Paddy, which makes George smile. Say it how it is.

He heads backstage, going over his material, focusing on his facial expressions and timing. He's in the middle of practicing his fake laugh when two comedians he hasn't worked with before walk in. He straightens up, introduces himself, and they respond with one-word answers—Joe, Pete—then go right back to talking to each other.

'You guys played here before then?' George asks, interrupting their conversation.

'Yeah, I'm pretty much a resident here,' Pete says.

Really? George thinks. I wouldn't know you from Adam. 'Oh right, and what about you?'

'Yes,' Joe replies. 'Been performing here regularly for the last four years.'

Fuck, they're smug. Completely full of themselves.

'I tend to do the Manchester Comedy Store more. Just finished a tour up there,' George says.

They glance at him, unimpressed, before turning back to their conversation.

Rude cunts.

A young woman bursts in and hugs Joe and Pete. She comes over and introduces herself as Suzie, practically vibrating with energy. The noise from the audience picks up as they start to pour in. Ade Charmers breezes backstage. Suzie squeals and leaps on him. Ade returns the gesture with showbiz kisses before sweeping around the room, shaking hands. *Pretentious prick.*

He stops when he sees George, giving him a slight sneer before joining Joe and Pete.

Another comedian swaggers backstage, exuding more arrogance than anyone else—Kevin Night from Comedy Roundup. No doubt he's headlining tonight. He struts around the room like a peacock, throwing high fives, exchanging showbiz kisses, and regaling the group with animated tales of past gigs. Where is Will?

'Right, all, the running order. First on, George Mailer,' the MC announces, pausing and turning to George. 'That you?'

'Yes, that's me,' George replies, trying to keep the fury from his voice. *First again, for fuck's sake!* 'Is there any chance I could go on later?'

The room falls silent, every comedian looking at him. The MC ignores the question, continuing, 'Then we have Big Paddy, who better get his big ass here soon, then Joe, Pete, Ade, and finally Kevin headlining. Have a good show, guys,' he says, pinning the running order to the door. As he walks past George, he adds, 'Don't go over your time. Ten minutes, not a minute more.'

Big Paddy turns up late, sweating, and greets Pete, Joe and Ade with enthusiasm, they return with frosty hellos. Good to note that he's not at the very bottom of the pecking order. George nods, but Paddy gives him an odd look, like he's smelt something nasty, and there's something else—wariness. George ignores him. He has bigger fish to fry. His stomach churns, like he's had a dodgy prawn salad in India.

In the toilet, George tries to vomit, but nothing comes up. He wills himself to get a grip—he hasn't been this nervous since his first gig. Nerves on the night don't make sense. He can be sweating and forgetting his words in front of thirty people at a back-end pub, yet as cool as a cucumber in front of three hundred.

He splashes his face, smiling at his reflection. 'It's your night!'

As he makes his way through the mounting audience, he's relieved to see Will at the bar. 'Fuck, you made it,' George says, grinning and high fiving him. He wants to hug him, never been so glad to see him in fact.

'How you feeling?' Will asks.

'Okay. Um, a bit nervous. The fuckers put me on first again. Every fucking time!'

'Don't worry, you'll be fine. You're a TV act now. Only a matter of time before you have your own show.'

'You're right. I don't know what I'm worried about. How was the rest of the tour?'

'It was fine. Shame you got kicked off though.'

'Kicked off? What are you talking about? I told Trent to stick the tour up his arse.'

'Right,' Will says. 'Look, never mind that. Concentrate on tonight. It could be your lucky break. Just go on and work your magic.'

George can't hold back anymore. He pulls Will into a hug. 'Thanks, mate. Honestly, you're the best. Right, I better get ready.'

'Knock 'em dead,' Will says.

Chapter 27

In the green room, the MC approaches him.

'Greg, you're no longer first, you'll be pleased to hear. You'll be on first in the second half.'

'It's George, not Greg.'

Relieved, George studies his material again. He's gone over it fifty times, but it helps calm his nerves. He stays in the green room for the first half of the show.

Big Paddy walks in, tossing Pete a packet of Rennie. 'No problem, my man.'

He strides over to George.

'Just grabbing a pint. Want one?'

'Yeah, that'd be great, thanks,' George replies, slightly puzzled by the change in attitude.

Paddy reappears five minutes later, handing him the drink.

'Cheers, mate.' George appreciates the kindness, but guilt creeps in over his previous alcohol spike stunt.

The first half ends, and the acts return to the green room for another round of complimentary chatter. George heads to the bar during the interval, looking for Will, but doesn't spot him.

Back in the green room, a tall man, with tinted oversized glasses and a suit enters. Joe and Suzie swarm him like a couple of bees. He chats animatedly with them. George edges closer, overhearing Avalon mentioned—the biggest agents in the South. The suited man leaves soon after, telling Suzie he'll talk to her later. She's up in the last section. He must be here for the whole show. This could be his chance. George takes another slurp of his pint.

The MC appears.

'Right, folks, the second half is about to start. Keep it down. Greg, you ready?'

'Yes,' George nods, too tired to correct him. He takes his place behind the curtain, eyeing the audience, waiting for his cue.

'Right now, we have a fairly new comedian to the Comedy Store.'

Fairly new? I'm not an amateur. I was filmed for telly a few days ago.

'I hope you'll give him a big Comedy Store welcome. Are we ready?' The crowd cheers.

'Introducing Scotland's newest comedian—Gre... sorry, George Mailer.'

The audience claps. Time to do it. George shakes the MC's hand and steps into the spotlight.

'Hello, ladies and gentlemen, how are we this evening?'

A mediocre response, followed by one bald man shouting, 'Better when you've finished!'

The crowd laughs. George braces himself, then ploughs on, studying the audience. They look ridiculously drunk for only half nine. It's like three in the morning drunk, the only thing missing is kebabs.

'I'm paid to act like a fool, what's your excuse?' George responds, forcing as much confidence into his voice as he can. A laugh. Good. That's all he needs. *Come on, G, this is your night.*

'My name's George and I'm from Glasgow. Has anyone here been to Glasgow?' Several hands go up. He scans the crowd for someone to improv with.

'You, madam,' he says, pointing to one of the hen-do girls. 'What's your name?'

'Liz,' she replies.

'Did you have a good time in Glasgow, Liz?'

'No, I ended up in a fight with this stupid bitch in a club.'

Fuck. Why her? Why can't they just say 'Yes, I had a great time?' His improv lines are shot to shit. He stumbles, looking around for someone else to work with. He spots another girl at the front. 'Did you like Glasgow?'

'Yes.'

'Did you get beat up or mugged?'

'No.'

'No, you didn't get off the coach, did you? Straight through.'

It gets a small laugh but not what he'd hoped for. The nerves kick in. His stomach starts gurgling. Something's not right. The stage lights burn him alive. They feel like they're melting his face off. The audience watches him with anticipation.

He pushes through, trying to salvage the set.

'You'll have to forgive me if I use the odd swear word,' he says, forcing a grin, 'but Glasgow is the only place in the world where Tourette's syndrome is seen as a gift.'

The laugh he gets is just what he needs, but George clenches his butt cheeks, certain he's about to shit himself.

'You know, I went to India. Didn't manage to find myself, but what I did find was a whole new way of releasing food at an astonishingly quick rate. Deli Belly,' he says, managing a smirk.

The irony isn't lost on him.

'It was horrible. I completely lost the confidence to fart,' he adds, pulling a face.

That gets a laugh. Relief—of a sort—floods through him. But then, a deeper movement in his bowels. He really needs to go to the toilet.

He powers through the rest of his set, but the words feel hollow. He misses three of his best gags. As he nears the end, he knows it's too late—he's shit himself. On stage. At The Comedy Store. His stomach churns with shame as he delivers his closer too quickly. Doesn't matter now.

He thanks the audience with a tight smile and leaves the stage, the lukewarm applause stinging more than he lets on. The MC pats him on the back, the touch as insincere as the applause. A sympathy pat.

Back in the green room, no one makes eye contact. Paddy smirks.

'Nice one, mate. What a gig. You'll probably be headlining tomorrow.'

George ignores him, making a sharp exit to the toilet. There's only one cubicle and it's in use. *Come on.* Finally, a very drunk man stumbles out, waving his hand in front of his face. 'Sorry, mate,' he slurs.

George rushes in, locking the door behind him. He sits on the toilet, not a moment too soon. How has this happened? He felt fine during the first half. He runs through the night in his mind. Paddy... the pint? No, he wouldn't. Would he?

He takes off his pants, tossing them into the bin. The door creaks open, followed by two men entering the bathroom.

'God, I'm pissed, I'll tell you, but I'd still be better than half the arseholes that are on that stage. The last guy was shite,' one of them says, laughing drunkenly.

'It was probably his first gig. Give the guy a break,' the other one responds.

'Fuck off, man, he was crap. My granny's funnier.'

George clenches his fists, feeling his blood boil as he finishes up. He waits in the cubicle until the two men leave.

'Pricks,' he mutters under his breath. He's blown any chance of a future gig. The agent from Avalon isn't going to sign him up any time soon.

He takes a deep breath, dreading the return to the green room, but his jacket and bag are still out there. He steels himself, opens the toilet door, and steps back into the world he wants to escape.

The Comedy Store is still buzzing, the crowd's energy spilling into the hallway as George walks past.

Will is waiting outside the bathroom, concern etched on his face.

'G.'

'Don't even bother,' George interrupts, holding up a hand. 'I was shit. Let's get outta here. I need a drink.'

'There's a bar across the road.'

'I'll get my jacket.'

'You want me to come in with you?'

The kindness of the offer catches George off guard, the weight of it almost bringing him to tears. He's tempted to take him up on it but knows it would make things worse. 'No. I'll be fine,' he says, walking back into the green room. He grabs his things quickly, avoiding eye contact with the other acts.

'Bye, George. See you around,' Paddy sings with a mocking tone.

A few of them laugh, and George can hear their laughter as he leaves, trying to keep his composure. Will waits for him, and they head toward the exit. George avoids looking at the audience, feeling the sting of humiliation burn through him.

They cross the road, and George follows Will into the bar. It's trying to be upscale, a bit pretentious, but it's quiet enough for George to breathe. Will orders, and George sits heavily at a table, his head sinking into his hands.

'I want to cry, Will,' he mutters.

'It wasn't that bad, G, come on.' Will sets the pints down.

'Not that bad? Come on, Will, it was a car crash.'

'What happened anyway? You looked confident when I spoke to you earlier.'

'I shit myself, Will, that's what happened.'

'Seriously?'

'Yeah,' George says, his voice tight. 'I actually shit my pants.'

Will leans in, confused. 'Really?'

'I think that fat fucker Paddy spiked my pint with some kind of laxative. The fat cunt,' George spits, his anger flaring.

'Why would he do that?'

'He's probably jealous that I'm going somewhere and he's not.'

'Seems a bit extreme. He's usually alright.'

'I don't fucking know, Will, but I know it was him.'

Jemma enters the bar, scanning the room.

'What the fuck is she doing here?' he mutters, nodding towards her.

'I told her I was coming to see you perform tonight and we'd be here after,' Will explains, glancing over at Jemma. 'She said she wanted to come along and support you.'

'Did she now? So, you're still seeing her?'

'Yeah. Why wouldn't I be?'

'Oh, I don't know, maybe because she thinks your best mate's a murderer?'

'She didn't say that, G.'

'She's got an agenda, that one. Trust me,' George replies, his gaze fixed on Jemma as she pulls out her phone.

'It would mean a lot if you could make an effort with her,' Will says, looking hurt.

'I could really do without her tonight,' George responds.

Jemma moves through the crowd of drunk suits and makes her way toward them. Will stands up to greet her, smiling and leaning in for a kiss.

'What do you want to drink?' he asks.

'Chardonnay, please, darling,' Jemma replies with a playful grin. Will throws George a pleading look before heading to the bar.

Jemma removes her coat and sits down, her posture cold but casual.

'Hi, George. How are you?'

George doesn't waste time.

'You can cut the bullshit, Jemma. Just say what you've got to say.'

'Okay, George.' She leans back, crossing her arms. 'I've tried really hard to be nice to you, even though you're rude, bad-mouthing me or just ignoring me. Honestly, I think you're a fucking moron. But you're Will's moron, so I've made the effort. But I'm done now! I doubt you two will stay close once you're in prison, so I'll bide my time.'

George leans forward slightly, his anger simmering beneath his neutral expression. 'And why would I be going to prison, Jemma?' He raises his hand to stop her before she speaks. 'And just before you answer that,' he continues, a sweet smile creeping onto his face, 'Can I just say I haven't made an effort with you because you're a jumped-up, snotty bitch. And I don't think you'll be around long.'

He takes a sip of his pint, maintaining his cool, before adding, 'So, prison, Jemma... why would you think such a ludicrous thing?'

'Prison's for morons and dodgy psychos. You belong there, with your drug deals and lies. Saying you hadn't gigged at Amusement House before, when you clearly had. And you did speak to that poor girl, and God knows what else.'

'Jesus, sorry about the wait, folks. Takes forever when people are ordering cocktails,' Will says, setting the drinks down.

'Thanks, darling,' Jemma replies.

'What are you two talking about?' Will asks, looking from George to Jemma.

'Jemma was just telling me she thinks I'm a fucking moron and a dodgy psycho.Lovely girl, Will. A keeper,' George says, taking a long drink of his pint.

Will looks confused and hurt. 'Jemma?'

'Just hear me out,' she says quickly, taking his hand.

'Hear you out? You called George—my best mate—a moron?' He pulls his hand away.

'Yeah, but with good reason,' Jemma says, her voice pleading.

'Why don't you tell him about the photofit? The one you had made up. It was like a portrait of me, Will. She told me the detectives were using it to find the killer, and it was going out on all the news channels,' George says, enjoying watching her squirm.

'You had a photofit of George? Why?' Will stammers, an angry edge creeping into his voice.

Jemma reaches for his hand. He pulls it away.

'He's a psycho. I can prove it. I've got evidence,' she says, pulling a video tape from her bag. 'It's all here.'

George feels his heart speeding up, beads of sweat forming on his forehead. Keep it together, stay calm.

'Oh right. That's a recording of George killing someone, is it?'

'Not killing someone, no. It's CCTV footage of him walking with Sharon Gallagher, in Manchester, on the night she went missing. You think that's just a coincidence?'

'Just get out of here, Jemma. I'm sick of the sight of you!' Will says, looking devastated.

'He's bad news. I'm telling you.'

'Go!' Will shouts.

Heads turn. Jemma's eyes well up with tears. She slips on her coat.

'I've handed a copy of this tape to the police,' she says, her voice sharp. 'I might have fabricated the photofit, but it got the truth out of you. You did talk to Shelly Daniels that night at the Amusement House, and you probably did kill her. You'll pay. I'll make sure of it.' She stands and leans over to kiss Will, but he pulls away. She smiles. 'It's not me who's been dishonest,

Will. This story's wrapped up now. No hard feelings,' she says, quickly leaving the bar.

'G, why are you on camera with the girl who was murdered in Manchester?'

George thinks quickly. He trusts Will, but he won't tell him everything.

'Just bad luck. She chatted me up at the bar at the Frog and Bucket. We had a few drinks at the van, then she left. That's it. The last time I saw her, she was fine—bit drunk, but alive. I went back to the hotel and slept.' George puts his head in his hands. 'I can't believe it's on tape... that and being at the same club as the other girl. Jemma's right, it doesn't look good. I'm going to be well and truly stitched up for this.'

'They'll need evidence, G. They'll see it's just a coincidence.'

'People have been charged for less. Something must have happened to her on the way home.'

'Did you see anyone hanging about when she left?'

'No, I don't think so.'

Will's phone rings. He talks for a minute, then hangs up. 'I hate to leave you like this, G, but I need to go. Nick's locked himself out. Are you going to be alright?'

'I don't know.'

'The first thing you should do is go to the cops, get it cleared up fast.'

'You're right. I'll go now. I'll grab a taxi.'

'Call me later, let me know how you get on,' Will says, picking up his jacket.

George watches him leave, his mind racing. There was no photofit, nothing solid to link him to Shelly. Was Jemma's story about the friend made up too? Where was the CCTV in Manchester? He was careful. He leaves the bar, heart pounding. This wasn't the night he'd imagined. He flags down a cab.

George steps out of the taxi, taking a minute before entering the police station. Repeating his story in his head. He met Shelly briefly, said hello, she wasn't interested, and that was it. Sharon, he met after the gig. They went back to the van, had a few drinks, then she left. The CCTV footage will probably show two people attracted to each other, hanging out. They don't have anything.

He hopes they don't get a search warrant for the whole building. The bedsit's clean, but the flat's a different story. The money, the film footage—his tools aren't hidden well either. He curses himself for being stupid. He could've ripped up a few floorboards to hide them. Running through various scenarios, he tries to anticipate their questions and devises a few of his own, hoping they'll reveal what they know.

Inside the station, he asks for Tanner, is escorted to an interview room, offered tea, and left alone. Scanning the room for a camera, he sees none. He practices different expressions—shock, sadness, indignation, confusion—he might need all of them. Should he call a lawyer right away? Would that look bad? George smiles as he plays the private performances in his head. It's all been worth it.

Chapter 28

DI Tanner and DCI Stone enter the interview room, taking seats opposite George. He's well-rehearsed and ready.

Tanner leads.

'Mr Mailer, thanks for coming in. Officers visited your home several times but couldn't reach you. We have a few questions. Tell us about the night you performed at the Frog and Bucket in Manchester.'

'Sure, what do you need to know?'

'Did you meet a Sharon Gallagher?'

'I met a woman called Sharon. Don't know her surname,' George says, trying out a bewildered look.

'And what happened?'

'She wanted a drink, but the pubs were closed, so we went for a walk instead.'

'For a walk?' Stone raises an eyebrow. 'Where did you walk to?'

George hesitates. He's reluctant to mention the van but knows it'll come up. If they search it, they'll find her fingerprints. Better to get ahead of it. 'We went back to my van and had a few drinks.'

'Then what?' Stone asks, jotting something down.

'That's it. She said she had work in the morning. I offered to walk her home, but she said she'd be fine— she lived nearby.'

'You let an inebriated girl walk home on her own, after midnight?' Stone sneers. 'Very chivalrous.'

'Women are independent these days. They do what they want.'

'Where did you last see her?' Tanner asks.

'My van was parked on Jury Street. She must have left around one.'

'She's been missing for a week, and the last person she was seen with was you,' Tanner says.

'As I said, we had a drink, then she left.'

'On Sunday, the 4th of March, you performed at the Amusement House. Is that correct?'

'Yes.'

'Did you see this girl?' Tanner asks, taking a photo from a folder and placing it on the table.

Jemma must have told them that he had admitted it.

'You showed me this picture when I came in for questioning before. I didn't recognise her, but now I think it might be the girl I spoke to. She looked different from that photo, though.'

'And it's just a coincidence that her body was found in the graveyard next door to where you live?'

He shrugs. 'Yeah.'

'And another coincidence that one woman is dead and another is missing, with you as the common denominator?'

'A terrible coincidence,' George says, rubbing his head, wondering if they had anything.Surely, it would have been on the table by now.

'What about Jade Emery?' Tanner asks, eyeing him closely.

Oh my God. George gulps and stops breathing, though his mask remains intact. 'Jade Emery? I don't think I know a Jade Emery.'

Tanner slides another photo in front of him. George looks at it, picturing the lovely Jade, safely tucked up in his freezer.

'Have you ever met or seen this girl?'

'No, I don't think so. Look, Sergeant, girls often chat up comedians after gigs. I can't

be expected to remember them all.'

'It must be tough with all these women throwing themselves at you,' Stone sneers. 'Do you like women, George?'

Indignant, he responds, 'Yeah, I like women.'

'Jade is an attractive girl. She was at your gig at...' He checks his notepad. 'The Comedy Cellar in Salisbury. And here's the kicker... she hasn't been seen since either. Her friend said they were given a lift by one of the comedians. Imagine.'

'I would like a lawyer now, please.'

'George Mailer, I am arresting you on suspicion of the murder of Shelly Daniels, and of the abduction of Sharon Gallagher and Jade Emery. You do not have to say anything, but it may harm your defence if you do not mention when questioned something you later rely on in court. Anything you do say may be given in evidence. On your feet, Mr Mailer.'

Tanner takes George to the custody desk. 'This is your custody officer, Sergeant Adams,' he says.

Adams, a short woman with lank hair and weary eyes, stands behind the counter. Another officer steps forward, searching George's pockets and emptying his wallet and phone onto the desk. The wallet is checked, and he's asked to remove his shoes, belt, and watch. Sickening thoughts cross his mind—when will he get them back? Is he going to jail? He feels detached, as if watching someone else's life unravel.

Adams turns to Tanner. 'What are the circumstances of the arrest?'

'He was last seen with both Jade Emery and Sharon Gallagher on the nights they went missing. Shelly Daniels' body was found near his home, and we have a witness who claims Mr. Mailer confessed to meeting her a few days before she went missing,' Tanner responds without hesitation.

'What's the purpose of detainment?' Adams asks.

'Prompt and effective investigation,' Tanner replies.

'Do you have a solicitor?' Adams asks George. 'If not, one will be assigned to you from the duty scheme.'

'OK.'

'We'll call one now. You'll be held until they arrive.' Adams steps forward, cuffs him, and escorts him to a cell. The key turns in the steel door, and George is left alone.

Sergeant Adams returns hours later to inform George that the duty solicitor has arrived. She leads him to an interview room.

'George Mailer,' she says, stepping aside to let him in and closing the door behind him.

A good-looking woman sits at the table. Tanned, with long dark hair, sexy specs, and a well-cut suit. A spread of notes is laid out in front of her.

She extends her hand. 'I'm Katherine Henning. I'll be representing you, unless you have someone else in mind?' She motions for him to sit.

'No, you'll be fine. Just a mix-up, I'm sure it'll be sorted out quickly,' he replies.

'Okay, George,' she says, locking eyes with him. 'The more truthful you are with me, the better I can represent you. No bullshit, no surprises. Understand?'

'Yes,' he answers, thinking... in different circumstances... maybe…

She flips through her notes. 'You're being charged with the murder of Shelly Daniels and the abduction of Sharon Gallagher and Jade Emery.' She looks up from her notes. 'How will you plead? Guilty or not guilty?'

'Not guilty.'

'The police have established that you were at the venues where all three women were.'

'I was at the three gigs, but I can't say for sure I met all three women.'

'Who did you meet for sure?'

'Sharon in Manchester. The girl Shelly, I can't be sure.'

'And Jade Emery?'

'I might have given her and her mate a lift after the gig, but I was back at the hotel less than an hour later.'

She flips through her notes. 'You told the police you didn't give anyone a lift after the Comedy Cellar gig.'

'I know, but I didn't want to be set up for it. You know what I think, Katherine? Is it okay to call you Katherine?'

'Yes, go ahead.'

'I think there's some weirdo following me around, killing women. Maybe a crazed fan or something.'

'Interesting theory,' she says, dismissing him. 'Let's focus on the facts for now. Alright, let's start at the beginning. I need you to tell me everything that happened on the nights in question, and I want the truth.'

'Okay,' he says, giving a brave soldier smile.

He recounts the three nights, telling the truth up until the important parts, ending each night with, 'I kissed them goodnight, and they went their own way.'

Katherine asks questions about every part of the story, pushing for more details at each step. He glances at her watch—it's well past midnight.

'Look, I'm done for the night,' George says, standing. 'I need my beauty sleep.'

'First thing tomorrow, you'll be questioned. Prepare for a full day. You'll likely go to court the day after,' she says, standing to shake his hand. George notices her elegant wrists, perfectly suited to silk.

'Thank you, Katherine,' he says, squeezing her hand before letting it go.

She bangs on the door and an officer takes him back to his cell. He lies in bed thinking about his up-and-coming performance in court. He might get a book, or a movie deal out of it. Shrugging off his earlier thoughts about going to jail, he snuggles down for a sound night's sleep.

He wakes to the sound of his cell door unlocking. Sergeant Adams enters, holding a sandwich wrapped in cellophane, and a cup of tea.

He devours the sandwich, feeling surprisingly cheerful despite the grim surroundings. After finishing, he puts on his trousers, folds the scratchy blanket, and waits.

Adams opens the cell and hands him his shoes. 'Put them on and come with me,' she says.

Taken to an interview room, George sits next to Katherine, facing the two detectives, DI Tanner and DCI Stone. A tape recorder sits on the table. Tanner presses record, and the questions start coming fast. George struggles to match his carefully rehearsed expressions to his answers. Katherine interrupts regularly, defending his rights and pointing out procedural details.

Stone asks where the van is. George glances at Katherine, who pauses the interview. Tanner stops the recorder, and both detectives leave the room.

'I don't know where the van is,' George says.

'What do you mean? Where did you leave it?' Katherine asks, her gaze suspicious.

'I sold it,' George responds, hoping it will give the police less to work with.

Katherine fixes him with a stern look. 'Are you saying that if the police search the area around your home, they won't find the van?'

'The buyer was from Essex. They won't find the van,' George says, confidently, thinking that they can't find it if they don't have the registration number.

'When did you sell the van?' she asks, taking notes.

'Two days ago.'

'Right.' Katherine stands up and calls the detectives back in.

The whole day is spent answering questions, often the same ones, repeatedly. Katherine draws a halt to the interview late in the evening. George thinks he's done well. He's delighted when Katherine tells him that he'll be going to court the next day, though is disappointed to hear that it's unlikely that he'll get bail. His surroundings are starting to get on his nerves. He is taken back to his cell. He sits there, bored, until he's tired enough to lie down and sleep.

The next morning, a young policeman hands him the same breakfast as before.

At the custody desk, Sergeant Adams holds up a sealed plastic bag containing his belongings. 'If you make bail today, you'll get these back. If not, they'll go with you to your next destination.' She gestures toward a large man with a shaved head and dark uniform.

The security man cuffs George's wrists, collects his belongings, and leads him through to the exit.

The van's doors swing open, revealing three small cages on either side of a narrow passage running between them. One cage is already occupied by a young man, his wrists handcuffed to the side. George is placed in the cage nearest the door and secured to the van's wall.

What if the van goes over a cliff? We're fucked. He takes deep breaths, thinking of the happy times that brought him here.

The journey seems endless, picking up prisoners from different jails. Proper scumbags, sneaking glances at the criminals around them.

When they finally arrive at the Magistrates' Court, the van doors swing open, the light stings his eyes. George's frustration grows as they're taken through the rear entrance—no media, no autograph hunters, nothing. He's led to a cell on the lower floor.

Soon after, Katherine arrives, dressed in a black cloak and wig. Calm and unfazed, though tired, she says, 'You won't be asked to say anything at this point. We'll be in and out of there quickly.' She leaves him alone again.

A security man comes to fetch him shortly after. A clerk announces George's name as he's placed in a box with a wooden base and a Perspex top. The courtroom is filled with half a dozen lawyers, all gowned and wigged. Two men and a woman sit behind a large bench, wearing plain clothing. A woman with a typewriter sits below them, not looking up. Katherine sits at a table in front of the bench. A man, concentrating on his notes, sits nearby. DCI Stone and DI Tanner are seated behind them.

The magistrate, sitting in the middle, says, 'Yes, Mr Shields.'

A man rises to his feet. 'Sir, two young women are missing, and another is dead. What these women have in common is they all met George Mailer on the night they were last seen. We have Mr Mailer's testimony stating that he was with two of these women. It is highly risky to let this man back onto our streets. We ask that you refuse bail.'

Katherine stands up. 'Sir, the prosecution has nothing but hearsay and circumstantial evidence. There's nothing to tie my client to the demise or disappearance of any of these women. He has no prior criminal record.'

The magistrate looks at George for the first time. George offers his most earnest look.

'Bail denied,' the magistrate says, promptly.

The security guard escorts him back to his cell. George sits down heavily. No bail—this can't be a good sign.

Katherine enters shortly after. 'We should receive your trial date in three or four weeks. After that, we'll have around two months to prepare your case. You'll be detained on remand at Belmarsh Prison. I'll see you there tomorrow afternoon, and we'll go over everything in detail.'

The door opens, and a guard stands in the doorway.

'I'll see you tomorrow,' Katherine says, walking out of the cell.

George leans over and vomits.

'Dirty bastard,' the guard grumbles, pulling him up by the arm.

Fear grips him. Three months—he can't do three months in jail. The guard escorts him to the van, and once again, he's caged, surrounded by loud and vile lowlifes. George keeps his head down for the rest of the journey, praying for a miracle.

His new home, Belmarsh prison, is surrounded by high walls topped with barbed wire. Six officers line up. Each officer unlocks a prisoner and hands them over, one by one. George is the last. He's led into the courtyard and brought inside, where a guard runs a beeping machine over his body, inches away. He's given a prison uniform and signs for his belongings in a sealed bag. His clothes and personal items are placed into a larger bag and added to a pile on the desk. He feels dazed, walking through the motions.

At every stage, doors are unlocked and locked as they go deeper into the prison building. He counts his breaths, eyes to the floor, ignoring the shouting calls from cells around him. Finally, he's stopped. His handcuffs are removed, and he's shoved inside a cell, the door clanging shut behind him.

The cell has a bunk bed, a small table, and a silver toilet pan in the corner. A minute window with bars lets in a sliver of light. He lets his eyes adjust to the space. The space. A box, an extension of the cage in the van.

'Welcome to paradise.'

George whips his head toward the voice. An old man with white hair and a matching beard sits up on the top bunk.

'Is it all you hoped for?' he asks, chuckling.

George ignores him and sits down on the bottom bunk. Three months of this? He'll lose his mind. He curls into a ball, pulling his knees to his chest, and closes his eyes, trying to block everything out.

Chapter 29

George wakes up to the sound of shouting. His eyes flicker open. Where the hell is he? The slot on the door opens and shuts, and the door unlocks. A small guard with thinning hair stands in the doorway.

'Rise and shine. Breakfast is served,' he says briskly.

A pair of feet dangle over the top bunk. A baton bangs on the door.

'Up and out, now!' the guard says, stepping into the cell. 'Mailer, Kesky, if you're not out of here in two minutes, you'll be spending the whole day here.'

George stands up, and the old man lands beside him. 'Don't think we've been introduced. The name's Kesky,' he says, holding out his hand.

'Get a move on, girls. There'll be enough time to get to know each other later.'

Kesky scurries from the cell, and George follows him to a canteen with long tables. Several guards stand around the perimeter, eyes fixed on them. They join a long queue with trays in hand.

'How was your first night in Hotel Paradise?' Kesky asks, not turning around.

'Fabulous,' George responds. 'The cocktails were superb.'

Kesky laughs. 'Keep your sense of humour, son. You'll need it.'

George is shocked to see a full fry-up: sausages, eggs, and bacon. He wasn't expecting that. He takes a portion of everything and sits down next to Kesky and two other inmates, eating quickly in silence. He still can't believe he's here.

Katherine arrives midday, entering the interview room looking sombre.

'Okay, we have a lot of work to do,' she says, removing pads and folders from her bag.

'Can you have the court date brought forward?' George asks. 'I can't spend three months in here.'

'If you are convicted, you'll be in prison for a lot longer than three months, more like the rest of your life.'

'That's not going to happen. They'll catch the real killer before then, and I'll be free to go. My fans will remain loyal, and I'll see to it that justice is done,' he says, imagining himself delivering his statement to a media circus.

'I need you to concentrate, to focus. I have questions which I need you to answer in as much detail as possible. Got it?'

'Yes. Fire away.'

Katherine asks him question after question.

'I looked at the CCTV footage of you and Sharon Gallagher in Manchester. It's a minute long… you both look relaxed… happy even. I don't think that it'll persuade a jury of any wrongdoing. You said you parked the van on Jury Street, where did you go from there?'

'Sharon said she lived nearby and would walk home. I just went back to the hotel and slept. Ask Will, my mate. We shared a room.'

'Will saw you arrive back at the hotel room?'

'Yes.'

'Why didn't you mention this before? This changes everything. If you were back in the hotel at the estimated time of death, then the prosecution's case is unstable.'

'I thought I did mention it already.'

Katherine flicks through her notes. 'No, you said you arrived at the hotel an hour after leaving Sharon, approximately 1:00 a.m., but you didn't mention sharing a room.'

George pulls his best puzzled look.

'Is Will happy to alibi you for that night?'

'Yes, I'm sure he will be.'

'Okay. I'll speak to him. Write down his number? This is good,' she says, gathering her bag and notes.

'Can I see Will? I'm allowed visitors, aren't I?'

'You are, but it'll weaken your defence if the jury finds out he's been here. They'll think you've both put your heads together and made this up. Just leave it to me. Now, I'm juggling a lot of cases. I won't be back for a few weeks. Write down everything you remember.'

'I will,' George says, feeling hope return.

Katherine bangs on the door, and the guard opens it. She leaves with a quick goodbye, and he's taken back to his cell. He hopes Katherine asks Will in a leading way about being his alibi.

Returning to his cell, he finds it less intimidating. He feels sure this is a temporary thing, like boot camp, he thinks. It might even be good for him. He will write great material and perfect his private audience ritual. He won't make the same mistakes again.

The door opens, and Kesky comes in. 'How did it go with your brief?'

'Great. Don't think I'll be here much longer.'

'Right,' Kesky says, smiling kindly.

'No, really. It's an open-and-shut case. I'll perform at the Crown Court, then I'm out of here.'

He stays close to Kesky in the following weeks. He likes him, he's a good listener. He's surprised at how quickly he settles into the routine and is even more surprised to find that he quite likes the rigidness of it, and the time he has for writing new material.

On Katherine's next visit, George is bright and enthusiastic. When the guard comes to get him, he picks up his pages of notes and takes them with him. At the interview room, Katherine's head is down, pouring over paperwork.

She looks up.

'Hello, George. How are you?'

'I'm great,' George says, meaning it.

'Sorry it's taken me a while, but I've been working on the case and it's good news. Firstly, Will says he can remember you coming back to the hotel and that he'll testify for you.' *Good old Will.* 'The other bit of good news is that we have a date for your hearing. We have exactly two months left to prepare. We're not out of the woods yet, there's still a lot of ground to cover.' She pauses, then notices his pad. 'I see you've got plenty of notes,' she says, pointing to it. She picks it up and reads. Her expression changes. 'What is this, George?'

'It's new material I've been writing. Some of my best stuff, the audience is going to love it.'

'George, your future is in the balance here. This really isn't the time for comedy. Think about names of witnesses who may be able to back up your statements—hotel clerks, taxi drivers? I would also like to call a couple of witnesses who can testify to you being of good character. Can you think of any?'

'Will.'

'Anyone else apart from Will?'

He thinks about it for a long time. 'Ron. My old boss at Stand and Deliver.'

'Anyone else?'

George racks his brain before answering. 'No.'

Katherine asks him questions for another hour. He's never been asked this many questions about himself. He enjoys it, knowing it's also great practice for future television interviews.

On the morning of the trial, George is taken to a room and given a suit. It fits perfectly, though the shirt is a little tight around the collar. The tie is polyester—he would have preferred silk. When he arrives at court, he's dismayed to be led to the back entrance again, like the bloody hired help.

The reporters will be disappointed to miss him—he looks good, he should be seen. He's taken to a cell, which doesn't seem right, now that he's in his finery.

Katherine enters and asks if he's ready. He assures her he is.

'Good. You won't be on the stand, but I want you to think and make mental notes of everything that the prosecution witnesses have to say.'

A long hour later, he's led into court by a guard and placed in the dock. The courtroom is crammed to bursting. He looks around for familiar faces. DI Tanner and DCI Stone are seated in the second row. Will is sitting behind them, looking worried and uneasy. More familiar faces—Ron and Dan the Man. *What the fuck is he doing here?* Then his old boss, Darren, sitting near the front, hoping to witness his demise, no doubt. *Pity.* There's a girl in the front row he recognises—Jade's drunk friend.

The media cluster together, notepads and pens at the ready. Two tables face the bench, Katherine at one and the barrister who was at the first hearing at the other.

'All stand,' the clerk announces as the judge enters, dressed in a wig and cloak. This is more like it, George thinks.

The clerk waits until the judge is seated and then reads the charges. The judge gives instructions to the jury. George looks at the jury as they're sworn in—quite a few females. That will work in his favour. He looks at each woman in turn and tries to make eye contact. He succeeds with one of the younger women and gives her a shy smile. She glares at him and looks away.

The swearing-in seems to take forever, but, eventually, the prosecutor stands and makes his opening statement.

'Milord, both the defence and the prosecution are agreed on the evidence from the postmortem regarding the victim, Shelly Daniels. Therefore, I don't propose to call any experts and will instead rely on the agreed statements.'

'Is this correct, Miss Henning?'

Katherine stands up. 'Yes, Milord.'

'Very well,' the judge says.

'With your Lordship's permission, I propose to call my first witness, April Scott,' the other barrister says.

April stands up and goes to the witness box. She was legless when George last saw her. She takes the oath.

'April, can you tell me, and tell the court, if you recognise anyone in this room?'

'Yes, I recognise him.' She points at George.

'For the record, you are referring to George Mailer, the defendant.'

'Yes. He gave me and my friend, Jade, a lift home from the Comedy Cellar.'

'The Comedy Cellar in Salisbury? That would have been on the 11th of March?'

'Yes.'

'And you're sure that the defendant is the man who gave you both a lift home?'

'Absolutely.'

'And was that the last time you saw your friend?'

'Yes,' she says, starting to cry.

'No more questions,' the prosecutor says, and sits down.

Katherine gets to her feet and adjusts her papers. 'Had you had anything to drink on the evening in question?'

April hesitates. 'Yes… a bit,' she says, looking down at the floor.

'A bit?' Katherine raises an eyebrow and turns to the jury. 'Weren't you so inebriated that you were sick before leaving the club?'

'That was a stomach bug.'

'A stomach bug that rendered you legless. So legless that you had to be carried into your home?'

April blushes. 'I might have been drunk, but he was definitely the one who drove us home.'

'No one's denying that, Miss Scott.'

'Oh,' she says, looking confused.

'George Mailer did indeed help you and your friend home. It's a testament to the sort of man Mr Mailer is—kind and considerate. Did you thank Mr Mailer for driving you home?'

'No. I mean, yes.'

'Could it be, Miss Scott, that you do not remember as you were too drunk?' Katherine smiles at the jury. 'And yet, you got home safely?'

'Yes,' she mumbles.

'And just to be perfectly clear, Miss Scott, did you witness any untoward behaviour towards you or your friend on the night in question?'

'No, but...'

'But?' Katherine fixes her with a hard look.

'Who else could have taken her?'

'Who says that she's been taken? Maybe she left of her own free will. It happens every day. No more questions, Your Honour,' Katherine says, taking her seat.

The prosecutor stands up. 'We would like to call Darcy Hills to the stand.'

George recognises her from the Amusement House—Shelly's friend. She takes the stand and is sworn in.

'Miss Hills, do you recognise anyone in this room?'

'Yes,' she says confidently, throwing George a venomous look. 'Him.' She points at George.

'Can you tell me about it?'

'Me and my friend, Shelly, were at the Amusement House. He was one of the comedians performing, and so was he,' she points to Will.

Will pales at the attention, looks at George for the first time, then looks away.

'Carry on.'

'He was staring at her.' She points to George again.

'And did the defendant approach her?'

'I don't know for sure. I went to the bar and the toilet. He could have then, but he had his eye on her. She was giddy when we left, which isn't like her.'

'No further questions.'

Katherine stands. 'You didn't, at any time, see the defendant speak to your friend?'

'Um, no...'

'Isn't it correct, Miss Hills, that Mr Mailer voluntarily took part in an identity parade, and that you did not pick him out as the man who had been staring at Shelly?' Katherine checks the document in front of her.

'I was ninety nine percent sure but just couldn't say for definite.'

Katherine turns to the jury. 'In a court of law, there cannot be one shred of doubt. No more questions, Your Honour.'

Chapter 30

After the recess, George is back in the dock as the prosecutor calls his next witness, Daniel Punt. Dan the Man—DTM)—takes the witness box and is sworn in. George stares at him, hoping to put him off. The prosecutor asks DTM to recount the evening that he first met the defendant.

‘We were having work drinks when he turned up,’ Dan says, casting an eye over at George. ‘Will introduced him to everyone, and then when I went to the toilet, he followed me. He said if he heard me giving Will any more shit at work, he’d hunt me down. He was very aggressive. I thought he might have had a knife on him.’

‘Speculation,’ Katherine says, standing up.

‘Then he threatened to snip my dick off, miming scissors. The look in his eyes was terrifying.’

Will’s mouth drops open, but he avoids making eye contact with George.

‘Yes, I’m sure that would have been an extremely frightening experience, Mr Punt. No more questions, Your Honour.’ The prosecution sits down.

Katherine stands. ‘Did anyone else witness this verbal exchange?’

‘No.’

‘It’s your word against Mr Mailer’s. Isn’t it true, Mr Punt, that you had it in for your boss, Mr Will Devon? I have several witnesses to support this observation.’

‘I wouldn’t say I had it in for him.’

‘Would you say you constantly undermined him and badmouthed him?’

‘Erm...’

‘Didn’t George just ask you to give Will a chance?’

‘No, he threatened me.’

'We only have your word for that. No more questions, Your Honour.'

Dan looks George dead in the eye as he leaves the stand. The prosecution calls their last witness for the day, Jemma Hatten. She confidently walks to the witness stand, wearing a smart dress and heels.

'Can you tell the court how you know Mr Mailer?'

'He's my boyfriend's best friend.'

George smiles at that, satisfied. *That's right don't you forget it.*

'And how long have you known Mr Mailer?'

'A few months.'

'How did you become familiar with this case?'

'I'm an investigative journalist for *The Times* and was looking into Shelly Daniels' death. When I learned that both Will and George had been at the venue where she went missing, I spoke to them separately. George lied, claiming he'd never been to the Amusement House. Will told me they both had been there and that made me suspicious.'

'Do you like George?'

'I hardly think that's relevant…'

'Then perhaps you won't mind answering.'

'No, I don't!'

'Can you tell us why?'

'I don't know. He just seemed overly dependent on Will. I tried to give him the benefit of the doubt at first, but I just had a feeling he wasn't trustworthy.'

'George and Will have known each other for a long time. Would you say that your actions—speaking to them separately and feeding them information—were driven by your personal feelings toward George, or were they solely in the interest of uncovering the truth?' Katherine asks.

'I was just doing my job,' Jemma says, though her voice wavers slightly.

'And about your conversation with Mr Mailer regarding the deceased, Shelly Daniels. How did that go?'

'He admitted he spoke to her and got her number,' she says, tucking her hair behind her ear.

Katherine leans forward, her tone sharp. 'Have you allowed your personal bias against Mr Mailer to colour your investigation, even to the point of twisting the facts to fit your narrative?'

Jemma's eyes flicker, and she shifts uncomfortably in her seat.

'I don't—' she begins, but Katherine interrupts, her voice growing more commanding. 'You see, Miss Hatten, you manipulated the facts to suit your story. And yet you expect the jury to trust you when you claim Mr Mailer's guilt? You went to great lengths to forge a photofit of Mr Mailer to back up a lie that the photofit was being aired on television. Would you say that you were compromising your integrity there to bring about distress and misery for Mr Mailer?'

'I knew something wasn't right and that he was lying,' Jemma says, her voice going up an octave and the cool cumber exterior melting.

Katherine turns, looking directly at the jury.

'No further questions, Your Honour.'

The judge nods, and Jemma is escorted off the stand. Katherine returns to her seat, her eyes scanning George. He feels a small flicker of hope, though it's tempered by the weight of the entire case still looming over him.

The court ends for the day, and George is taken back to his cell. Katherine joins him to tell him about the next stage of the process but refuses to give him any assurances on the outcome.

The next day begins with Ron taking the stand as the first witness for the defence. He tells the court that he found George reliable, honest, and hard-working.

The prosecutor rises. 'You said you sold a van to Mr Mailer?'

'Yes.'

'And did you ever see his driving licence?'

'No, I asked him for it, but he kept forgetting it.'

'If I told you that we checked with the DVLA and found that George Mailer has never taken a driving test, never mind passed one, would you be surprised?'

'Yes,' Ron replies, looking disappointedly at George.

'Not quite the solid character you described. No more questions.'

Ron steps down, dismissed. George feels guilty and avoids making eye contact.

Katherine calls Will as her final witness. He confirms that he's known George for over twenty years and praises him. Katherine asks him a series of questions, and Will avoids making eye contact with his friend. She goes through all the dates in question, and Will doesn't falter. Katherine eventually takes a seat.

The prosecutor stands. 'Just to get the facts straight. You've known Mr Mailer for twenty years. In that time, have you ever known him to lie?'

Will remains silent.

'Mr Devon?'

'No,' Will says, looking at the floor.

'And you say that on the night of Saturday, 11th March, you saw Mr Mailer enter the hotel room where you were staying. Is that correct?'

'Yes.'

'Are you sure, Mr Devon? Remember, you are under oath.'

'Yes, he did come back to the hotel.'

'And what time was that?'

'About 2:00 a.m.'

'Are you sure?'

'Yes,' Will mumbles.

'If I told you we have a witness who says you were in a hotel room with several other comedians until 5:00 a.m., what would you say to that?'

Will looks close to tears. He glances desperately at George, then hangs his head.

'I can't remember exactly what time it was.'

'It was not before 5:00 a.m., Mr Devon, not according to three other witnesses. No further questions.'

The court is adjourned for the day. George knows his alibi is dead and buried. He's fucked.

George is escorted to a cell in the court's basement. He's devastated—his alibi is gone. He replays the jury's expressions during the trial, particularly the shock when Dan claimed George had threatened to cut his dick off. Maybe someone will step forward to take responsibility for Shelly's death. You hear about that happening. Maybe he should advertise for it? *Man wanted to take responsibility for two abductions and one murder. Bed, breakfast, and dinner served daily, for life, in return.*

The cell door opens. Katherine enters, her mouth set in a tight line, her eyes flashing with anger. 'I told you from the beginning that I needed you to be honest with me. You haven't been. You'll be convicted, and then the jury will deliver their verdict after the closing speeches.'

'Something'll turn up,' George says weakly.

Katherine meets his gaze. 'Your alibi is gone. Several witnesses testified you're a liar and a bully. What do you think's going to turn up?'

He looks at the floor, the crushing weight of hopelessness sinking in. 'You think I'm going to prison?'

'It's a foregone conclusion, especially when they find the van. If there's hair, blood, or any body fluids linked to the three women…'

George thinks of the blood from Sharon's head when she rolled off the bed.

'I already told you that Jade and Sharon came back to the van.'

'So, there may be hair and fingerprints. Anything else? Will there be blood, George?'

'No,' he lies.

She looks at him wearily. 'I'll see you on Monday morning.' She bangs on the door. The guard appears, and she leaves.

He's driven back to Belmarsh, feeling low enough to want to curl up and cry. Kesky's on his bunk, reading a letter. George lies down on his own bed.

'How did it go?' Kesky asks.

'Not good,' George says, struggling to keep it together.

'Got a letter from an old mate today. He's in Broadmoor security hospital.'

What the fuck does this have to do with me? George wants to scream in frustration.

'He was convicted of two murders a few years back. Was a head shrink himself—smart guy, eh?' Kesky chuckles.

George's patience is thin.

'Anyways, he was sentenced to thirty years. At court, he started acting out—shouting, saying he could hear voices, see things that weren't there. The judge called a halt to the trial and sent him for tests. He knew exactly what to say and do to convince them he was mental. Ended up in Broadmoor. He says it's nice there. Good food, and a room of his own. Time's easier spent, he says.'

A guard comes to take them for dinner. George tells him he's not hungry and stays in his cell. He picks up the letter from Kesky's bed and reads:

My gardening's come on a lot. Big gardens here... They even have arts and crafts, and workshops for woodwork and ceramics, if you can believe it! The hospital's also got a café, a shop, a bloody hairdresser—I'm bald as a coot now, but still. Plenty of free therapy, and they're big on rehabilitation. I'm playing the part beautifully, a model patient.

He's interrupted by the guard opening the slot.

'Mailer, you have a visitor.'

A visitor. Who could it be? Katherine with a get-out-of-jail-free card? George puts the letter back on the bed. The guard escorts him to the visitor's room.

He's shocked—though unexpectedly pleased—to see Sammy. She stands, taking a step toward him, arms outstretched.

'No physical contact. Please sit down,' the guard commands, settling into a chair behind him.

Sammy lowers herself into the seat. Her voice trembles as she asks, 'How are you?'

'Been better. What are you doing here?'

Tears well up in her eyes. 'George, I know what happened.'

His jaw clenches so tightly his teeth ache, and his hands ball into fists at his sides. 'Nothing happened.'

'I know what that bastard did,' she spits.

A dark wave of shame washes over him. 'Shut up,' he snarls, his voice ragged as he struggles to keep his emotions in check.

'Listen to me,' she says, her voice rising in frustration. She glances at the guard and lowers her tone. 'It's not your fault. You were just a kid.'

'I don't know what Mum's been saying. She's gone mental.'

He shuts his eyes, forcing himself to breathe through the rush of memories. The screams of his mother—her eyes wide and full of terror, the ropes digging into her skin. Tears streaking down her face as his father towers over her. The smell of his own piss running down his leg. Fleeing like a coward.

'George,' Sammy says, her voice softer, trying to reach him. 'He was a fully grown man. And you were just a wee boy.'

George freezes and cocks his head, brow furrowing. 'A wee boy? I'd hardly call eighteen a wee boy.'

Sammy stares at him, confusion flickering in her eyes. 'What are you talking about?'

His mind spins. *Dad's return, me running?* 'Erm... What are you talking about?'

Sammy takes a long look at him, several expressions fleeting by on her face. 'God, what do you remember about our dad?'

Fuck, fuck! This isn't on the table. It's buried, locked away, battened down behind the hatches, never meant to resurface.

'She always said he did a runner, but it turns out our dad likes wee boys,' Sammy says as she reaches out for George's hand, fighting off tears. 'He abused you for years. You were probably too young to remember, George. That's why he went to prison. But he escaped and came back to the house. You were lucky you weren't there. My ma's lucky to still be alive. The bastard was caught and put back inside, where I hope he rots!'

His breath catches, and the world spins around him. His body stiffens as the floodgates open in his mind. 'No... don't!' His voice cracks, desperate to shove the memories back where they belong.

He stands abruptly, unable to sit still, his legs shaking. 'I want to go back to my cell now.'

'Please, George,' Sammy pleads, her hand reaching out to him, her eyes raw with pain. 'I just spoke to Katherine. She said you should tell the jury. Tell them what happened. She thinks you'll get a lighter sentence.' Sammy's sobs break through, her body shaking as she tries to make him understand.

Ignoring her, George moves toward the door, his body heavy with shock. The guard leads him away.

Back in his empty cell, he collapses onto his bed and curls into a ball, his chest tight, struggling to breathe. His hands grab the pillow, clutching it as he screams into it—his voice muffled but raw, filled with pain and fury, the weight of the dark truth threatening to engulf him completely.

George is exhausted after a fitful night's sleep.

Katherine arrives at Belmarsh early, sitting with her arms crossed and lips pale. It's the angriest he's seen her.

'They located the van,' she says, her voice sharp. 'Do you want to know what they found inside, George?'

He stays silent.

'There's hair and fingerprints from Jade Emery and Sharon Gallagher. And blood—Sharon Gallagher's blood. Why is her blood there, George?'

'She had a nosebleed,' he answers, not missing a beat.

'It's likely you're going to prison for a very long time. Your sister spoke to me. I suggest you take the stand and tell the jury about your father. It won't get you off, but it might reduce the sentence.'

'You don't want to take what Sammy says too seriously. She makes things up.'

'Okay, George. Your call. Court proceedings have been halted to examine the van further, and the findings will be presented in court when they're ready. I'll be in touch.' She stands and leaves the cell.

Three weeks later, George steps back into the dock. The courtroom is packed, the air thick with anticipation.

'All stand,' the clerk announces. The judge takes his seat, and all in the room sit back down. The prosecution rises, launching into a tirade against George. The findings from the van are damning. His only option now is an easier time at Broadmoor. It's time to step up.

'He's a devil!' George shouts, his voice cutting through the courtroom.

The room falls silent, all heads turning toward him. George raises his hands in a praying position, holding them high above his head. Murmurs ripple through the court.

'He has been sent by the devil to test us!' George bellows, raising his voice even louder.

'Mr Mailer, you will be removed from court if you cannot control yourself,' the judge warns.

He smiles widely, then barks. 'I told you this would happen. You're a very naughty boy,' he says, slapping himself across the face. He erupts into loud, hysterical laughter.

'Guards, take him down,' the judge orders.

George begins screaming, pointing at imaginary threats. Two guards rush forward, manhandling him from the dock and dragging him back to his cell. They take his shoes, belt and tie, leaving him alone. Has he done enough to earn a spot in Broadmoor Hospital?

A while later, a guard arrives to escort George. He's taken to an interview room where two guards stand inside. Katherine is already sitting at the table.

'Are you okay?' she asks, concern in her eyes.

'I'm fine,' he replies, offering a smile. 'Why do you ask?'

'George, you've been found guilty of murder and two counts of abduction. The charges could increase if bodies are ever found. Do you know where they are?'

'No, Katherine, don't be silly,' he smiles again, trying to mask the growing unease.

Katherine stands, her expression hardening. 'The judge has decided to send you to a secure hospital for further tests and assessment. But regardless of the results, I must warn you, it's likely you'll be locked up for a long time.'

Without another word, Katherine leaves the room, the door clicking shut behind her.

Two guards come to get him. They don't give him his shoes back, leading him out to the van in nothing but his socks. As he's escorted to the vehicle, he notices there are no journalists around. He'd thought there'd be a high demand for press interviews. It's disappointing!

Chapter 31

The van comes to a halt outside a red brick building, boxed in by high walls. It's more visually pleasing than Belmarsh, though George had imagined something grander—a statue or a pond at the entrance maybe. The guards lead him inside. Behind the counter, two staff members are dressed in civilian clothes. Perhaps he'll get to wear casual clothes too. One of the guards handsGeorge's sealed bag of belongings to a tall lady with glasses. Her name badge, sewn to her top, says '*Grace'*. She peers over her specs at George.

'Mr. Mailer. These are your items. I'll ask you to check that they are all present and correct,' she says, holding up the sealed bag. He sees his phone and wonders if they'll give it back now. 'Is everything there?' she asks.

'Yes,' he replies.

A man with jet-black hair and a matching moustache puts down his clipboard and walks over to search him. His name badge reads '*Bert'*. He asks George to take off his jacket and hands him a pale blue two-piece set, not dissimilar to children's pyjamas, and a pair of white slippers. *Slippers are a good sign.* Hopefully, there will open fireplaces to heat them up next to.

He's taken to a room to change into his new outfit. Back at reception, Bert takes his suit and shirt from him, bags them, then leads him down a long corridor. He unlocks a door and walks George through another long passage lined with doors, each with small windows. A face appears behind one, eyes piercing and lips curled in a sneer. Loud banging from the opposite door startles him, followed by a high-pitched scream. He feels uneasy. The nurse stops at the next door and unlocks it.

'This is you,' Bert says, holding the door open.

George peers inside. It's a bare white room, no bigger than his last cell. A mattress with a pillow and sheet on top is the only furniture.

'It's a little stark.'

The nurse smiles sarcastically. 'You're a card, I'll tell you.' He takes two steps toward the door and locks it behind him.

George is overcome with exhaustion. He lies down on the bed and drifts into a nap, only to be jolted awake by a large woman with a no-nonsense expression, banging on the open door and demanding he follow her to see the doctor. George knows what's required to keep his cushy spot here—genuine madness. They walk down a long corridor, the sound of their footsteps echoing, and stop in front of a door. She knocks firmly.

'Come in,' a voice calls from the other side. They enter, and behind a desk sits an attractive man in his fifties, who gestures to the chair opposite him.

The woman leaves quietly.

'Hello, I'm Dr. Ramsey,' the man says, offering a warm smile. 'I'll be conducting a number of tests while you're here at Broadmoor. All I ask is that you be as honest as possible. Can you do that?'

'No problem,' George replies.

'This is just an informal meeting for us to get to know each other. Would you mind if I ask you a few questions?'

'That'd be just fine. I'm an open book.'

'Would you say that you lie easily, with some difficulty, or never?'

'Never. Don't see the point in lying.'

'And do you care about other people?'

'I do.'

'I hear you're a stand-up comedian. That must be a difficult job?'

'Not really. If you're funny and know about timing and delivery, you've got it made.'

'And how would you describe your career at present?'

'Excellent. I've just completed my first tour and a TV gig. I've received quite a bit of interest from some agents. I suspect they might get into a bidding war, but that's fine by me. More interest, more money.'

'And how do you feel about being convicted for abduction and murder?'

'How do you think I feel? I'm devastated. I wouldn't hurt a fly, and anyone who knows me knows that. I'm a good man in the wrong place at the wrong time. Would you like to hear my theory on what's been going on?'

'Yes, I would,' Dr. Ramsey says, raising an eyebrow.

'I think I have a fan who's a bit of a stalker. Probably a woman. She goes to all my gigs, and when she sees these women come on to me, it drives her crazy. She waits until I've said goodnight to them, then goes in for the kill.'

'You think these women are dead?' Ramsey asks, jotting something down on his pad.

George looks up at the ceiling. 'Really, should I tell him?' he mutters to the sky, then smiles at the doctor. 'I'm afraid those women are dead. God just told me. I'm tired now. Didn't get much sleep last night. Can I go?'

'Of course,' Ramsey replies, pressing a buzzer. The matron enters and leads him back to his room.

Chapter 32

As George nears his one-month mark in Broadmoor, he's settled into the routine. He's found his rhythm—writing new material and making notes for a book. The confinement takes some getting used to, but he spends much of his time in the gardens, staying occupied with various activities. He's volunteered for everything—arts and crafts, even the woodwork class, where he's surprisingly excelled. The teacher is impressed with his progress, laughing at his jokes, which he enjoys. *In different circumstances...*

His room—minimal as it is—feels nicer and cleaner than his old bedsit, free of cockroaches too. He reads voraciously, spending hours in the library studying a range of topics, including British law, miscarriages of justice, and test cases with precedent.

He misses the stage, the thrill of private performances, and, of course, lager.

A guard informs him of a visitor, and George is led to the visitors' room. Will sits across from him, a nurse just two feet away. Will looks unwell—dark bags under his eyes, guilt evident in his glance as he meets George's eyes.

'Hey, George. How are you?' he asks, his voice tentative.

'I'm alright.'

Will studies him quietly. 'Are you really?'

George leans in, lowering his voice to a whisper. 'I'm not mad, Will, if that's what you're asking.'

Will exhales with relief. 'Top acting skills in court, G,' he whispers.

After a brief silence, Will adds, 'Listen, G, I'm so sorry. Sean Philips told the police I was with those lot.'

'You did your best. I appreciate that. And you're here.' George's eyes soften.

Will glances at the nurse before lowering his voice again. 'What's it like?'

'It's not too bad. And I'm planning an appeal. I'll get out soon.' George says, his voice steady.

'Really?' Will looks stunned. 'You think you have a chance?'

'Yeah. There's a barrister in here—he's helping me with it. He won tons of cases before coming here.' George glances at the nurse, who remains absorbed in her magazine, unaffected.

'A barrister? Amazing. What's he in for?'

'Probably best not to go into that,' George says, shrugging. 'But he says miscarriages of justice are big business. And if I write a book about my experience, it could be a bestseller. With that, and my comedy skills, I might do rather well—TV interviews, newspaper articles...' He trails off, noticing the look of disbelief on Will's face.

Will's brow furrows. 'They still haven't found the guy who killed those women, though. Surely that'll make it difficult?'

'Matter of time,' George says, his voice flat. 'He'll turn up. They always do.'

Will shifts uncomfortably in his chair. 'Terrible business with your dad, G. Sammy told me what happened. The evil bastard.'

'I don't want to talk about that, Will. Ever!' George's voice rises sharply, and his fists clench at his sides.

The nurse coughs, reminding them of her presence as she shifts in her seat. George takes a breath, trying to steady himself.

'Look, Will,' he says, 'It's showtime!' He winks and then starts barking loudly.

Will sits back in his chair, shaking his head admiring Georges acting skills.

The nurse, startled, springs to her feet. 'Time's up,' she says curtly.

Bert appears at the door. 'Come on, George.'

A half-smile pulls at Will's lips. 'So good to see you, G. Keep up the writing,' he shouts.

'Ayy!' George replies with a wide smile, flashing a thumbs up—the classic Fonz gesture.

Thank you

A huge thank you to my fellow author friends from my earlier writing group, Jules Grant and Ish Duval, for working through countless drafts with me, allowing George to seep into their lives, and encouraging me to pursue an MA in Creative Writing. I'll be forever grateful.

Thanks also to book designer Amanda Ripley and book editor Paul Swallow, whose expertise helped me finish this book, and to fellow author Paul Marriner, whose unwavering support and generous feedback have been invaluable. A special thank you to author Elly Griffiths, whose insightful feedback was greatly appreciated.

Above all, heartfelt thanks to all the readers who chose this novel. I know you had countless options, and I'm incredibly grateful that you picked this one. I truly hope you enjoyed it. If you feel inclined to leave a review on Amazon or Goodreads, I would be very appreciative.

Printed in Dunstable, United Kingdom

67400124R00129